DAVID SHERMAN
Author of MAIN FORCE ASSAULT

Tango Niner takes on everybody—corrupt
friends and vicious enemies
THE NIGHT FIGHTERS, BOOK 3

OUT OF
THE FIRE

Ivy
BOOKS
0104-3 $3.50

Attack!

"It looks like someone's in the wire," Randall said. "Charlie's coming to Tango."

"Pop a flare over the west wire," Burrison ordered. Slover adjusted the angle of his mortar when a rocket-shaped round shot almost straight up, arced downward, and made a small bang when its flare burst open. In the sudden glare, six Vietcong could be made out crawling down the hill under the cover of the incoming fire. The wires they were pulling led to explosive charges.

"Hit them!" Randall yelled. "Take them out before they blow the wire." He sighted on the closest VC and pulled the trigger. The bullet hit the communist's head, bursting it like a ripe melon hit by a hammer. On his left, Pennell led three PFs in gunning down two more VC who were between the middle and outer rows of concertina. One of the bodies fell against a trip wire—an explosion in the middle bank of wire brightly lit the night for a second.... Nights were getting interesting at CAP Tango Niner.

Also by David Sherman
Published by Ivy Books:

KNIVES IN THE NIGHT

MAIN FORCE ASSAULT

OUT OF THE FIRE

David Sherman

IVY BOOKS • NEW YORK

Library of Congress Catalog Card Number: 87-90996

ISBN 0-8041-0104-3

Manufactured in the United States of America

First Edition: January 1988

For Sergeant Rock, Corporal Baba Louie, Corporal Boots, Eggy, both Jean-Jacques, McLain, Saole, Doc Gordon, and the others

AUTHOR'S NOTE

The U.S. Marine Corps' Combined Action Program was real. A small number of Marines—usually one fourteen-man rifle squad plus one Navy Medical Corpsman—would be put into a village to train and work with the local Popular Forces (civilian militia) platoon to rid their village of Vietcong activity and make the people safe. Not many people ever heard of the CAP Program and some who did didn't like what we were doing. For example, the U.S. Army didn't think the Marines should be involved in the kind of civic action the CAP units did, and they thought the troops assigned to the program were wasted resources that could be put to better use on battalion operations searching for Main Force VC units and NVA regiments. The Marines believed the way to win the war was to win the people and went with their own program. Another group that didn't like us was corrupt South Vietnamese officials. When we set out to make the villagers safe, we didn't care whom we made them safe from. If that meant a corrupt official wasn't allowed to rip off the people, well, "Sorry about that."

While the events depicted in this novel are fiction, there is nothing in it that could not have happened. Combined Action Platoon Tango Niner is loosely based on the CAP unit the author served with several miles from Chu Lai in the summer of 1966.

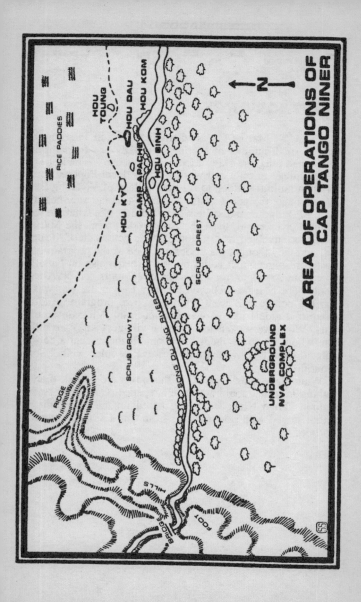

AREA OF OPERATIONS OF
CAP TANGO NINER

N

RICE PADDIES

HOU
TOUNG

HOU DAU

HOU KOM

HOU KYO

CAMP APACHE

HOU BINH

SCRUB FOREST

SCRUB GROWTH

SONG DO DANG RIVER

RIDGE

HILLS

BRIDGE

FOOT

UNDERGROUND
NVA COMPLEX

RICE PADDIES

0 MILES 5

HOU TOUNG

TO RIDGE — HOU KY

CAMP APACHE

BULLDOZED EXTENSION

HOU DAU

MAIN ROAD

HOU KOM

SONG DU ONG RIVER — HOU BINH

SCRUB FOREST

THE FIVE HAMLETS OF BUN HOU VILLAGE

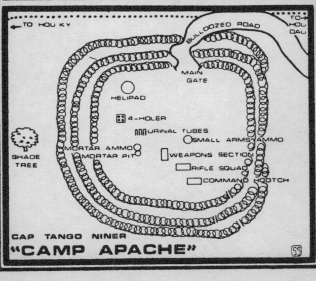

TO HOU KY

BULLDOZED ROAD

TO HOU DAU

MAIN GATE

HELIPAD

4-HOLER

URINAL TUBES

SMALL ARMS AMMO

MORTAR AMMO
MORTAR PIT

WEAPONS SECTION

RIFLE SQUAD

SHADE TREE

COMMAND HOOTCH

CAP TANGO NINER

"CAMP APACHE"

PROLOGUE

This is what happened before:

Lieutenant Houng arrived at Tango Niner shortly after
10:00 A.M. with a visitor—Vien Phoung, an elder from one
of the hamlets in the neighboring village of Bun Anh. This
wizened ancient stood stoop-shouldered in front of Lieutenant Burrison and Sergeant Bell while Houng made the
introductions. Burrison bowed courteously and studied the
old man's face. The man's expression could have been sad,
anxious, or resigned; the lieutenant couldn't tell. In old age
the peasants' faces all looked like carved mahogany masks
and were usually impossible for the Americans to read.

"Many people Bun Anh dau, sick," Houng said. "Vien
Phoung say Ma-deen bac si, doctor, come Bun Anh, fix
dau people." Houng's eyes pleaded with Burrison. The
Popular Forces lieutenant knew what Bell's response would
be, but he wasn't sure about the American lieutenant.

"What do you think, Sergeant Bell," Burrison asked, "can we get away with it?"

"Yessir. We can get away with it and we'll score a lot of points with the peasants in the district if we do. Going to Bun Anh might be the first step in pacifying the entire district."

"It's 'Doc' Rankin's turn to do a med-cap, isn't it?"

"That's right, sir."

"Tell him to pack his med-kit, we're going for a ride."

Sergeant Bell led the med-cap patrol while Burrison stayed behind.

A crowd of curious villagers surrounded the Americans but maintained a respectful distance while Vien Phoung explained who the foreigners were. The old man's shouted voice was thin and reedy. At first no one moved toward the makeshift aid station, but eventually, under the old man's urging, a few did.

Suddenly an ARVN jeep careened into the hamlet, narrowly missing the people scattering out of its way. It screeched to a stop in front of the Marines' jeep. The man in its passenger seat stood up behind the windshield and shouted in a demanding voice, "What you do here, Ma-deen. This not Bun Hou, this Bun Anh. You not belong here, you dee dee mau."

"Well, well, if it isn't our ti-ti friend, Phang," Corporal Zeitvogel said softly.

Bell walked over to the ARVN jeep. "Hello, Captain Phang. It's been a while since the last time we saw you. I was beginning to hope maybe your friends in the NVA wasted you for fucking up their gig so badly."

"You salute me, Sergeant!" Phang screamed. "Me captain, you salute me."

"Fuck you, Phang." Bell turned from the assistant district chief but stopped when he heard the sound of a .45 hammer being cocked. He turned around. Phang was pointing his automatic at Bell's head.

"You salute me, Ma-deen."

"Look past me, Phang," Bell said in a cold voice.

Phang's eyes flicked past the sergeant and widened. Zeitvogel and Hempen both had their rifles in their shoulders aimed at him. Doc Rankin had pulled his .45 from its holster and was also aiming at the Vietnamese official.

"Is me not saluting enough for you to die for, Captain?" Bell asked.

Phang swallowed and slowly lowered his sidearm. "You live this time, Sergeant," he said in a voice shaking with fear, "but you not belong here. You stay away Bun Anh."

Bell looked around. The few people who had been waiting to be treated by Rankin were gone. "Well, Doc," he said, "it looks like you don't have any more patients today. Pack up and let's go home."

Phang screamed, "You not belong Bun Anh, you stay away."

"You know, Phang," Bell said conversationally, "I thought this place was awful poor. Now I know why. How much are you taxing these people? Twice the official rate? Three times the rate?"

"You never mind. Taxes not your business. You dee dee mau, not come back."

"Phang, don't you even try to tell me where I can go and not go. Now move that jalopy of yours, it's blocking my jeep."

When the Marines and Lieutenant Houng were in their jeep and ready to leave Phang started screaming at Bell again, "You stay away from here, Ma-deen. You come back Bun Anh, I get you."

Bell stared at Phang with the flat eyes of a cold-blooded killer. "Phang, you're slime," he said. "You stay out of my way or I'll step on you and squish you like the slug you are." He shifted into gear and drove away with Phang screaming incoherently in the background.

The Marines ran another med-cap in Bun Anh the next day. This time Lieutenant Burrison went along. Captain Phang was already there, helping an absentee landlord collect rent.

Phang leaped to his feet when he saw the Americans enter the hamlet and stood leaning forward with his knuckles on the table. "What you do here, Ma-deen?" he shouted when Bell dismounted from the jeep. "I say you no belong Anh Dien, I say you stay away Anh Dien." The Chinese landlord remained sitting, impassively watching the scene.

"And I told you not to come around when I'm here," Bell said calmly. He looked at the people standing in line at the table. Each had a piece of colored paper in his or her hand. Looking back along the line, the sergeant saw that the people were loading sacks of rice onto the trucks and were given the slips of paper after loading the rice.

"You dee dee mau, Ma-deen," Phang screamed. "You no belong here."

Burrison stepped over to the table and introduced himself. "I'm Second Lieutenant Burrison, commander of CAP Tango Niner," he said to the livid ARVN officer. "Who are you?"

Phang spun from looking at Bell to glare at this new American. He took a couple of deep breaths to calm himself, then said in a lower voice, "Me Captain Phang, assistant district chief. You are commander, you are second lieutenant?"

Burrison nodded.

"You second lieutenant, me captain. You salute me," Phang shrilled.

Burrison shook his head and said, "I'm sorry, sir, but Marines don't salute in the field. It draws the attention of snipers."

"This not field, this secure area, pacified!"

"That's not what I've heard, Captain."

Phang's jaw muscles worked. "This is not your village," he said abruptly. "What you do here?"

"There are sick people here and no doctor," Burrison said. "We have come to provide some medical treatment."

"Lie," Phang screamed. "There bac si here. People no pay bac si, he no bac si them."

Burrison looked at the rice bags that now nearly filled the trucks. "I wonder why they can't pay," he said.

While everyone's attention was distracted by Burrison and Phang, Bell positioned the rest of the med-cap group on a line facing the ARVN soldiers at the trucks. They stood with their weapons held casually ready.

"You no bac si people Anh Dien," Phang said with ice in his voice. "You dee dee mau. You go now or you die."

Burrison blinked involuntarily. Then he put his hand on his holster and said in a voice he tried to make as cold as Phang's, "Do you think your men can kill all of us before we kill enough of them to make the survivors break and run?"

Phang looked beyond Burrison and saw how the other Americans and the Popular Forces lieutenant were deployed. Instead of giving the order that would lead to a bloodbath he said in a quieter voice, "You dee dee. You go now, not come back."

"We are here on a med-cap," Burrison said in a calm voice that belied his internal shaking. "We will leave after treating all the sick people who ask for it."

Houng shouted for Vien Phoung to come and help line up the sick and injured. The hamlet elder did not appear. No one stepped forward to receive treatment.

Bell stood behind Phang and the Chinese and looked at the notepad.

"You know, Phang, I can't read Vietnamese," he said, "but the numbers are written the same in both languages. I know what the legal maximum rent for farmland is. It looks to me like you're helping Mr. Landlord here collect double what he's due." He shook his head slowly. "That's a no-no, Captain."

The Chinese turned languidly to Bell and said with a heavy French accent, "You are a troublemaker, Trung Si. Luck does not last forever. Take care that you are not making trouble when your luck runs out."

"Oh, I'm not a troublemaker, Mr. Landlord," Bell said. "I only make trouble for the bad guys when they cross my path."

The Chinese looked impassively up at Bell. "I own this land. Do you say I am a bad guy, Trung Si?"

"The amount that can be charged for rent is established by law. Are you collecting only what is legal?"

"I am collecting what is mine."

"If you are doing it within the law, then you are not a bad guy and I am not a troublemaker." Bell smiled.

During this time Houng was walking around, talking to people, inviting them to come for treatment. Many of them ignored him, others spoke briefly—mostly saying they weren't hurt and no one in their families was ill. But a few said a little more. Houng returned to the jeep after a few minutes and said, "We go now. No one want bac si."

Houng waited until they were outside the hamlet before saying anything. He let it pour out. "Phang numba fucking ten," he said vehemently. "Vien Phoung, him dead. Phang tell people Vien Phoung killed by Ma-deen. Phang say he collect money from Ma-deen for kill Vien Phoung. Phang lie. Me say Phang bang-bang Vien Phoung."

"Shit!" Bell pounded on the steering wheel and slammed on the brakes. "I'm gonna get that son of a bitch. Now he's killing innocent people to keep us away. His ass is mine. I'm going to get him. Phang's going to fry for this."

But corrupt ARVN officials and greedy landlords weren't the only problem the Marines of Tango Niner had —there were Vietcong to contend with as well. Recently they had intercepted a large number of VC supply runs and the Tango Niner compound had come under mortar attack. They thought Charlie was going to hit them hard. They went to work beefing up their defenses. And one man had a funny feeling.

"I want to take a few men out for a walk, Jay Cee," Lance Corporal "Billy Boy" Lewis said to Sergeant Bell. "I don't want to get out of any work, or anything, it's just I'd feel a lot better if I knew Charlie wasn't watching while we're doing it. We'll be back in an hour or so."

"Take Big Red, Wells, and the Kid with you," Bell told him.

They found someone—a seven-man recon squad with a mortar. Six of the VC sat in a semicircle around the mortar; the other was up a tree hidden in a blind, watching the Marine compound through binoculars.

"I'll start off by evening the odds," Lewis told his men. He reached into the inside pocket of his utility shirt and pulled out a plastic bag. He unfolded the oil-soaked cloth that he took from it, exposed his ninja throwing stars, and selected two of them. Folded again, the cloth went back into its plastic bag and the bag returned to the inside pocket. "Their backs are to us," he said. "I'll take out the two closest to us. When the second one gets hit, that's when we fire. Pick targets from right to left. When your man goes down, take the next one if he's still up. Everybody got it?"

The others nodded. Wells and Robertson had the tense look of adrenaline-pumped men ready for action. Tucker looked scared—no matter how many firefights he had been in and won, he still suffered from the same gut-wrenching fear he had felt the first time he came under fire. As for Lewis, he had never thrown the stars in combat before. He didn't show it, but he was uncertain about whether or not he could actually kill a man with one.

When he was satisfied they were ready, Lewis held a star in each hand, twisted his body far to the right and swung his right arm in a sidewinding motion at the back of the closest VC. In one smooth action, he followed through on the swing, came back, plucked the second star out of his left hand, wound back and twisted forward. He followed through by falling forward into a prone firing position.

The first VC felt a sudden pain in his back and gasped. He reached around to his ribs to claw at the red pain that was suddenly becoming his entire universe, and fell forward. The second Cong heard the gasp and turned his head to look, but never completed his turn because the second star struck him in the neck, scraping the side of a vertebra, slashing his jugular, and tearing his carotid artery and nerve.

Three Marines fired as one and Lewis's shot came a split second behind the others. All four remaining VC pitched to the ground. The Marines put another round in each of them to make sure. Then the watcher dropped out of his tree.

"Get him!" the lance corporal shouted. The Marines opened up on the fleeing VC. Eight rapid rounds pounded into his back and propelled his corpse into a tree.

The expected attack came with a rush that night.

A fusillade of fire came from the east of Camp Apache. Bullets zinged overhead or slammed into the earth of the hillside, kicking up clods of dirt. There were a few tense minutes of silence, then a machine gun swept the south face of the hill.

Bell jumped out of the command post and ran to the position overlooking the back gate. "Where is it?" he asked when he dropped into the trench. The machine gun had stopped its fire.

"At the edge of the trees, right over there."

Bell reached for the field phone to direct the mortar to drop a high explosive round on the gun's position, but before he could, heavy fire erupted in the west.

"What do you have out there, Tex?" Burrison asked from the CP.

"I see movement. It looks like someone's in the wire," Randall said. "Charlie's coming to tango."

"Pop a flare over the west wire," Burrison ordered. Slover adjusted the angle of his mortar and dropped a round down the tube. The rocket-shaped round shot almost straight up, then arced downward, made a small bang when its flare burst open, and swung down underneath its parachute. Six Vietcong were crawling down the hill under the cover of the incoming fire. They were pulling wires after themselves from the explosive charges they had set to blow holes in the barbed wire.

"Hit them!" Randall yelled. "Take them out before they blow the wire." He sighted on the one closest to him and pulled the trigger. The bullet hit the Communist's head and burst it like a ripe melon hit by a hammer. On his left, Pennell led the three PFs with him in gunning down two more VC who were between the middle and outer rows of concertina wire. The bodies bounced under the impact of the bullets and collapsed against the outside wire. Trip-wire tangled with one of the bodies and was jerked by the tumbling body. An explosion in the middle bank of wire brightly lit the night for a second. When its dust cleared, a ten-foot gap in the wire was visible. In the corner trench near the helipad, Lewis opened fire with his automatic rifle. Six rounds slammed into one of the Vietcong soldiers, lifted him from the ground, and threw him down, bent like a broken doll. More fire blasted from the Marines and PFs defending the west side of the hill, and the last two VC died. The VC in the wire were dead, but in their dying they had detonated five of the twelve charges they had set—three holes gaped in the middle bank of wire and two more were in the innermost.

The VC surrounding the hill had increased their rate of fire while their comrades who set the charges were being killed. Enemy fire came from everywhere except the north, where the Marines had their machine gun.

Burrison raised Slover on the radio and told him to light up the open area between the hill and the trees on the west. The mortar *carumph*ed twice and the two shells popped open a hundred meters apart. The blue light illuminated a line of a hundred men trotting toward the hill with their rifles held at the ready.

"Holy shit, we got company coming!" Randall shouted into his phone. "Lewis, Pennell, put some fire out there." The three Marines, the corpsman, and nine PFs on the west side of the hill started firing at the advancing VC.

Burrison ordered Slover to fire high explosive rounds at the charging VC and told Randall to direct the mortar's fire.

"How far out are they, Tex?" The range was the only information Slover needed to fire effectively.

"Seventy-five meters and closing," Randall answered.

Five high explosive rounds shot out of the mortar tube

before the flares went out and Randall had to call for another illumination round. "They're pulling back," he shouted when the new flare opened up high above the battle ground. Ten or fifteen bodies lay crumpled on the ground under the flare's light.

The fire from the east halted, and the defenders on the other side of the hill gradually stopped firing at the withdrawing VC as they stopped seeing targets. Silence returned to Camp Apache. It didn't last long.

"They're inside the wire!" Randall screamed over the phone. Without waiting for orders, Slover fired two illumination rounds. A few VC were inside the outer row of wire, running around, looking for the lines that would set off the charges to open the remaining holes in the Marine defenses. More black-clad enemy soldiers were pouring through the gaps in the outer wire.

"How many are there?" Burrison asked.

"I don't know, but it looks like more than before," Randall answered. The twelve men with him in the three trenches facing the west side of the hill were firing as fast as they could at the VC between the outer and central wire.

"Wall," Bell said into the field phone, "get your gun and all your men over to Lewis's position and put some enfilade fire in that wire." He jumped out of the hole covering the south gate and ran to the north side of the hill to shift men to cover the main gate and then he went to the west side to direct the defense there.

While Bell was strengthening the lines under direct assault, Burrison was on the radio calling for air support. In minutes two gunships were on their way, ETA Camp Apache, about ten minutes. Then Burrison told Slover to fire high explosive rounds into the wire. The big corporal was already doing it.

After shifting people to cover the main gate, Bell gave all his attention to the west defenses. Now twenty-three defenders were shooting at what looked like two hundred attackers.

Two more explosions ripped through the night, cascading dirt and debris into the sky and tearing more holes in the middle bank of concertina wire. Some VC were searching for the openings in the inner wire, and others were looking for the lines that would set off the last charges in the inner wire, breaking down the last barrier to their assault. Some of them fell under the rifle fire from the Marines and PFs in the trenches, more were scythed down by the mortar rounds exploding in their midst, but there were too many VC to stop.

"Louie," Bell said into the phone, "we need more fire. Use both tubes."

"Roger that, Jay Cee," Slover said. To his men he added, "Keep firing the same pattern until I get back." Then he ran the few meters to the pit dug for the mortar Lewis had captured earlier in the day and, standing as tall as he dared and using dead reckoning, fired it alone. In less than two minutes he fired all twenty rounds that had been captured with it. By then it didn't matter that he didn't have any more rounds to fire because most of the Vietcong who didn't die in the wire had penetrated the inner bank and were running across the hilltop. He dove back to the .81's pit.

Burrison talked into the field phone and the PRC-20 radio at the same time. "Everybody, keep down," he said. "They've gotten inside. Stay in your holes and fire across the hilltop. Anyone above ground is the bad guys."

Close to a hundred and fifty VC ran across the hilltop screaming, "GI, you die tonight! Marine, another man fuck your girlfriend! GI, I will cut off your balls! Marine, say prayers to your god!" The first ones inside the compound weren't sure of what to do. They ran screaming toward the middle of the compound and were gunned down by the Marines and PFs before they could cause any damage. The ones that came after them carried hand grenades and satchel charges in addition to their rifles. They looked for defensive positions to throw their explosives into.

Pennell, Knowles, and four PFs poured point-blank fire into the VC trying to run through a hole in the inner wire thirty meters to their right front, and stopped that part of the human flood cold. They kept shooting at the forms trying to rush through the opening until there was a wall of bodies higher than the stacked concertina had been.

Slover pointed his mortar tube straight up and dropped three rounds down it. Seconds later the three shells burst overhead and three flares sputtered to life, spilling their eerie blue light on the forms of the VC running across the ground below them. "Doc" Tracker looked toward the middle of the compound and saw a black-clad form running toward him, swinging a pack at its side. The corpsman threw his rifle into his shoulder and pulled the trigger three times. The bullets slammed into the VC's chest, stopped him, stood him straight up and flipped him backward. But he was already slinging the satchel charge forward and it sailed out of his hand into the trench.

"Bail out," the corpsman yelled and scrambled out of the trench. The charge went off with an eruption like two freight trains colliding and violently shook the ground he lay on. Clods of dirt thudded onto him. He rolled over to knock the dirt off himself and shook his head to try to get rid of the ringing in his ears. When the ringing eased enough so that he thought he could hear again he called out, "Everybody okay?" When he didn't hear anybody answer, he realized he couldn't hear any gunfire. "I can't hear," he shouted in case any of the others in the trench with him had survived the satchel charge and could hear him. He rolled back into the hole and landed on something soft. He groped with his hands, found a body and checked it for wounds. His hands came away from a body's head covered with blood and brains. He checked the length of the trench for living casualties and found Bell sitting dazed from the concussion outside the hole. A quick examination didn't reveal any bleeding or broken bones. "Looks like you got your bell rung, Jay Cee," he punned. "You'll get over it." He pulled him back into the trench and kept looking. A few feet farther on he found a PF sagging against the side of the trench, bleeding from a hole in his side. He applied a compress bandage to the wound and kept going. He reached Randall, who was shaking his head and blinking. Randall mouthed words and pointed to his ears—he couldn't hear either. Tracker nodded and pantomimed the same message back. The corporal nodded and stopped blinking so he could start looking for more VC. The other two PFs had seen the VC with the explosive early enough to get safely away from the trench before it went off and were all right.

McEntire and Foster rained belt after belt of ammunition at the figures in the wire and Lewis added bursts of automatic rifle fire to the machine gun's cacophony of death. McEntire hated having to stop firing the gun long enough to change barrels, but if he didn't, the barrel would melt and the gun would be worthless. They kept firing into the wire until there was no one left in it to shoot at, then they turned around and looked for targets inside the compound.

To kill its light-making ability so the VC could operate more safely in the darkness, one twenty-man VC platoon advanced on the mortar pit by fire and maneuver. The remaining VC divided into two groups and went in opposite directions—one group continuing across the hill to where Zeitvogel's fire team and nine PFs were firing at them, the other group heading back to where they had come through the wire to wipe out what they thought were only a few defenders.

One squad heading to the east side of the compound saw the command post and diverted to it. Houng and Swarnes blasted away with their rifles, while Burrison stood in a one-handed range stance and blew three attackers away with his .45.

Slover saw the group advancing on his mortar pit and took a chance firing a high explosive round at them. Shrapnel from the explosion hit a few of the VC, but the round was far enough off that Slover didn't want to risk firing again. He and his mortarmen used their rifles. The big corporal sighted on a man swinging back to throw a grenade and pulled the trigger. At the same instant he saw the Charlie collapse backward, he heard a grunt from someone in the mortar pit and a thud as someone fell. He didn't have time to look to see who it was.

Then Burrison heard a new voice on his PRC-25, the

radio he used to call for air support. "Blazing Trail, this is Blue Turtle, over."

"Blue Turtle, Blazing Trail, go," Burrison answered.

"Blazing Trail, Blue Turtle. I have two platforms here and your lights are in sight at my twelve o'clock. What's your situation? Over."

"We are being overrun, Turtle. How soon can you be here? Over."

"Blazing Trail, that must be one hell of a firefight if you can't hear us. We are a half klick east of you and orbiting. Over."

"I'm mighty glad to hear that, Turtle. Victor Charlie is inside the compound. How can you help us? Over."

"Trail, how high is your hill? Over."

"About twenty feet above the plain, Turtle. Over."

"Blazing Trail, tell your friendlies to get into the bottom of their holes and stay there. We are going to give you a crew cut. Blue Turtle out."

Burrison shouted the news about the gunships into the field phone and the PRC-20. He looked to the east and could now hear the drone of the helicopters. In seconds he was able to make out their shapes as black holes against the background of stars. The two birds flew to the north of the hill and dropped down until they looked like they were going to land below it. Then their guns and rockets opened up on the hilltop.

When the gunships opened up on the hilltop, Tango Niner's machine gun was firing madly at a Vietcong platoon that was frantically charging it. The charging platoon crumpled under the withering fire from the birds. Its closest men had penetrated to within ten feet of the trench before being cut down. The Marines and PFs in the trench ducked down to get out of the way of the helicopter's rounds. It was the right thing to do under the circumstances, but it was also a mistake. One of the VC who had almost reached the trench wasn't dead yet. He cocked a chicom grenade and tossed it at the machine gun before he died.

The VC who were still alive and fighting realized that

with the gunships on the scene they had lost the battle. They tried to run out of the compound through the openings they had blasted in the wire. Some of them made it.

And then the fight was over.

Burrison asked for a casualty report. Athen, from the mortar squad, had to be medevaced but would return. Bell, Randall, and Tracker would be examined for burst eardrums. Foster, the machine gunner, had earned a trip back to The World—if he lived that long. McEntire was down, but not badly hit. One PF was dead and two others wounded.

The men in the trenches on the south side of the hill climbed out to look over the carnage in the compound. They shouldn't have, because now they were silhouetted against the sky. The machine gun that had been forgotten since it had stopped firing early in the fight opened up from southeast of the hill. One of the gunships saw its muzzle flash and buzzed over to take it out. But it was too late.

A ricochet tore Kid Tucker's abdominal wall open. One of the PFs with him had the top of his head blown off. Pancho Carrilo was drilled through the heart. Steven Lam, the Chinese lance corporal from Seattle who had thought the Marine Corps was too smart to send a Marine of Oriental descent to fight a war in Asia, had his throat ripped out. The PF standing next to Lam had his shoulder shattered by the same burst. The war that he thought he had no business in suddenly became very personal to Corporal Jesus Maria Ruizique; a bullet blasted through the meaty part of his left arm.

The two gunships continued circling the hill, firing random bursts into the trees east, south, and west of the hill until Rankin and the still-deaf Tracker finished patching up the wounded as well as they could. Then the birds landed and the ten Marine casualties and three wounded PFs were put aboard to be med-evaced. They flew off and the thirty-eight survivors waited tensely for dawn.

The sun finally rose and the Marines and PFs of Tango Niner started repairing damage to the defensive positions. Then the first wave of helicopters arrived.

Slover ran from the PFs he was supervising to get his orange paddles to lead the choppers in, but before he even reached his squad tent, one of the choppers landed near the main gate long enough for its cargo of grunts to jump off and another was touching down on the helipad. The other seven birds in the wave deposited their grunts onto the open area west of the hill and then all but the one that landed on the helipad took off again back where they had come from. By the time the second wave of eight helicopters arrived minutes later and landed their cargo of infantry east of the hill, Burrison, Slover, and Zeitvogel were greeting the men who had arrived on the hill.

A lieutenant colonel led the contingent off the bird that landed on the helipad. He was followed by Captain Hasford and Staff Sergeant Suddick and another Marine, Captain Ronson, who was a stranger to everyone on the hill except Zeitvogel.

The lieutenant colonel looked around the hilltop and made a quick estimate of the number of VC dead. He said, "It looks like you had yourself quite a party last night."

"Yes, sir," Burrison said. "It was quite a blast."

The lieutenant colonel started walking around. He nodded with approval at the trench segments that had been dug and the beginnings of the bunkers. After a quick visual review he asked, "Is there anything other than the radios and the .81 that you don't need to have replaced now?"

Burrison looked at Swarnes and Rankin, who had almost completed an inventory. They shook their heads. "No, sir," he said, "we need just about everything, including some new men."

The lieutenant colonel nodded. "In the next week you'll get everything you need—including the new people." He looked over at the navy blue jeep he knew wasn't authorized to Tango Niner. Except for Burrison, everyone in the platoon knew Bell and Zeitvogel had stolen it from the Air Force at Da Nang a week and a half earlier, then had it painted blue. "Your jeep has a flat. Make sure you put a new tire on your equipment list."

After a few more minutes of conversation the lieutenant

colonel said, "Get me a full inventory of what you need by this time tomorrow, and I'll get it to you ASAP. Captain Ronson and his company will stay here and help you mop up and complete your defenses. Good job, Lieutenant." He spun on his heel and strode to his waiting helicopter.

The Marines set about burying the dead Vietcong, digging a trench network and bunkers, erecting new tents, a new four holer and a new shower, scouring the area for able-bodied Vietnamese to assist with the digging and construction. They restocked ammunition in the mortar and small arms bunkers. It took about the week that the lieutenant colonel said it would to get all the equipment they needed.

"Company's coming," Swarnes said, relaying a message he received on his radio. Then Swarnes called Captain Ronson's radioman to let his skipper know VIPs were arriving. The reply came back that the grunt company commander was already on his way.

Three helicopters appeared in the eastern sky. When they reached the hill two circled while one touched down. Slover took his usual place with his back to the wind at the helipad and guided the bird in with his orange paddles. Burrison and Bell stood aside to greet the visitors and were surprised to see a squad of riflemen run out first and stand in formation nearby. The chopper that brought them took off again, and a second one touched down at the same time Ronson and his company first sergeant arrived on top of the hill.

The lieutenant colonel stormed off his command ship, his face looking like a thunderhead about to burst. Captain Hasford was the only man to debark with him. "Glad to see you're here already, Captain," the lieutenant colonel said to Ronson. He ignored Burrison's greeting. "Sergeant," he snapped at the NCO leading the Marines who landed on the first helicopter, "get your men over there and upend that shithouse." He pointed at the newly constructed four-holer that replaced the one lost in the mortar attack nine days earlier.

Followed by the lieutenant colonel, the squad trotted to the wall-less outhouse, removed its roof, and turned over the box. Hasford, Ronson, Burrison, Bell, and the first sergeant trailed after him. The senior officer watched while the sergeant reached inside the box and yanked on something attached to the inside near one of the holes. The sergeant handed first one, then a second package to the captain from intelligence, who displayed them to the lieutenant colonel.

The older man stared at the two clear plastic packages and their white powder contents for a long moment before turning to Burrison. "Lieutenant, I hope, I sincerely hope that isn't what I think it is. If it is, you and some of your men are going to spend a long time breaking big rocks into little rocks. I take drugs very seriously—and two kilos of heroin are very serious. As of this moment you and your NCOs are relieved of all command and leadership duties and are under house arrest until such time as that powder is analyzed." He turned to Ronson and continued, "You are in command. These men are not to leave the compound except under guard. Take their weapons and return them only in the event of an assault against this compound, and then only if you are convinced that you need the extra rifles to keep from being overrun. You'll be hearing from me." He spun away and walked with long strides back to his helicopter. Hasford looked at Burrison and Bell as though he couldn't believe what was in his hands, then followed the lieutenant colonel.

CHAPTER ONE

Overnight, November 7, 1966

Lance Corporal Billy Boy Lewis scanned the familiar landscape with practiced eyes and picked a route through the trees that would let the patrol watch for movement in the open area north of the narrow strip of woods and keep an eye on traffic on the river to the south. He glided soundlessly through the night even though he was in the light brush that grew everywhere under the trees except on the well-beaten paths. The noise to his rear told him the ten men of Corporal Cauldron's squad didn't have much practice at night movement. When he listened carefully he could make out two holes in the line of noisemakers behind him: a small hole was where his good friend and fellow Combined Action Platoon Marine, "Jesse James" Wells, night-walked near Cauldron; the other was a larger hole where the Popular Forces squad leader the Marines called Collard Green glided with four of his PFs.

Lewis sighed silently. There was no help for it, he'd have to move the patrol onto a path. He didn't like to go on paths at night because that's where booby traps were most likely to be laid and ambushes set. But he thought with as much noise as those grunts were making every VC in ten klicks could probably hear them and get ready to 'bush their asses. He turned and led the way to a path.

A minute later a rough hand grabbed his shoulder from behind and a voice grated in his ear, "What the fuck are you doing on this trail? Get off it and stay off it." Corporal Cauldron didn't like to go on paths for the same reasons Lewis didn't.

"I'll get off the fucking trail as soon as you and your men learn how to move quietly," he snapped in a low voice that didn't carry beyond the squad leader. "You're making so goddamn much noise back there every Vee Cee in the district can hear us. You got to move quiet on a night patrol."

Cauldron stared for a long moment at the dim blot that was all he could make out of Lewis's face in the inky darkness under the trees. Finally he said, "Don't trip any booby traps," and motioned Lewis to move out again.

Lewis grunted and turned his back on the squad leader. He cradled his M-14 in his arms and his hands went to his face and twisted. When they came away the right end of his mustache pointed straight out to the side and the left end curled aggressively upward. Gripping his rifle firmly in both hands and pointing its muzzle wherever his eyes looked, he stepped forward. Out in the open the moon and stars gave enough light for a man with good eyes to read a paperback book—but here, under the trees, the night was so black, vision was limited to mere yards. Lewis looked hard at every shadow, every dimly seen shape, but he relied more on his ears and his nose than on his eyes. And he relied on a sixth sense he had that sometimes told him someone he didn't know was there.

The path he followed was a familiar one that he had walked countless times during the day and either walked or paralleled many times at night. He knew these woods like he knew the streets and alleys of his own neighborhood in the Bronx. So he was surprised when he suddenly froze and held a hand out to the man behind him indicating no one should follow him. But he wasn't surprised that he found the ambush before it spotted him. After the ass-kicking the Marines of Tango Niner had put on the reinforced Vietcong company that had tried to overrun Camp Apache a week and a half earlier he was surprised to find anyone out here. He glanced back once to make sure his signal was being obeyed and melted into the trees.

Lewis thought himself as light as a feather, quiet as a soft breeze, and more slender than a stalk of grass. Crouched over, he silently toe-heeled through the underbrush until he came to the first man. He breathed through his open mouth while he studied the squatting form five meters away. The black-clad VC was watching the trail through a break in the trees. Lewis could barely make out a string that trailed from his hand into the trees along the path. A tug on that string would alert the rest of the ambush that someone was entering its killing zone. He moved on and counted the ambushers until he found another VC with a string in his hand, watching the trail in the other direction. Then he returned to the squad he had left behind.

Cauldron was waiting for him. He pitched his voice very low but anger came through in his words. "Where the fuck did you go?"

"Come" was all Lewis said and led the patrol leader away from the ambush. Cauldron signaled for his fire team leaders to join him and Lewis. When they were far enough away for Lewis to feel secure in talking he said in a low voice, "Charlie's got a twelve-man ambush up ahead. Let me take Jesse James and the fay epps and we'll go waste them."

"No way," Cauldron snapped. "I let you do that and I'll have two dead Marines and a seventeen-gook ambush to deal with."

"Bullshit," Lewis snapped back. "Me and Jesse James and those fay epps can waste these Charlies." He could barely see Cauldron shake his head. "Come on, Honcho, we're silent, sudden, and deadly. Let us do it."

Cauldron shook his head again. "I'm not sending two Marines out with a bunch of gooks who might turn on them as soon as the shit hits."

Lewis gnawed on his lower lip to keep from shouting at this dumbass grunt who wasn't listening to him. When he got his anger under control, he said softly, "They aren't gooks, they're fay epps—the same fay epps who've been helping us put Charlie in a hurt locker every time he's come around for the past few months."

"Where's the ambush and how's it set?" Cauldron asked. Lewis explained how the VC were set, less than ten meters deep in the woods from the trail with the first man fifteen meters from where he had stopped the patrol. "How did you know he was there if he was that far away?" Cauldron asked.

Lewis shrugged. Maybe he heard some sound, maybe he smelled a faint scent, maybe it was just a feeling of something wrong. "They're at two- or three-meter intervals," he continued. "They probably expect an eight- or ten-man patrol like we usually put out and want to hit it hard and fast and then dee dee. They're like all them dumbass Charlies, they think we can't fight at night."

Cauldron turned to one of the fire team leaders and said, "Leave Jerome with the gooks. Tell him to waste them if they try anything. The rest of the squad will get on line and we'll roll up the flank of that ambush." He reached for his radio to call in a report.

"What the fuck do you mean, waste them," Lewis stopped him. "They may be gooks, but they're our gooks."

"Only good gook's a dead gook," Cauldron snapped.

Lewis glared at the corporal's dimly seen shape. "Corporal Cauldron, I live in Bun Hou," he said slowly. "Collard Green and his fay epps are my home boys."

"Then you stay with them while some real Marines go waste that ambush. I don't want any fucking gook lover alongside me when the shooting starts. You might not pull the trigger because you're afraid you'll shoot one of your buddies and that might make me die." Cauldron pushed the speak button on the side of his PRC-6 radio and went through the I speak–you speak routine of radio communications. He didn't mention the fact that he was leaving the PFs behind under guard. The corporal gathered the men of his squad together, got them on line, and moved into the brush to hit the ambush from its side.

Jerome checked to make sure his M-14 was set on full automatic and the safety was off. He positioned himself where he could cover all five PFs, who squatted together wondering why they were being treated this way, not understanding why these Marines, unlike their friends in Tango Niner, didn't trust them. Lewis sat on the ground. He wished his good buddy Wells was with him instead of with the squad. He casually swung his rifle's muzzle around so it pointed at Jerome. The other Marine saw the movement and swallowed. They waited with the PFs looking at Lewis for guidance. He didn't move when the shooting started, so neither did they.

Cauldron saw the VC observer where Lewis had said he was a half-second before the Vietcong soldier saw him. As the small man spun toward the Marine he yanked hard on his string and tried to whip his SKS rifle around to fire. He never made it. Cauldron shot three rounds rapid fire from the hip. One round shattered the VC's shoulder and one splattered his head. The third round flew wide of its collapsing target.

"Hit the deck!" Cauldron shouted. The squad dropped to a prone position and opened fire. Confused voices came from their front, but few shots were returned—the VC were afraid of shooting each other. It was over in less than a minute. "Cease fire," the corporal called. He listened to the sound of silence from where the VC ambush had lain and the sound of fleeing bodies crashing through the trees. He rose to his knees. "Team leaders report," he shouted. "Any casualties?"

The three fire team leaders checked their men and reported everyone was all right.

"Second and third teams, stand by to move," Cauldron said to his men. "First team, when I get the rest of the squad in position to cover you, check that ambush site for bodies, weapons, and prisoners." He stood up. "Second and third teams, let's go." Cauldron quickly positioned his men to the rear of where the VC ambushers had waited. "First team, move," he shouted.

The Marines of Cauldron's first fire team didn't try to be quiet sweeping through the ambush site. They talked and shouted to each other, making sure they all knew where each of the others was, and letting the rest of the squad know as well.

"Here's one," someone shouted. The position of the voice changed slightly as the Marine dropped to a knee to examine the body he found. "He's dead. Shit, his chest is so fucked up it looks like Jimbo's blooker made a direct hit on his ass." He made grunting noises for a few seconds while he patted the ground around the body, then he said, "I found his weapon."

"Check his pockets for documents and grab his pack," Cauldron ordered.

"No pack," the still unidentified voice called back. "And he must be wearing his mama-san's clothes because he doesn't have any pockets, either."

The only other thing the searching Marines found was a wet spot on the ground. A Marine felt the wet dirt, then touched his fingers to the tip of his tongue. "Blood," he said. "We got at least three of them." He patted the ground some more to see how large the spot was. "He lost this much blood, if he ain't already dead he's going to die soon."

After radioing in his report Cauldron got the squad together and led it back to where Lewis and Jerome maintained an uneasy truce over the PFs. "We got three of them," he told the CAP Marine. "Think they might have been buddies of any of your gooks?"

Lewis glared at the NCO, biting off his reply. Instead of saying, "Fuck you, Cauldron," he said, "These fay epps don't have buddies in the Vee Cee."

Cauldron snorted. "Let's move it out," he said. "We're setting our own ambush."

The patrol moved a hundred and fifty meters farther down the trail and set in an L-shaped ambush on the river side of a bend in it. Cauldron assigned two Marines to watch the trail in each direction, three to watch the water, three to keep an eye on the forest opposite them and two to cover the PFs. Three hours later they pulled out and returned to the hill where the compound the Marines of Combined Action Platoon Tango Niner called Camp Apache was located. Cauldron and his squad stopped at their platoon's area, slightly southeast of the hill. Lewis, Wells, and the PFs continued up the hill and entered the compound through the narrow openings that were staggered through the three banks of concertina wire that surrounded it.

CHAPTER TWO

Early morning, November 7, 1966

Lewis stomped into the squad tent that was erected between the two new bunkers that had been built as living quarters for CAP Tango Niner's rifle squad. He found his cot in the darkness and plopped his rifle onto it. He wrenched off his cartridge belt, threw it onto the boards of the wood pallet floor, and noisily kicked it under his cot. "Goddamn mutha-fucking cock-sucking asshole grunt," he swore.

Across the narrow aisle through the middle of the tent, Wells was making the same noises. "Fuckfaced prickhead had best get his shit straightened out before somebody stuffs his balls down his throat," he swore. PFC George E. Wells was an eighteen-year-old from the corn country of Indiana, where he was always getting into trouble with the sheriff's office. He thought of himself as an outlaw and wanted everyone to call him "Jesse James." Lance Corporal Billy Harold Lewis, better known as "Billy Boy," was nineteen years old and claimed to have learned night movement and escape and evasion tactics while running white lightning for moonshiners, and he sometimes affected a Southern accent. Almost nobody believed Lewis's tales of running 'shine because he also admitted he had never left his native Bronx before enlisting in the Marine Corps. Lewis was Wells's hero and he aped everything the older Marine did. Lewis was also the only one of the Marines who called Wells Jesse James.

"You two shut the fuck up," a sleep-sodden voice said in the darkness. "Some people are trying to cop some Zs in here."

"Hey, Short Round," Lewis said, excited, to the voice, "wake up, old buddy. We got to talk, you and me." He rushed to the cot of Lance Corporal John Hempen and shook his shoulder. "C'mon, Short Round, get up. We got us a problem."

"Charlie coming through the wire?"

"No!" Lewis snapped, impatient.

"It can wait until I wake up."

"Bullshit. You're awake now. Get up." Lewis shook Hempen's shoulder again.

"I am not awake, you dipshit. And you aren't going to be awake anymore, either, you don't stop shaking me."

"C'mon Short Round," Lewis said, shaking Hempen again, "drop your cock and grab your socks. We're taking too much shit from the grunts and we gotta straighten it out—now."

"No shit, Sherlock," Hempen murmured. "'Bout fucking time you noticed. It can wait until I wake up. Dee dee." He flopped onto his side facing away from Lewis and faked a snore.

Lewis rocked back on his heels, momentarily at a loss for words. His hands went to his face and twisted. When they came away the right end of his mustache jutted toward his left eye and the left end curved out and up like the horn of a Spanish bull looking for a toreador to gore. "Fuck you, Short Round," he muttered. "I'll grab some sleep and then go straighten out the grunts by my own self." He went back to his cot, stripped down, and pulled on clean skivvy drawers. Then he made sure his rifle and cartridge belt were exactly where his hands would fall on them if he suddenly woke and had to come up fighting. Mumbling to himself about Hempen's lack of cooperation, Lewis lay down and fell asleep.

"REVEILLE, REVEILLE, REVEILLE," the voice shouted inches from Lewis's ear. The wiry lance corporal with the mismatched handlebar mustache instantly rolled from his cot to the tent floor. His right hand landed on the forestock of his M-14 and his left grabbed his cartridge belt. He rolled over once, looping the belt around his neck and one shoulder as he rolled, and came up with his rifle in both hands ready for action—he had a round already in the chamber. His head spun around as he looked and listened for where the trouble was. The squad tent filled with laughter.

Hempen squatted on the far side of Lewis's cot with a broad grin on his face. Wells, Lance Corporal Tim Webster, and PFCs John Robertson and Willie Pennell were at what they hoped were safe distances from Lewis. They were all laughing at him. These six junior men were all that remained of Tango Niner's rifle squad after the reinforced Vietcong company tried to overrun Camp Apache and the squad's NCOs were placed under house arrest for suspicion of heroin smuggling.

"What the fuck?" Lewis demanded and shook his head in confusion.

"Drop your cock and grab your socks, Billy Boy," Hempen chortled. "We're taking too much shit from those grunts and we gotta straighten it out—now."

Lewis looked at Hempen and screwed up his face. "What do you mean," he demanded. "Last night you didn't want to."

Hempen shook his head. "I didn't want to do it last night," he said. "Last night wasn't the time to do anything. Today is. Come on, get dressed and grab some chow. I went to the Top and requested mast. You and me're seeing Captain Ronson in half an hour."

"You're crazy, Short Round, you know that? You're fucking dinky dau."

Hempen grinned. "No I'm not," he said, "I just got my shit together better than you, that's all. Get dressed and chow down so we can go see the Skipper."

Lewis slowly rose to his feet, trying not to look foolish. He brushed himself off and dressed in his least dirty utility uniform. He dropped the front of the ammo crate on legs he used as a table and pulled out his field stove and a box of C rations. Then he took his canteen cup from the nail it hung from on the side of the table. A few minutes later he was outside the tent sitting with Hempen and Webster on stools made from more discarded ammo crates.

Camp Apache had originally been built with everything except the ammo bunkers and perimeter fighting holes above ground. A week and a half earlier, a reinforced Vietcong company had tried to overrun it. The day before that night assault the Marines and PFs of Tango Niner, along with civilians they hired, had started to dig bunkers and trenches. Nearly everything aboveground when the VC hit was destroyed or damaged, and the partially completed defensive works had saved the Combined Action Platoon from worse casualties than it suffered. Now all three squad tents, the fifty-five-gallon drum shower, the wall-less outhouse, and the mess table the daily hot meal was served from had been replaced. Nearly all of the new bunkers were finished and a new fighting trench circled the perimeter, and connecting trenches were being dug between the bunkers and trenches. The Marines weren't content with just improving the defensive positions of Camp Apache— they decided that since they had to work on their compound anyway, they might as well make it a more pleasant place to live. One of the improvements was tables and chairs in the open. The chairs were low stools made from ammo crates and the tables were galvanized metal sheets supported on sandbags.

Lewis put his field stove—it was a C-ration can with

three triangular holes cut on the bottom of its sides and its top bent so it didn't form a perfect circle—on the table, lit a heat tab in it, and put his canteen cup half full of water on it to boil. While the water was heating he looked to see which meal he had drawn. Spaghetti and Meatballs. Not the best C-ration meal, but one of the better ones. It would fill him.

"How come you didn't want to help last night but you do today?" Lewis asked Hempen.

"The way we have to do this is go to Captain Ronson and tell him the kind of shit that's coming down," Hempen replied. "We have to go to the Top first if we want to see the Skipper. Last night the Top was sleeping and he would have been boo-coo pissed off if we woke him up." His coffee water was already boiling and he removed it from his field stove to add powdered coffee, creamer, and sugar to it, then put a partly open can on the stove to heat up. His meal was Beans and Franks.

Webster had gotten the short end of the stick. He was stuck with Ham and Limas, the most universally despised meal in the military cuisine. Nobody ever ate Ham and Limas if there was something else available.

Lewis stirred cocoa into his now hot water and put his Spaghetti and Meatballs on the stove to heat. He shook his head. "You sure gave me a hard time last night, Short Round," he said.

"Not as hard as the Top gave me this morning," Hempen said. "He didn't want to let us see Captain Ronson unless I told him what it was about." Every enlisted Marine has the right to "request mast," to meet with his commanding officer to discuss a grievance. He cannot be refused this right, though he must take it up the chain of command starting with his company commander and each level of command will try to talk him out of going to the next higher level. And at no level below the commander he wants to talk to must he divulge what he wants to talk about, although pressure may be brought to make him tell.

"Did you tell him?" Lewis asked.

Hempen shook his head. "Wouldn't do any good," he said.

"What are you going to do if the Skipper likes things the way they are?" Webster asked.

"Go to the lieutenant colonel," Lewis answered.

"Or Captain Hasford," Hempen added.

"Hasford's okay," Lewis said, "but he's a staff officer; he's not in our chain of command."

"But he believes in what we're doing. He'll help."

"And he doesn't believe Jay Cee and the others were smuggling heroin, either," Webster said.

"Maybe," Lewis agreed, "but the first thing we got to do is see Captain Ronson. Then we take care of that heroin shit." He swirled the remaining cocoa in his canteen cup and drank it down. "Time to go yet?"

Hempen glanced at his wristwatch. "Yup," he said. "Let's go. I want my honcho back, I need somebody I can hide behind." Short Round Hempen topped the scales at five foot four and was the shortest Marine in CAP Tango Niner. Corporal "Stilts" Zeitvogel, at six foot five, was his fire team leader and the tallest man in the CAP. "You come too, Malahini," he added to Webster.

Lewis twisted the ends of his mustache. When he took his hands away from it the right end drooped down Fu Manchu style and the left tapered to a sharp point out to the side.

The three lance corporals rinsed their canteen cups out with a small amount of water, wiped them dry, and cleaned their mess forks with a piece of clean cloth. After ducking into the squad tent to drop their mess gear on their cots they twisted their way through the offset openings in the south face of the three banks of concertina wire surrounding the Marine compound on top of the hill. They wore camouflage bush hats and carried their M-14s in their hands. Their cartridge belts and other gear were left behind in the tent, though each of them carried a K-bar knife hanging from his belt and had an extra twenty-round magazine in a hip pocket or inside his shirt. Only Webster had taken the time to shave. The grunt company's command-post tent was seventy-five meters from where the path down the side of the hill reached the floodplain. They headed toward it.

"Just a minute there," a big voice boomed at them as they started to enter the CP tent. They turned to the voice. It belonged to the first sergeant, a huge bear of a man whose size fit his voice. "So you're all here to waste Captain Ronson's time, are you." He strode to the three CAP Marines and glowered down at them from his commanding height. "You fuckfaces got a problem? What makes you think I'm going to let you in to see the Skipper if you haven't shaved?"

"I shaved, Top," Webster said.

"I wasn't talking to you, dipshit," the first sergeant snapped at him. "I'm talking to these two fuckfaces that didn't bother to shave like it's Saturday morning back in The World and they're a couple of sloppy civilians. Well?" He waited for an answer.

"We're in the field, Top," Hempen said, "we shave every other day. Today isn't shaving day."

"Is that a fact, short round," the first sergeant said. He didn't know Hempen's nickname was Short Round, but automatically called him that because of his height. "Well, I'm just as deep in the field as you are and I shave every day." That was true. He had a very heavy beard and in garrison he shaved twice a day. In the field he only shaved once a day, but set his Gillette Adjustable to shave so closely that he scraped his face raw each morning. Every day his face went from pink and raw-looking in the morning to a heavy five o'clock shadow by sunset. He changed blades every other day. "If I can shave every day, so can you."

"No can do, Top," Lewis said, "we've got to conserve water."

The first sergeant's eyes bugged. "What do you mean 'conserve water,'" he bellowed. "You go down to that goddamn river there and you've got more running water than you'll need in a lifetime."

Lewis shook his head and said, "Can't use river water, Top. There's too many fish pissing in it, it's not clean."

Hempen and Webster flinched. They knew Lewis didn't like first sergeants and was seeing how far he could bait this one without getting into too much trouble. From the expression on the first sergeant's face, Hempen thought Lewis had just gone too far.

"Top," Hempen said before the first sergeant could say anything, "what Lance Corporal Lewis means is people upstream use the river for a head and the water is too polluted by the time it gets here." Hempen knew that wasn't true, he knew there were no hamlets between this part of the river and the mountain lake it flowed from. He hoped the first sergeant didn't know that.

The first sergeant seemed to mull over what Hempen said. Then instead of lighting into Lewis for it, he snarled at all three of them, "You will shave, every day, starting today. The next man I see from that CAP unit who hasn't shaved, his ass is mine. Now..."

"Top," a company clerk interrupted. He was standing in the entrance to the CP tent. "The captain says he's ready to see them."

The first sergeant's jaw worked while he stared at the clerk for a moment. He had wanted to send Lewis and Hempen back to their hill to shave before they saw the company commander, but Captain Ronson wanted them now. He turned back to the three and said in a lower voice, "In one hour I'm coming up on that hill for a face inspection. Any swinging dick I find who isn't clean-shaven is in a world of shit with me. Do you understand me?"

"Yes we do, Top," they told him.

"Now get in there," he said and jerked his head toward the tent.

CHAPTER THREE

Request mast

They stepped into the small cubicle within the tent that was Captain Ronson's office and stood at attention. "Lance Corporal Lewis reporting, sir," Lewis said. Hempen and Webster announced themselves the same way. The company first sergeant followed and stood behind them.

Captain Ronson sat erect at his tiny field desk. His chair was turned to face his visitors directly. His face was set in stone when he looked at them. He stared at them until they began to make small, uncomfortable movements. "At ease," he finally said in a cold voice, and continued to stare at them while they shifted to parade rest. "Do Lieutenant Burrison and Sergeant Bell know you've requested mast with me?"

"Nossir," Lewis answered. He had appointed himself spokesman. Hempen shot a glance at Lewis. After the

34

cracks Billy Boy had made to the first sergeant, he wasn't sure he wanted him talking to the captain.

"Then you're going over their heads, jumping the chain of command."

"Nossir," Lewis said. "Our leaders were all relieved of duty. We report to your Top now. We, that is, Lance Corporal Hempen, went to him to request mast." Hempen relaxed slightly—Lewis didn't sound like he was going to get out of line with Ronson.

Ronson looked at Hempen. "Did you discuss your problem with the first sergeant and try to get it resolved with him before coming to me?" he asked and looked over Hempen's shoulder at the senior NCO.

"Nossir."

"Then you decided to waste my time with something that you might have been able to resolve with the first sergeant?"

Hempen swallowed and felt himself starting to sweat. This meeting wasn't going the way he thought it would, Ronson didn't sound at all inclined to give them a fair hearing. He opened his mouth to speak but Lewis was already talking.

"Nossir, we don't want to waste your time," Lewis said, "but I think maybe we're wasting ours."

"You watch how you're talking to an officer," the first sergeant barked and stepped toward Lewis.

Ronson held up a hand to stop him. "How are you wasting your time?" he asked.

"We've got a serious problem that needs to be taken care of, and if you won't listen to us somebody's going to get hurt," Lewis said. "If you won't help us we should be going to someone else to stop it."

Ronson leaned back in his chair. "All right, what is this mysterious problem?"

"It's those damn fucking grunts of yours, sir."

Ronson raised his eyebrows and did nothing to stop his top sergeant from clamping a huge hand on Lewis's thin shoulder. "What about those damn grunts of mine?"

"Sir, let me explain," Hempen blurted before Lewis could make the situation any worse.

"Go, Lance Corporal," Ronson said. "Let me hear what you can say that's better than what your buddy already did." He sounded as if anger seethed just below the surface after Lewis had spoken.

Hempen took a deep breath before starting. "Sir, your men don't know our fay epps, they don't trust them on patrols. They don't want them out there and it shows. The fay epps don't know what's wrong, but they're getting to a point where they don't want to go out with your men. They're afraid of them."

The captain cocked an eyebrow. "Why do the PFs think my people don't trust them?"

"Because your men call them gooks and bunch them together in the middle of a patrol formation instead of treating them like patrol members like we do." He hesitated before going on, "Last night Lance Corporal Lewis was on the point and discovered a Vee Cee ambush. The patrol leader left the fay epps behind under guard while he took his squad to flank the ambush."

Ronson turned to Lewis and asked, "Is that true?"

"Yessir," Lewis said hotly. "That damn grunt . . ." What he was going to say was cut off by the first sergeant's hand squeezing hard on his shoulder.

"You were with Corporal Cauldron, weren't you?"

"Yessir."

"Cauldron's a good Marine, and a good squad leader, he's won a Bronze Star. Did he say why he left the PFs behind?"

"He said he was afraid the fay epps would turn on his Marines when the shooting started."

Ronson looked at his first sergeant. "Is that true, Top?" he asked.

"I don't know what happened last night, sir, but, yes, it's true our men don't trust the PFs."

"Why not?"

"They've seen too many civilians helping Charlie—hiding him, supplying him," the first sergeant said. He shrugged. "So far every Vietnamese they've seen except for the Arvins have been Vee Cee. And they just came off a tough operation where they lost too many buddies. Too many of them think the only good gook's a dead gook."

Ronson looked back at the CAP Marines and said, "So you think one of my Marines might hurt one of your PFs." He thought, but didn't say, Or one of your PFs might hurt one of my people.

"Yessir," Hempen said, "if your people don't change their attitude that's what I think is going to happen." He thought, but didn't say, Or one of us might waste one of your damn grunts.

Ronson's eyes unfocused for a moment while he thought about what he had just been told. If the situation was as strained as they said, it was very bad and would have to be straightened out in a hurry. His company would be leaving Bun Hou soon and these Marines, or some other Marines, would probably stay to work with the Popular Forces in the Combined Action Platoon. Antagonisms between the men of his company and the indigenous forces could endanger the Americans left behind when they moved out. When he spoke, authority and command were clear in his voice. "What do you suggest I do about it?"

"Sir, I think we should stop sending us and the fay epps with your men for a while," Hempen said. "I think you should use your men for ambushes and send us and the fay epps out on roving patrols. That way we do what we do best and your men don't have to go where they don't know the area. If Charlie's out there we'll catch him or he'll walk into your ambushes."

"We know this area, Captain," Lewis cut in, "we know where we've caught Charlie, where he's likely to go. Let us pick the ambush sites and our own patrol route."

"I haven't said I was going to do what Hempen suggested," Ronson said.

"Sir," Webster spoke up for the first time, "if we do what Lance Corporal Hempen said, that'll show your grunts that our fay epps are good fighters and can be trusted on patrol with Marines."

Ronson thought for a few seconds, then said, "I'll consider what you've said and make a decision later. You're
dismissed." He turned to his desk, picked up a piece of
paper, and looked like he was reading it. But he didn't read
it, he was thinking. In a few minutes he'd have the first
sergeant get Corporal Cauldron and his platoon leader in
here. If Cauldron verified what Lewis and Hempen said
about the previous night he'd talk with more of the squad
leaders. If they were making the PFs feel untrusted he'd
have to take action. He wouldn't let the CAP Marines draw
the patrol routes for his company, but maybe Hempen was
right about not sending out joint patrols for a while.

The CAP Marines hesitated for a moment, then came to
attention and said, "Thank you, sir." The first sergeant followed them out of the CP tent.

"Forty-five minutes," the Top said, looking at his
watch, "and I'll be on your hill for a face inspection. Remember what I said before." He stood and watched them
walk back to Camp Apache.

First Sergeant Graves had been in the Marine Corps for
more than twenty years. He was holding on hoping to
make sergeant major before he retired. He also liked the
idea of getting more campaign ribbons to wear along with
the three he had from World War II, two from the Korean
conflict, and two other expeditionary medals he had for
service in Lebanon and the Dominican Republic. But campaign medals and the Good Conduct Medal weren't all he
had been awarded. He was a big man, over six feet tall and
two hundred and forty pounds of muscle. He looked the
hard-assed combat Marine.

As a private on Guadalcanal he had charged up Carl-
son's Ridge with a machine gun to help beat off a banzai
charge—the fifty bodies piled up in front of his position
when the battle was over were enough to win him a Bronze
Star. On Peleliu he got his first Purple Heart. He was a
sergeant on Okinawa and found himself commanding his
company after all of its officers and senior NCOs were
killed or too badly wounded to keep fighting—they gave
him the Navy Commendation Medal for the way he led his

understrength company along the narrow-gauge railroad
between Half Moon and Sugar Loaf hills, distracting the
defenders enough for other companies to take those objec-
tives; he won a Silver Star for single-handedly taking out
three bunkers that had his company pinned down on Kuni-
shi Ridge. The Korean government awarded him, along
with the rest of the First Marine Division, its Presidential
Unit Citation for heroics during the division's withdrawal
from the Chosen Reservoir. The company of which he was
then the gunnery sergeant was awarded both the Presidential Unit Citation and a Meritorious Unit Citation, and a
potato masher grenade thrown by a Chinese soldier gave
him his second Purple Heart. There was no doubting his
valor, his bravery under fire in two wars.

But the twelve years of garrison duty, twelve years of
sitting at desks and paying attention to spit, polish, and
inspections rather than to tactics and maneuvers since he
had last fired a shot in anger had made changes in First
Sergeant Graves. He had added ten pounds of fat to his
frame and fifteen pounds of muscle had given way to fifteen more pounds of fat. He had forgotten what it was like
to shoot at living targets and have them shooting back at
him. Garrison details were important to him now, they
were the things that made a man a Marine. What men
needed to do to keep their morale up while trying to stay
alive in combat had taken a backseat.

"Asshole," Hempen muttered when they were far
enough away so that the first sergeant couldn't hear him.

"Which one?" Lewis asked.

"You, Shit-for-Brains," Webster said. "First you mouth
off to the Top and make him pull some mickey mouse shit
on us, then you swear at Captain Ronson about his damn
fucking grunts. If Short Round didn't take over you might
have got us all thrown in the fucking brig." The three were
walking side by side with Webster in the middle. He spat to
the side—Lewis's side. "Shit-for-Brains. Now I understand why Tex didn't want you and Wells in his fire team
and why Short Round wouldn't do anything last night.
You'd fuck up a wet dream."

"I didn't do nothing," Lewis said, suddenly defensive. "We don't have enough water to shave every day and I'll be damned if I'm going to use that river water..."

"Fucking river comes straight down from the mountains," Hempen interrupted him. "I bet we could follow it all the way to the top and not find anybody living along it. That river's cleaner than the well water we use to shower with."

"And those damn fucking grunts are why we had to go see Captain Ronson," Lewis said, ignoring Hempen's interruption. "I didn't do nothing."

Hempen reached behind Webster and cuffed the back of Lewis's head. "You hear that, Malahini," he said. "You're right, there is shit sloshing around inside his gourd. Listen." He cuffed Lewis's head again.

"Hey, cut that out," Lewis said and rubbed the back of his head.

"Did you hear that?" Hempen asked.

"Yah, I heard it," Webster said, "shit sloshing around." He waited for Lewis to move his hand from his head and cuffed him again. He and Hempen nodded sagely to each other. "Shit-for-Brains," they agreed. Lewis dropped back so they couldn't hit him again. He glowered at their backs.

"What do you think he's going to do?" Webster asked.

"I think that prickhead is going to inspect us for shaves, just like he said," Hempen answered.

"I didn't mean the prickhead, I meant the Skipper."

"I don't know. Jay Cee and Stilts said they thought he was okay. Maybe he'll tune his troops up." They were at the foot of the hill and didn't say anything more until they were halfway up it. "Well," Hempen said slowly, "let's go tell Jay Cee about the shaving inspection." Suddenly he staggered forward. So did Webster.

"That's what I thought," Lewis said. "Both of your heads are full of shit." He had gotten close to them, slung his rifle over one shoulder, and smacked them both on the back of the head. "You forgot we have to tell Jay Cee and Scrappy about our request mast."

Two minutes later they were in the command hootch

tent. The tent was divided into three parts: one end was the radioroom, with the radios used for communicating with the patrols and higher headquarters; the other end was a combination storage room and living space for the two Navy Medical Corpsmen serving with the platoon; in between was a room shared by Second Lieutenant "Scrappy" Burrison, the platoon leader, and Sergeant J. C. Bell, who was both the squad leader of the rifle squad and the platoon sergeant.

"Can't go the fuck in there," PFC "Swearin'" Swarnes, the platoon's radioman, told them. Swarnes earned his nickname the old-fashioned way, he earned it by being the most foul-mouthed man in the platoon. A cot opposite the bench the radios sat on was his sleeping area.

"Bullshit, we can't go in," Lewis said. "Why the fuck not?" Lewis was the platoon's general-purpose goofball and always tried to outdo everyone else.

"Lieutenant Houng's telling Scrappy and Jay Cee what he found out about that goddamn Phang and the fucking reparation money he's collected. Scrappy told me to tell any motherfucker who wants to see him to go fuck themselves until he's through."

Hempen looked at his watch and jittered. "Shit, we only got forty minutes," he said. "Come on, let's go tell everybody about the Top."

"Whoa, wait one, Short Round," Swarnes said. "You go running around too much people're going to think you're a shit beetle and stomp on your young ass. What about the Top?"

Hempen and Webster looked at each other with the same idea occurring to each of them—telling Swearin' Swarnes about the face inspection would get the word around faster than trying to tell everybody themselves.

"That prickhead first sergeant thinks we're in garrison or something," Lewis said before Hempen could. "He's coming up here to inspect our shaves."

Swarnes looked blankly at Lewis for a long moment before saying, "You're shitting me, aren't you, Billy Boy.

Ain't no dumbass first sergeant fucked up in the head bad enough to think men in the field gotta shave every day."

"Swearin' Swarnes, Billy Boy wouldn't shit you, you're his favorite turd," Hempen said. "That dumbass first sergeant down there does think we should shave every day and he's coming up here to inspect our faces."

"He says anyone who isn't clean-shaven when he comes up here, well, that man's ass is his," Webster added.

Swarnes's face wore an expression of disbelief at this improbable news, but his eyes were concerned as their gaze flicked between Hempen and Lewis. "The man's fucking dinky dau," he finally said. "You two scuzz balls had best get your faces shaved." First sergeants were the only men in the Marine Corps who scared Swarnes, and the news of the coming face inspection shook him up badly enough he forgot to swear as much as he normally would. He rubbed his own chin while he watched Hempen and Lewis leave and decided that, to be on the safe side, he should shave again himself, even though he only needed to shave two or three times a week and had already shaved this morning. He suddenly noticed Webster still standing there and demanded, "What the fuck are you gawking at? You better go shave before your scuzzy ass belongs to the Top." He rooted in a box under his cot for his razor, soap, and canteen cup. No one saw Swarnes leave his radioroom or talk to anyone else, but fifteen minutes later every Marine in CAP Tango Niner except Lieutenant Burrison and Sergeant Bell was shaving.

CHAPTER FOUR

Background

The twenty-five Marines and two Navy corpsmen of the Combined Action Platoon designated CAP T-9 had been assigned to Bun Hou village in June 1966, five months earlier. Their compound, named Camp Apache because it was deeper in Indian Country than any other Marine camp, sat on top of a low, flat-topped hill west of Hou Dau, the principal hamlet of the six hamlets that made up the village of Bun Hou. To its west was Hou Ky, the westernmost hamlet of this farming village. South of Camp Apache's hill ran the Song Du Ong River. In June Bun Hou had been controlled by a Vietcong company that had been there for a long time and had grown complacent. The Marines had the job of destroying that VC company and returning control of the village to its people. Also, in June, Sergeant Phao Houng of the Army of the Republic of Vietnam, a native of Bun Hou who had been decorated many times for valor in

combat and who was proud of having killed many Viet-
cong and North Vietnamese soldiers, was released from the
ARVN, given a lieutenant's commission in the Popular
Forces, and assigned to his home village to raise and lead a
PF platoon. The Marines knew they had a tough job; they
thought Lieutenant Houng had an impossible one.

The Marines' job wasn't as difficult as they had thought
it would be because the local VC weren't prepared to take
on and beat men as well-armed and -trained as they were.
They quickly broke the back of the VC company in Bun
Hou. The Vietcong then sent in a second company to do
what the first company hadn't been able to do. Unfortu-
nately for those VC, not only were the Marines better
armed, better trained, and better fighters than they were,
but by now the Marines knew the area of Bun Hou village.
The new VC didn't.

The second company failed more quickly than the first
one had. The success of the Marines in fighting the VC
showed the villagers the insurgents could be beaten, and
Lieutenant Houng quickly got his Popular Forces platoon
organized. But a major infiltration and supply trail followed the Song Du Ong floodplain and the Communists
weren't going to give up it up. The Marines and PFs of
Tango Niner successfully ambushed supply runs and infiltration groups several times a week until the Communist
cadre felt they were in danger of losing their hold over the
people of Bun Hou. So a specially trained platoon of North
Vietnamese Army soldiers was sent south to wipe out CAP
Tango Niner. In ones and twos and small groups, the NVA
managed to kill a dozen members of Tango Niner before
the Marines found their hidden base camp and wiped them
out, with only Major Nghu, the NVA commander, escaping
with his life. Tired of losing every time they tried to wipe
out the small patrols the Marines and their PFs sent out
every night, the VC tried a different tactic—they sent a
reinforced main force company to overrun Camp Apache.
The Marines were ready for the attack when it came. The
Americans and Vietnamese of Tango Niner just about
wiped out the reinforced company. They were now repair-

ing, rebuilding, and reinforcing Camp Apache following that assault.

But the Vietcong and NVA weren't the only foes the Marines had to concern themselves with. The assistant district chief was an ARVN officer, Captain Phang. When the Marines, and then the PFs, started killing Vietcong and NVA soldiers, Phang tried to collect indemnities from the Americans. He claimed the dead enemy soldiers were innocent farmers, woodsmen, and fishermen. The Marines refused to ante up and eventually, worried about exposure that would cost him his other lucrative scams, Phang disappeared from Bun Hou. Three days before the assault on Camp Apache, the Marines discovered that Phang was filing and collecting on fraudulent claims. These claims said the Marines of Tango Niner were killing people and livestock and destroying property in villages other than Bun Hou, villages none of them had ever heard of. They got names of people who Phang claimed to be collecting for and decided to get the hard evidence they needed to convict Phang of corruption and remove him from office—Lieutenant Houng and his squad leaders were going around the district talking with the people named in Phang's claims. Phang learned the Marines were on to him and decided to rid his district of these meddlers before they could catch him.

The Marine infantry company, commanded by Captain Ronson, that had been brought in to help mop up any VC remaining from the assault and to help in the rebuilding was assigned to remain in Bun Hou indefinitely.

This is why Lewis, Hempen, Webster, and the others were patrolling with their PFs and infantry squads. And it's why they went to Captain Ronson with their problem without talking to their own leaders first. And why Burrison didn't want his meeting with Houng and Bell interrupted.

CHAPTER FIVE

IN-spection, FACES!

"What's going on over there?" Lieutenant Burrison asked. His meeting had finally broken up and he stepped outside the command hootch with Sergeant Bell and Lieutenant Houng. Thirty meters away the fifteen Marines and two corpsmen of CAP Tango Niner were lined up in two rows facing First Sergeant Graves, who was walking through their ranks closely peering at their faces. Everyone was there except Swarnes, who was with his radios.

"Face inspection, sir," the radioman said. "The Top wants everyone in Tango Niner to shave every day and he's out to get anybody who doesn't."

Burrison looked at Bell's lightly stubbled jaw and rubbed his own. They were both in the habit of shaving every other day just like their men. "I think I'm going to put a stop to that," he said. "He has no right to issue orders and inspect my men without going through me first."

"Scrappy," Bell said slowly, "I don't believe you should. Not until after he's finished." He shook his head. "That first sergeant looks like the type who likes to have second lieutenants for breakfast." He paused and eyed Graves for a moment longer, then added, "And uses three-stripe sergeants for toothpicks."

Lieutenant Houng observed them with amusement. As a married man with children, he had a mustache. Shaving his chin once a week until he became head of his family would clean his face of the few whiskers that grew there. He had never seen a westerner with a beard, but the amount of hair his Marine friends could grow on their faces in two days amazed him. And it was not only on their upper lips and chins where it belonged, it grew all over the sides of their faces and their cheeks and necks. An American with a full beard must look very formidable indeed.

Burrison reconsidered and decided to wait until after the first sergeant's inspection before confronting the man. "Swarnes," he said, "when the Top is through over there tell him I want to see him in my quarters."

Swarnes swallowed. "Aye-aye, sir," he said reluctantly. He had hoped to avoid contact with the first sergeant. Even though he had shaved twice in the past half hour he was afraid he might have missed a spot and didn't want it to be caught.

"Me go now," Houng said. There was nothing more he could do here now and he wanted to think more about what he had told Burrison and Bell and the ideas they had about it, and the new searching he and his squad leaders must now do. He turned and headed toward the main gate of Camp Apache before he could be invited to stay to join them at noon chow. It was good to sometimes eat their food with his American friends, and their C rations had been novel at first. But he had eaten too many C-ration meals in the past week or so and they were far too bland to eat as a steady diet, and sometimes caused constipation. He walked through the truck-sized opening in the wire, past the crudely hand-lettered sign that read

CAMP APACHE
USMC
Home of Combined Action Platoon T-9
It Takes Two to Tango
Charlie Gonna Die Here
Barry Sadler, Eat your Heart Out

—turned left, and headed for his home in Hou Ky hamlet, where his wife, Cao Lin, would soon feed him rice with nuoc mam sauce.

Burrison and Bell gazed after Houng's receding form but didn't really see him leave. They were thinking of his report.

A few days before the Vietcong had attempted to overrun Camp Apache, Burrison had gone to Da Nang with Corporal Tex Randall to see what information they could get on the death of Vien Phoung, an elder from Anh Dien hamlet who had come to Camp Apache looking for some medical assistance for his hamlet, which was a few miles east and north of Bun Hou. According to Captain Phang, the old man had been killed by Marine Harassment and Interdiction fire. The Marines and PFs of Tango Niner didn't believe Phang—they hadn't heard any artillery explosions near Anh Dien on the night Vien Phoung died.

On their arrival at Da Nang, Burrison and Randall discovered that Tango Niner had a reputation. Phang had been submitting at least one indemnity claim a week for some time, claims for things he said the Tango Niner Marines did. Bobbie Harder, a civilian clerk working for the Department of Defense and assigned to the Marine records unit, went over the records with Randall. All of the claims were for incidents in villages the Marines of Tango Niner had never visited. Randall and Bobbie quickly became attracted to each other and Burrison let the corporal stay at Da Nang for another day after he left himself. Bobbie surreptitiously made a list of a dozen incidents, giving date, time, location, type of incident, and recipient of the indemnity money and gave the list to Randall. Houng and his three squad leaders knew at least one person in nearly every hamlet of each village on the list. They had spent as much time as possible since getting the list visiting those people, trying to find out whether or not the claimed incidents had actually happened and if the named people had been paid the money collected by Phang.

Everyone the PF leaders knew had now been visited. Every report had been exactly the same:

"Him say samee-same—no talk, no talk. Them say all samee-same—no talk, no talk. Me think them afraid they talk Phang come bang-bang them."

Except for one. Yesterday afternoon the PF squad leader the Marines called Collard Green visited the last person on his list, a middle-aged woman to whom he was distantly related by marriage through his mother-in-law. At first she didn't want to talk about the incident he was interested in, but eventually—because Collard Green was, after all, a relative and a man she knew to be honest—she let loose in a torrent of anger all the impotent rage she had been holding in for weeks.

A friend of hers, a woman who had been a childhood playmate, grew weary of paying taxes to both the Saigon government and the Vietcong. These taxes, coupled with the illegally high rents being assessed by their absentee landlord, left her family with too little after their labors. They were hardworking farmers tilling rich lands and bringing in large crops. But the taxes and extortion paid to feed the greed of others kept them poor. So one day she stood in the hamlet square and denounced at length the Saigon government, the Vietcong, and the landlord. She concluded her denunciation with a declaration that in the future she would only pay taxes to one government and would only pay the landlord the legal rent. Since the Saigon government was the legal government and the Vietcong were insurgents, the taxes she would pay would be to the Saigon government. Two days later three strangers wearing the conical straw hats and black pajamas of peasants, but wearing red armbands and carrying AK-47 rifles, walked up to her where she was weeding a bean patch with other members of her family and shot her to death. The three strangers then went to her oldest son and their leader told him, "You will pay taxes to us."

A few days later this distant relative by marriage of Collard Green's mother-in-law was passing by a house in her village that was owned by Captain Phang and overheard him boast to another ARVN captain how he was collecting indemnities from the Americans. He had told the Americans that this woman, killed by the VC for refusing to pay taxes to them, had been killed by American Marines. Phang bragged he was giving one-fifth of the money he received from the Americans to the family and keeping the rest for himself. Discreet questioning by Collard Green's relative disclosed that the dead woman's family had been paid, by Phang, one-fifth of the normal indemnity amount for accidental death. Then she, being the good Catholic she was, had gone to the main church in the district town and asked the priest for assistance. He had refused, he told her what she was saying couldn't be true because he knew Phang was an honorable man—and a good Catholic besides.

Collard Green had listened to this tale patiently and with great interest. When it was over he asked his distant relative if she would be willing to testify against Phang in court. She told him don't be dinky dau, she wasn't crazy enough to do something like that. Phang would surely have her killed, and probably other members of her family as well, if she did any such thing. Collard Green understood. He thanked her ten thousand times and returned to Hou Ky, where he passed his information on to Lieutenant Houng. By then it was too late in the day for Houng to go to Camp Apache; this news would have to wait until morning.

"We've got one we can burn Phang with now, Jay Cee," Burrison said when Houng had left. "We tell the lieutenant colonel and he starts an investigation that starts with asking the family about the money they received from Phang."

Bell followed the lieutenant into the command hootch. "If we can manage to get to the lieutenant colonel before our asses get hauled in front of a court-martial," he said. "If we can't get to him before then, we may never have another chance."

"You don't have any doubt that's really heroin Phang planted, do you?" He sat on the chair at his small field desk.

Bell shook his head. He sat on his cot. "No doubt about it, Scrappy. I've told Phang we're going to get him and he told me if we fuck with him he'll get us first. We're fucking with him." He wished he had his rifle to clean so he'd have something to do with his hands, but he and Burrison and all five corporals in the CAP had been disarmed when they were placed under house arrest. "If all he wanted to do was scare us he would have put two pounds of talcum powder there and let us know about it so we could see that he could do things like that. No"—he shook his head again—"if he got the lieutenant colonel involved, it's real and he wants to get rid of us permanently."

Burrison nodded. "I think you're right," he said. "Let's hope Houng and his squad leaders can find whoever planted those bags. It had to be somebody in that mob we hired to fix up Camp Apache after the attack."

"You wanted to see me, Lieutenant?" a gravelly voice asked.

Burrison turned his head and saw First Sergeant Graves standing in the entrance to his quarters. "Yes I do, Top," he said. "Come on in and have a seat." He gestured toward his cot. Out of the corner of his eye he noticed Bell had stood up at the first sergeant's appearance. Bell remained standing after Graves sat down. The young lieutenant studied the first sergeant for a moment before speaking to him. He decided this was not a man to be put at ease with small talk. "What were you doing with my people out there, First Sergeant?" he asked.

The ghost of a smile flickered across Graves's face, but his expression hardened a touch. "Those scumbags don't like to shave," he said. "I was making sure they do." He lowered his eyes to Burrison's chin, then looked back at his eyes.

Burrison struggled with himself to not flinch or blush when Graves looked at his unshaven face. Instead he held his face stony and asked, "By whose leave did you inspect my men?"

Graves slowly shook his head, "Sorry, Lieutenant," he said, "but they aren't your men anymore. They are now a special scout section that reports to me. I was inspecting my people."

The first sergeant's statements stunned Burrison. He blinked, trying to collect his thoughts. "I've been temporarily relieved of command duties, Top," he finally said. "I haven't been relieved of command of Tango Niner."

"Now I don't know anything about that, Lieutenant," Graves said, shrugging. "But I do know the lance corporals and PFCs who were in your platoon are now my scout section."

Burrison chewed on the inside of his lip for a moment. He suddenly realized something that Bell had known since the first sergeant walked in—he hadn't been called "sir." He didn't notice it at first because in the field enlisted Marines normally call officers by name rather than calling them "sir" for the same reason they don't salute them, to reduce the chances of enemy snipers zeroing in on the leaders. Now Burrison understood the first sergeant was addressing him in a way to let the young officer know that he, Graves, was in charge. Then he caught the last thing Graves had said. "Be that as it may, First Sergeant," he said. "Who gave you permission to inspect my corporals?"

Graves leaned forward and rubbed his hands on his thighs, elbows akimbo. He smiled; he knew the young officer was now in a corner he couldn't get out of. "Tango Niner is attached to my company," he said. "I'm the first sergeant of Echo Company and the welfare of the men is my responsibility. For their morale, I have to make sure they keep themselves clean—and clean-shaven."

"Bullshit," Burrison snapped. He shook himself. "We're in the field here and don't have the time or resources for garrison mickey mouse. What's important for morale out here is what is going to keep these men alive and well."

The first sergeant smiled wider and shook his head. "It's not like we're on an operation," he said. "No place in this country is a real rear area. The only distinction for a grunt is if you're on an operation or not. We're not on an operation."

"The distinction is how close the bad guys are," Burrison countered. "They're right outside the wire here. One of our patrols last night found a Vee Cee ambush. There's a good chance one or more patrols tonight will kill some bad guys. And a week and a half ago there were more than a hundred of them inside the wire." This wasn't getting anywhere. He took a deep breath and tried to stare down Graves's smile. When he couldn't he said, "I don't want you inspecting my people without clearing it with me. Do you understand, First Sergeant?"

"I understand, Lieutenant," Graves said, getting to his feet, "you don't want me to inspect your men without telling you first." He started to leave but turned back before leaving the tent room. "One more thing, Lieutenant," he said, "that country boy with the mustache that isn't squared away?"

"Lance Corporal Lewis." Burrison nodded.

"The next time I see him that mustache had best be trimmed to military length. If it isn't I'll shave it off right then and there with my K-bar." And then he was gone.

Burrison sat looking for a long moment at where Graves had stood. Bell sat down and didn't look anywhere in particular. Finally Burrison asked, "What's his problem, Jay Cee?"

"I do believe he doesn't like us."

"I could tell that," the young lieutenant grunted. "But why not, do you think he believes that smuggling frame?"

"Maybe," Bell said and shrugged, still looking nowhere. "But he's been a first sergeant sitting behind a desk in the spit-and-polish Marine Corps for a long time. I think he doesn't like the men who are enlisting now because their country's at war and they want to do their duty to their country by fighting as one of the best but don't want to stay in after the war—just be combat Marines and go back to the real world without ever thinking of being lifers. These new Marines don't know anything about spit and polish and don't want to learn. He was in World War II and Korea, where Marines fought in regiments, divisions, and amphibious corps, not like we fight here. I don't think he likes CAP units doing things their own way instead of the way he learned to do things. Or maybe it's just because he's a first sergeant. Nobody likes first sergeants, so maybe he doesn't like anybody in return."

Suddenly Swarnes stuck his head through the opening in the canvas wall separating his radioroom from the center room. "Excuse me, Scrappy. Sorry, Jay Cee. Short Round, Malahini, and Billy Boy want to see you."

Burrison sighed. "Send them in."

Swarnes ducked out and seconds later the three lance corporals filed into the room.

"Billy Boy, didn't I tell you to square that mustache away the first time I saw you," Bell said before any of them could say anything.

Lewis started. He had something important to talk to Burrison and Bell about. Why was Jay Cee giving him the same kind of hard time First Sergeant Graves had? "I don't know," he said. "Did you?"

Hempen elbowed Lewis in the ribs. "He sure did, Billy Boy," he said. "That was the same time he didn't believe me and Stilts were card-carrying Little Guerrilla Killers."

Bell groaned. He remembered very well his first day with Tango Niner and the confrontation he almost had with Corporal Stilts Zeitvogel, the six-foot-five-inch black Marine who had told him he should hand the squad's training over to him if he wanted it to be the best night-fighting unit in this "Bad Green Machine" because of his own counter-guerrilla training—he called himself a "Little Guerrilla Killer." Hempen had defused the confrontation by producing his own Little Guerrilla Killer card. Inside the card's black border a cartoon Pancho Villa figure with crossed bandoleers puffed out its chest and held a pop-gun that fired a flag emblazoned with the words LITTLE WARRIOR. Corporal Dennis Lanani, a Hawaiian whose patrol was wiped out by an NVA sapper platoon three months later, also had a Little Guerrilla Killer card. "Short Round's right, that's when I told you to square your mustache away. You didn't. Today, First Sergeant Graves told you to. If you don't, he's going to cut it off. You understand that, don't you?"

Lewis grimaced and twisted his body from side to side like a high school boy being chewed out for something he didn't believe was wrong. At nineteen and with little more than a year and a half in the Marines, he wasn't far beyond being a high school boy. "Ah shit, Jay Cee," he said, "the Top don't mean that."

"If you want to believe that, you try him," Bell said in a level voice. "Personally, I believe him."

"What do you want?" Burrison finally asked the three lance corporals. All three tried to talk at once and it took a moment for them to sort out who would be their spokesman. Hempen finally won the job of explaining, around Lewis's interruptions, to Burrison and Bell about the problems they were having with the line company grunts and their request mast with Captain Ronson. When he was through, the lieutenant and the sergeant stared at them for a long moment. "Why didn't you come to us first?" Burrison finally asked.

"I hope you dumbasses didn't fuck things up too bad," Bell told them.

"But we thought . . ." one of them started to say but was stopped at a gesture from Burrison. All three looked sheepish.

"Let's go see the skipper," Burrison said to Bell, "try to straighten this business out." The two stood up and reached for their weapons before remembering they didn't have them anymore.

Swarnes was completing his end of a radio transmission when they walked through the radioroom.

"We're going down the hill to see Captain Ronson," the lieutenant said to his radioman.

"Glad to hear that, Scrappy," Swarnes replied. "That was the skipper's radioman I was just talking to. Captain Ronson wants your ass in his hootch most ricky-tick."

CHAPTER SIX

New orders

It took Burrison and Bell less than two minutes to reach the company CP tent. Graves was waiting for them at its entrance. "Your boys sure know how to stir up a bucket of shit," the first sergeant said when they reached him.

"My boys?" Burrison said. "A little while ago you were telling me they were yours."

The beefy senior NCO shrugged. "My boys, your boys —what's the difference? We all report to the same boss." He led the way into Captain Ronson's office.

"Lieutenant Burrison, Sergeant Bell." Ronson acknowledged their presence. He was sitting at his field desk. "Sit down, please."

There were two folding chairs and a locker box. Burrison sat on one of the chairs and Bell took the locker box so Graves could have the other chair. The first sergeant remained standing in the doorway, arms folded across his chest. A faint smile lay on his face. By not sitting on the chair the CAP sergeant had left for him, Graves knew he was making Bell and his officer uncomfortable and exerting his power over the younger men.

"You know about your men coming to see me this morning," Ronson said with no attempt at small talk. "I talked to some of my squad leaders and they verified what your people told me. We do have a problem here. Did they tell you the solution they proposed?"

"Yessir," Burrison said.

"What do you think of it?" Ronson's expressionless face gave Burrison no clue to what the senior officer thought.

"Given the nature of the problem I think it's a generally good solution. But even though they could do a good job of drawing the patrol routes I don't think they should do it. I'd rather draw them myself with Sergeant Bell and my own patrol leaders helping me."

Ronson nodded. "I thought you'd say something like that. I agree that for a few nights your men should go out with the Popular Forces and my people should go on Marine-only patrols. But what do we do about a patrol leader for your people, do your lance corporals have experience running their own patrols?"

"Nossir, they don't," Burrison said. "But I think any of the three who came to see you could do a professional job of it." He turned to Bell. "What do you think, Jay Cee?"

"I think you're right," the sergeant answered, looking at Ronson. "Short Round is probably the best of them, even though Malahini is senior to him."

"Without your corporals do you have enough men to put out two patrols?"

"No problem. If we need to I can add Knowles and Reid to the six men in the rifle squad."

Ronson studied the two CAP Marines for a moment, considered what they said. Then he said, "Tonight we're putting out four patrols. Two of them will be rifle squads from my company, they'll set ambushes. The other two will be CAP patrols. The radio call signs will be Wiley Coyote One and Two for the rifle squads, Road Runner

One and Two for the CAP rovers. Base is Painted Desert."
He picked a map up from his desk and opened it on his cot.
He laid a clear sheet of plastic over it and drew a felt-
tipped pen from his shirt pocket. "Let's get these routes
drawn," he said.

"This is no shit," Bell said to Webster and Hempen, "tonight your patrols follow their fucking routes. There'll be a
grunt squad set in an ambush here"—his finger jabbed at a
map point two thirds of the way from Camp Apache to the
cleft in the hills to the west where the Song Du Ong River
came down from the mountains onto its floodplain—"and
another one over here"—he pointed to another spot overlooking the rice paddies northwest of the hill Hou Dau
hamlet sat on. "There's no way you're getting together
with the grunt squad leaders to work out alternate routes.
Anyway, I showed these routes to Stilts and Tex. They say
they're good and you should catch Charlie if he's out there
tonight." Bell watched his lance corporals closely while
giving them their orders. He couldn't tell whether they
were nervous about leading their first night patrols or excited about getting the chance to show what they could do.

A few feet away Billy Boy Lewis sulked. He wanted to
be a patrol leader and didn't quite accept Bell's explanation
that the other two lance corporals both had time in grade on
him. "You'll get a chance to lead a patrol later," Bell had
told him, but that didn't make Lewis feel any better. In his
disappointment he almost forgot to make the ends of his
mustache point in different directions.

"Any questions?" Bell asked Hempen and Webster.

The two stared intently at the lines drawn on the acetate
map overlay. After a moment they shook their heads. They
knew the areas they'd be patrolling the way they knew
their own neighborhoods back in The World.

"Then do what you have to do," Bell said, dismissing
them.

Webster and Hempen rose and returned to the squad
area to brief their men before evening chow.

"Come on, Billy Boy," Hempen said to Lewis. "Let's go give Big Red the scoop."

Lewis clenched his hands in front of his face and twisted. When his hands came away the right end of his mustache pointed straight out to the side and the left jutted to the side before abruptly shooting upward before reaching its end. Then he got to his feet and, with a dour expression, followed his patrol leader for the night.

Half an hour after sundown Hempen would take Lewis and "Big Red" Robertson out of the main gate, turn left and meet a half-dozen PFs in Hou Ky. They would then take their time following the treelines separating the rice paddies from the scrub forest between the paddies and the river until they reached the ridge coming down from the western mountains. After sitting in an ambush for an hour they were to move three hundred meters to a second ambush site and stay there for another hour before heading east through the scrub until they reached a point near Hou Ky, where the PFs would be dropped off and the Marines would return alone to their compound. An hour after Hempen left, Webster would take Wells and Pennell out and turn right and meet their PFs near the southwest corner of Hou Dau hill. They would rove through the scrub south and east of Camp Apache as far as the high bend in the river before turning west to a place where they could overlook the small island where the deserted hamlet of Hou Binh sat in a wide place in the river. Webster's patrol was scheduled to return an hour before Hempen's.

After they had all eaten, Corporal Stilts Zeitvogel met with Hempen and his men to help prepare them for their patrol. Corporal Tex Randall did the same with Webster and his two Marines.

The tall black corporal sat cross-legged in front of the three Marines and shook his head sadly. "Goddamn," he swore softly, "it's a fucking conspiracy to keep me off the courts. Give me Wilt Chamberlain and Bill Russell with the three of you and I'd still have trouble fielding a basketball team that could play decent against high schoolers."

"Fuck you, Stilts," Hempen gibed back. "All roundball

is, is a bunch of tall guys who aren't coordinated enough to do anything else running up and down a gym trying to throw a beach ball into a peach basket without tripping over their own damn feet."

Zeitvogel leaned toward the chunky Marine who stood more than a foot shorter than he, narrowed his eyes, and stage-whispered, "Want to go one-on-one against me in tackle football?"

"Shit no, man."

Zeitvogel straightened back, looking smug.

"You'd probably trip over those size-fifteen clodhoppers of yours, fall down, and hurt yourself, and I'd get blamed for it," Hempen said and jerked backward to avoid the playful roundhouse the tall man swung at him.

"Big Red's the only one of you could stand a chance on the court," Zeitvogel continued. "And that's only because he's big enough to knock people down." He shook his head again. "Dumb fuck'd probably foul out in the first period."

"If I was playing against these dudes they'd wind up in the hospital before I fouled out," Robertson said, grinning and indicating Hempen and Lewis.

"Take you off at the kneecaps, fucker," Hempen joked back.

Lewis didn't say anything. He sat slightly apart from the others looking down and to the side. He looked surly.

Zeitvogel picked up a different ball. "Cut the crap, Billy Boy."

Lewis slowly turned his head to look at the man who had been his fire team leader before being relieved from duty pending the results of the smuggling investigation. "What crap?"

"Acting like some schoolboy who can't get a date for the junior prom, that's what crap."

The accusation stung. "I'm getting fucked over, Stilts," Lewis said in an agitated voice. "When I captured that mortar Scrappy said he wished he had a fire team to give me. Now we need two patrol leaders and he lets Jay Cee make Short Round and Malahini the patrol leaders instead of me. How come for why? What did I do to fuck up so I don't get to be patrol leader?" He jittered while talking, seemed to become more upset as he spoke.

Zeitvogel studied Lewis for a moment, then asked, "You trying to say Short Round and Malahini can't do the job?"

Lewis squirmed and looked away. "No, that's not what I'm trying to say."

"They senior to you?" Lewis didn't respond. "Answer me."

Lewis nodded.

"Did Jay Cee tell you you'd get a turn as patrol leader?" Another nod.

"He said you'd get a turn even though the others are senior to you?"

"Yes." Lewis still didn't look back at Zeitvogel.

"Then you're calling Jay Cee a liar."

"Bullshit," Lewis snapped and looked up. "No way I'm calling Jay Cee a liar."

"Then what the fuck's your problem, Billy Boy?"

Silence.

Zeitvogel cocked his head. "Now you telling me you ain't got a problem?"

Lewis fidgeted. He had to admit to himself that he wasn't being treated unfairly, that his feelings were hurt because he wasn't picked first over men with more experience than he. It didn't make him feel any better, but it took away his excuse for pouting. "I ain't got no problem," he said and turned more toward the others.

"Good. Now let's review your patrol orders one more time."

The sun set rapidly the way it does in the tropics, and the stars formed a speckled backdrop for the gibbous moon. The light was so bright that a newspaper could have been read by it.

Thirty minutes before his patrol was scheduled to leave, Hempen looked again at the camouflage paint on the backs of his hands and his forearms, checked his face in his field mirror one last time, picked up his rifle, and, with his arms held out to the sides, hopped in place. The only sound he made was the thudding of his boots when he landed on the tent's wooden floor. Then he visually inspected Lewis and Robertson. They had used two different shades of green stick paint to draw lines on their exposed skin—lines that disguised the highlights of their foreheads, noses, cheeks, chins, and knuckles, and lines that confused outlines. Neither man's rifle had its sling, and the front sling keeper was taped to the stock. Billy Boy's automatic rifle had its bipods closed. They each carried one canteen stuffed inside a cut-off cushion-sole sock before going into its carrying cover. A twenty-round magazine was in each rifle, and Robertson carried four more on his cartridge belt; Lewis had six, the same as Hempen. They had first aid kits on the backs of their belts and Lewis and Hempen carried K-bars while Robertson had a bayonet. Their straw-camouflage bush hats were crushed down on their heads. They looked ready.

"Let me hear you, Big Red," Hempen said. While the redhead with the bull's build hopped in place to demonstrate how quiet he was, Lewis left the tent to inspect himself; he was the only man in the patrol units who didn't have to hop for his leader, he was the quietest of them all. When he was satisfied with Robertson, Hempen said, "Let's go join Billy Boy." They blew out their kerosene lamps and lashed the door flaps open on their way out. Later someone else could roll the tent sides up for ventilation. They found Lewis squatting in the shadows by the side of the tent looking into the darkness of the night, letting his eyes adjust to the night light. "I'll be right back," Hempen said to them. He turned and walked up the slight slope to the command hootch and poked his head inside the radioroom—the red light bulb that provided its illumination wouldn't damage his night vision.

"Swearin', tell the honchos we're ready to go."

"No shit," Swarnes replied. "Don't fuck up too bad out there. Wait one."

While he glided across the radioroom to the flap separating it from the next room Hempen went back outside. It takes the eyes twenty minutes to become fully acclimated to the dark and he didn't want to risk having to start his twenty minutes over again.

"Where are the others?" Bell asked, joining him.

"Over by our hootch."

Bell led the way. Zeitvogel was already there when they arrived. They stood or sat quietly for several minutes, waiting for the time for the patrol to leave. Finally Zeitvogel broke the silence by saying quietly, "It ain't going to be no sweat out there, Short Round. Just pretend you was me."

"Bullshit, Stilts, I ain't going to do that," Hempen said. "I don't want to go banging my head on the tops of trees."

The tall Marine punched his short buddy in the shoulder. "You know what I mean."

Bell looked at the luminous face of his watch. Hempen caught the motion out of the corner of his eye and did the same. "Time to go," the chunky lance corporal said and stepped toward the main gate. The others followed him without words. They reached the gate and Hempen stepped aside to let Lewis take the point. Bell clapped each of the three on the shoulder as they left, then he and Zeitvogel stood watching until they disappeared into the night.

"Wish I was going with them," Zeitvogel said.

"They'll do all right," Bell replied.

"I know. I'm just going stir crazy staying in my hootch every night."

CHAPTER SEVEN

Occupation, class clown

When John Hempen entered high school, a whole new world of possibilities was opening to him; he was in tenth grade, he was one of the big boys, and he could do all the things the big boys did.

The first big boy thing he did was go out for the football team. The coach looked down at the chubby boy, who was stretched to his highest five-foot height, and boomed in a voice calculated to intimidate him right off the gridiron, "Kid, this school doesn't have a midget team, and it doesn't carry enough insurance to cover the costs when Badman Bombozsky hits you with his full one hundred and eighty-seven and one-half pounds and flattens your tail on the grass." But John Hempen didn't intimidate that easily. He kept after the football coach until the coach finally relented and let him be water boy. Somehow being water boy didn't satisfy Hempen's desire to do the big boy things, even though he did get to go onto the field during games.

The next big boy thing he did was go out for the basket-ball team. The basketball coach was a former college star who'd been drafted by the Knicks in the fifth round but didn't last through his first training camp. He went to work as a high school coach and forever after took his embarrassment out on his players. After ignoring Hempen until he couldn't stand the pestering any longer he said, "Kid, I can't look down far enough to see you," turned his back, and went back to ignoring him.

Our hero went out for the fencing team. The fencing coach was uneasy about having someone so small on the team, but let him try out anyway. The other boys all had reaches so much longer than Hempen's that they often scored multiple points on him before he could get close enough for a touché. But the coach admired his grit so much that he let him spar with the girls' team in practice. This didn't do much for John's macho self-image, but it did teach him how to talk to girls without getting flustered. The other boys couldn't understand how he got so many dates with the best-looking girls in the school. Not even when he explained, "They're people just like everybody else. They pull their silky, sexy lace panties on one leg hole at a time almost the same way we do."

He still wanted to be on a team but by then it was too late to try out for the wrestling team and his school didn't have a swimming team or a tennis team or a golf team. So he figured you don't have to be big or tall to play baseball and tried out for that team. He wasn't fast enough to shag flies in the outfield, his range wasn't far enough to play shortstop (the other infield positions were filled by return-ing letter men), his knees weren't flexible enough for a catcher, and he couldn't throw straight enough to pitch. The coach looked at Hempen, looked at the equipment bag, looked back at him, and shook his head. "You can't be manager either," the coach said, "because the equip-ment bag's too big for you to carry."

They never told him, but the coaches secretly admired

John Hempen's guts. He was a little guy, still hardly more than five feet tall at the end of his first year of high school, but the way he acted it almost seemed that nobody had ever told him he was little and he hadn't noticed it on his own.

Then it was summer and there weren't any more school teams to try out for. John Hempen grew some during that summer, but was still not bulky enough to make the football team or tall enough for the basketball coach to be able to see him and his arms still weren't long enough to fence with the other boys. But he tried out for the wrestling team on time. The only problem there was the team didn't have any other members his size for him to practice with. He lost every match.

During his senior year John Hempen tried a different tack. He became class clown. He was still a little guy, John Hempen was. At the beginning of his last year of high school he had grown to five foot three. Out of the entire class of 482 seniors that graduated with him at the end of that year only two of the boys and fewer than a dozen girls were shorter than he. Being so short he had to be careful about how he cut up, of course. He developed his wit to get away with things. And he managed to pull off almost everything he pulled on the teachers at Westmont Senior High in East Gulf Beach, Florida.

Except for old Mrs. Cranmer. Old Mrs. Cranmer was a special case. It was well known to all the students at Westmont that when Ponce de León discovered Florida and started searching for the fountain of youth he met a little old lady who knew where it was—but she didn't want this foreigner to find it so she gave him such godawful bad directions that he never did stumble across it. The students knew that little old lady was Mrs. Cranmer—she was certainly old enough. She carried a steel yardstick to poke unruly students back into line with, and it was rumored that she had black belts in both judo and karate. Nobody messed with old Mrs. Cranmer.

John Hempen wasn't nasty or vicious in what he did. He wasn't the one who flushed the cherry bombs down the toilet in the boys' room and cracked the soil line, or the one who balanced the bucket of water over the door of the teachers' lounge. But he did install the specially made whoopie cushions under the seats in the boys' room stalls, and he did turn a live goose loose in the teachers' lounge. He was best known for making strange noises in class and coming up with silly but logical answers to the question he was asked in class. Most of his teachers stopped calling on him before Thanksgiving. He wore the funny glasses with Groucho Marx eyebrows, nose, and mustache until they were confiscated. Then he sent away for a pair of the glasses advertised in the back of comic books, the X-ray vision glasses that were supposed to let the wearer see through women's clothes. He let the girls try on the glasses to assure them they really didn't work, then stared at the women teachers through them. It took the women teachers two weeks to figure out why the other students giggled so much when he looked at them with those funny glasses. Then they were confiscated, too.

He was also imaginative in some of his more elaborate jokes.

Young John knew a little about how audio equipment worked and put that knowledge to good use at the school assembly right before Christmas break. He wired a timer into the auditorium sound system and added a record player and switch box to it. The principal stepped up to the stage lectern to give his annual "Let's all have a safe and enjoyable vacation and come back ready to study even harder" speech. He got a few sentences into it when his mike went dead and the hall was filled with the strains of "Deutschland Über Alles" and Adolf Hitler's voice boomed out in one of his more acerbic speeches. By the time the school's electrician found the record player, timer, and switch box and was able to get the stage mike working properly again, nobody could take the principal's speech seriously.

In the spring term, when the biology teacher opened a formaldehyde jar full of dead frogs, twenty live frogs leaped and clambered out of the jar. The last of them wasn't recovered until three days later and for a month the biology teacher kept checking his classroom for escapees.

The art teacher gave one of her classes a lecture on early Italian Renaissance religious paintings. She used slides to illustrate the lecture she gave facing her class. After listening to several minutes of tittering from her pupils she turned to the screen to see if she had inserted the slides in the projector upside down. That's when she discovered that every other slide was a photo of a nude woman.

There were other such incidents and the faculty of Westmont High was very glad to see John Hempen graduate, even though they couldn't prove he had done any of the things they knew he did. Twelfth grade had been fun but, like being water boy for the football team, sparring partner for the girls' fencing team, and the only wrestler in his weight class, it didn't do anything for his masculine self-image. So right before graduation he did something none of the other boys in his class did. As a matter of fact, none of the boys from Westmont High had done it during the three years he had been there. John Hempen enlisted in the U.S. Marine Corps. Everyone in his class looked at him in awe and disbelief. Other boys craned their necks forward and looked at him out of the corners of their eyes. "You'll never make it," several said. He smiled back at them. "Watch me." The girls looked at him wide-eyed. "Can I write to you?" they asked. He grinned at the girls. "Sure you can," he said. "And if I have time, I'll write back."

He was an intelligent boy and scored very high on the enlistment test, high enough to be offered the options of a three-year enlistment or guaranteed aviation mechanic school. But he needed to do something for his self-image, so he signed up for a four-year hitch and hoped for assignment to the infantry. Since he didn't have any office skills and didn't tell the Marines about his knowledge of audio equipment, they obliged his desire for the infantry.

Hempen reported to boot camp at Parris Island, North Carolina, in July. In November during Infantry Training Regiment he found out about Marine Recon and requested assignment to a Recon unit. He was told to wait until he reported to his first duty station, then request a transfer.

After boot leave he reported to duty with the Eighth Marines at Camp Lejeune, also in North Carolina. He started to wonder if he was ever going to get out of the South. The company gunnery sergeant looked at him quizzically and said, "Boy, don't you understand, we're getting ready to go to war. We need grunts more than we need recon. You're staying right here." He stayed right there for eight months, then got orders to report to Vietnam as a replacement.

Battalions running around the boonies with sixty to eighty pounds of ammunition and gear per man in hundred-degree-plus temperatures didn't seem to him to be quite the way to fight a war against guerrillas. Especially since the guerrillas traveled light and could stand off at a distance to snipe and run. The Vietcong seemed to catch the Marines in ambushes a lot more often than the Marines caught them, even though the casualty counts always had the Marines killing anywhere from two times as many VC to ten times as many as the VC managed to kill. So he wasn't too reluctant when his company was ordered to give up enough men to form a rifle squad for a Combined Action Platoon and his platoon sergeant told him he was volunteering for it.

CHAPTER EIGHT

Late night, November 8, 1966

The north gate to Camp Apache was wide enough to
drive a truck through, and a bulldozed road wound through
the opening in the three banks of concertina wire that surrounded the compound. At night, plugs of the circular
barbed wire were rolled into the openings to close the gate
—except for a narrow passage left open for patrols to enter
and leave through. An M-60 machine gun guarded the
main gate at night. Lewis twisted his way through the narrow, zigzag openings in the wire. A few meters beyond the
wire he stepped off the truck road and paralleled it to the
foot of the hill. At the bottom the bulldozed road turned
east and a footpath ran west from its corner. Lewis turned
left and looked back over his shoulder for directions. Hempen pointed and the point man stayed between the path and
the hill, heading for the scrub forest that began two
hundred meters beyond the corner of the hill.

The three Marines had removed the safeties on their rifles when they went through the gate. Now they held their weapons ready and walked slowly, slightly bent over, their eyes and ears probing the darkness, and maintained silence for any sight or sound that didn't belong, any sight or sound that could indicate danger. They walked quickly and entered the trees less than six minutes after turning toward them. Then they slowed down and moved more deliberately through the trees. The Hou Ky gate was a quarter-mile from the northwest corner of Camp Apache's hill. The three Marines took fifteen minutes to go the rest of that quarter-mile from where they entered the trees. It was a much faster pace than they would use on a night patrol anywhere else, but Bun Hou was their home—they knew the land and they owned the nights here.

Once inside the hamlet, they flitted from the shadow of one hootch to the shadow of the next, staying in darkness as much as possible, not exposing themselves to the light of the moon and stars. When the Marines of Tango Niner had first arrived, nearly all of the hootches in Hou Ky had been thatch shacks. The only masonry structures were old French buildings. After the Marines arrived, they freed the people from the yoke of Vietcong taxation and made sure the landlords and government tax collectors didn't take more than was legally due. The Marines hired villagers to work for them: cleaning the compound, bearing water for the shower, disinfecting the four-holer with lye, digging a new pit for the four-holer when necessary. The Marines used the Hou Ky barber and tailor. All of this gave the villagers of Hou Ky enough freedom so that two families where able to pool their resources to start a business at the river's edge making sun-baked adobe bricks. Now more than half of the hootches in Hou Ky had been rebuilt from those bricks.

Lewis reached the largest of the old French structures and glided along its side until he reached a corner. He stopped there and listened. The melodic sound of several voices softly singsonging came to him. He looked back at Hempen and nodded. The patrol leader held up a hand and stepped around Lewis and the corner. In the middle of the small square was a bench. In the shimmering night light he saw a half-dozen PFs sitting on the bench. Two of them were smoking cigarettes. In the few steps it took him to reach them they were all standing and he was able to recognize them as the bandy-legged little squad leader named Willy and five of his men; Long, Mai, Hien, Butter Bar, the Marines called him that because he was the fattest man in the platoon, the fattest Vietnamese peasant any of them had seen—and the one they called Pheet because his feet looked several sizes too big for his ankles. The two smoking crushed their cigarettes beneath their feet.

"Chao ong, Willy," Hempen murmured and nodded to the other PFs.

"Chao ong, Shor' Roun'," Willy said back. His teeth almost gleamed in the dark when he grinned and held up a thumb. "Ma-deen numba one," he said, obviously glad to be patrolling with only the CAP Marines again. "We go kill boo-coo Vee Cee."

"You got that right, Willy," Hempen said. He quickly got his patrol organized and they moved out in a westerly direction through Hou Ky. Lewis kept the point followed by two PFs, Hempen, two more PFs, Robertson, Butter Bar, and Long. Stronger now, the patrol didn't stay in the shadows but went straight along paths until it left the hamlet. On the north side of Hou Ky the rice paddies came down to the edge of the hamlet and curved around it on both sides. One path led to where the paddies reached the thin scrub that covered the area between them and the river. A tree line separated the paddies and the scrub. Lewis stepped up into the tree line and blended into its shadows.

The patrol moved slowly for two hours through the tree lines that sometimes angled to one side or the other but mostly went west toward the mountains. Moon and star light glinted off the paddies on the right and shadows flickered in the scrub on the left. Then Hempen signaled Lewis to turn left. Not far from the edge of the paddies they reached a trail. This trail came down a ridgeline from the mountains and went through Hou Ky to Hou Dau. This ridge trail was a major infiltration route for supplies, rein-forcements, and replacements for main force Vietcong units operating on the Song Du Ong floodplain downriver from Bun Hou. Once a week and sometimes more often, a patrol lying in ambush near the bottom of the ridge would catch a few VC coming down it with supplies or weapons.

Hempen broke squelch on his PRC-6 walkie-talkie and murmured into it, "Arizona Desert, this is Road Runner One. Arizona Desert, Road Runner One. Over."

Swearin' Swarnes was monitoring the transmissions on the radio even though Captain Ronson's command post was running the patrols. He forgot himself for a moment and answered, "Road Runner One, this is Arizona Desert. Go, over."

"Desert, Road One. Be advised, am at Checkpoint Bravo and going down. Over."

"Roger, Road One. Desert out," Swarnes said. He re-leased the speak lever on his handset and heard another voice on the air saying, ". . . zona Desert out." He swore colorfully when he remembered that he wasn't the radio base, but calmed down when he realized the radioman in Ronson's CP must not have realized he had been cut off the air by his transmissions. Just then the radioman in the grunt CP was looking at his handset and shook it, wondering why the beginnings and endings of the transmissions he had just received from Road Runner One had been garbled while the middles were fine.

A hundred meters from the foot of the ridge Hempen smiled to himself; he understood what had happened. Using hand signals, shoulder taps, and words softly spoken into ears, he led his men across the trail and set them in their ambush. The site he selected allowed them to cover the path in both directions and see movement on the lowest reaches of the ridgeline. They lay on the back side of a low ripple in the ground fifteen meters from the trail. The rip-ple gave them cover from gunfire and the weeds and trees concealed them from view. He arranged his men at an angle slightly toward the ridge; a PF was on the end closest to the ridge, then Robertson, two more PFs, himself, two PFs, Lewis, the last PF. This effectively gave him three three-man fire teams of one Marine and two PFs each. If he needed to move an element, he could tell a Marine, who could take his two PFs with him. Because the hour was still relatively early and the patrol would only be lying in ambush for two hours, Hempen decided not to establish a sleep rotation. Everyone would stay awake.

The passage of time was marked only by the moon's sliding across the sky and Hempen's half-hourly murmured radio reports of, "Desert, Runner One. Situation as before. Over." And the CP's brief acknowledgment. His situation reports were followed immediately by Webster's Road Runner Two and the two grunt ambushes Wile E. Coyote One and Two. Then another half hour of the moon inching its way across the sky and silence unbroken except by the occasional *fuk-yoo* cries of hunting lizards. A little before the fourth and final sitrep was due, with the moon dropping rapidly toward the mountains, Hempen was studying his watch and wondering if he could stretch the ambush another half hour when Mai nudged him and pointed at the ridge. Hempen unfocused his eyes and pointed them slightly to the left of the trail. His peripheral vision immediately picked up what Mai had seen; a dim spot of orange light was making its way down the trail.

They don't ever seem to learn, Hempen thought. That little lamp their point man carries on the ridge isn't bright enough to give them any real illumination to help them get down the ridge, but it sure lets us see them a long way off. The group of VC, probably a supply run of four to eight men, was far enough away that the lance corporal felt secure enough to go from position to position, making sure each man saw the light and knew to hold his fire until Hempen sprang the ambush by firing. He returned to his position and watched the dim, bobbing light drop lower down the ridge, waiting for it to blink out before it reached the flat land. In a few minutes he realized the lamp wasn't going out, but was left lit after whoever was carrying it reached the foot of the ridge. Something was wrong. He passed the word up and down the line: "Hold your fire, let them go through."

In a few more minutes a black-pajama-clad figure wearing a slouch hat came into view. His Ho Chi Minh tire-tread sandals made soft slapping sounds on the hard-packed earth of the trail. He carried an AK-47 assault rifle in his right hand and a small oil lamp dangled from his left. Hempen could feel the tension along the line as his men tried to hold their breaths and sink deeper into the earth. Five more men carrying huge packs supported on their backs by "A" frames followed the first man. They were unarmed. Another armed man brought up the rear of the short column. Now Hempen felt a different tension on his line. It was the tension of men who knew they just blew a perfect ambush opportunity that might cause them harm later on. He tapped the men to each side and, using hand signals, told them to hold tight and pass the word to wait quietly.

Hempen knew the VC sometimes used a small lamp to light their way down the ridge. He also knew the lamp was always put out before the Cong reached the bottom of it. If the supply run was keeping its light on and continuing on the main trail to Hou Ky it had to be a decoy. Two minutes later he knew he was right.

A figure dressed and armed like the first man who walked through the ambush's killing zone glided silently into sight. His weapon was held at the ready and his head swiveled from side to side. Another followed him, and another and another and another. Hempen waited until he thought the point man was probably in Long's sights, aimed at the man directly to his own front, and pulled the trigger. The Communist soldier was hit by a five-round burst; the first bullet hit him in the hip, the others climbed his body until the fifth tore into his temple, shattering his head. The lifeless body crashed to the far side of the trail. A wall of sound exploded to Hempen's sides before he released the trigger from his first burst and started looking for a second target. There weren't any. All eight Vietcong who had entered the killing zone were down, dead or dying.

"Hold your positions," Hempen shouted in the sudden silence when the shooting ended. "Keep alert, there might be more." His radio lay forgotten by his side and he didn't hear its tinny voice start to chatter at him.

They waited alertly for a moment, then Robertson shouted, "I hear someone," and fired into the trees at his flank.

"Billy Boy, move up to Big Red's right," Hempen shouted. Then he tapped Mai and Willy and ran with them to Robinson's left side. A whistle shrilled and fire came from their flank before he covered half the distance. They dropped to the ground and scurried ahead on elbows and knees. They heard the two PFs with Robinson start firing. Billy Boy's automatic opened up and Hempen took advantage of the heavier fire to lunge forward the few additional yards to a position where he could fire to the flank. The Marines' three M-14s, two of them on automatic, and the PFs' six carbines blasted out a wall of fire and broke the VC flanking maneuver.

"Keep firing," Hempen shouted over the screams of the retreating enemy and cries of the wounded being left behind. The CAP patrol poured more fire after the fleeing Cong. When he couldn't hear any more noise from the running VC he called cease-fire. "Big Red, take your fay epps out there and see how many we've got." He looked around. "Where's my radio, I've got to tell Big Louie to pop some illum out here." Then he remembered where he left it and scrambled back to where he had lain in the ambush.

"Road Runner One, Road Runner One. This is Arizona Desert. Can you hear me? Over," a voice was saying over the radio when he picked it up. "Road Runner One, Road Runner One. Somebody come in, please." There was a strain of anxiety in the voice that had been calling for close to two minutes.

"Arizona Desert, this is Road Runner One. Over," he said, breathing heavily.

"Runner One, what's going on out there? Over."

"Desert, Road Runner One just bagged us boo-coo Charlies. Have the piss tube pop me some light so I can get a good body count. Over."

"Runner One, Desert. Wait one."

Hempen waited impatiently. "Find anyone?" he shouted to Robertson.

"Three so far," Robertson called back in an excited voice. "Two wounded, one wasted."

"Hot damn. Willy, take Mai onto the trail and count the bodies there."

"You bet, Shor' Roun'," the PF squad leader shouted back. Hempen heard the two run to the footpath and their jabbering while they checked out the bodies on it.

"Road Runner One, this is Arizona Desert Actual," a new voice spoke on the radio. The "Actual" identified the voice as belonging to Captain Ronson. "Talk to me slow and calm and tell me what you've got there, over."

"Desert Actual, Runner One. We caught a Victor Charlie squad in our killing zone." He released the speak button and called to Willy, "How many you got?"

"Got eight, Honcho. All die."

"Eight KIAs in the killing zone," he continued on the radio. "Then more of them tried to flank us. We're counting those bodies now. Request illum to assist in count. Over."

"How many friendly casualties? Over."

"None," Hempen said quickly, then realized he hadn't checked. "Anybody hurt?" he called out to his squad.

"That's the dumbest fucking thing I ever heard you say, Short Round," Lewis shouted back. "There's eight dead Charlies on the trail and Big Red's found two more dead and three wounded out there and you want to know if anyone's hurt? Shit." His head shake on the last word could be heard in his voice.

"Not *them*, numbnuts. I mean *us*."

A few more shouts determined that no one in the CAP patrol was hurt.

"Are you at your designated ambush site? Over," Ronson asked.

"That's an affirmative, Desert Actual, over."

"I'll give you a flare round. Can you direct? Over."

"Can do. Over."

"Wait one."

Less than a minute later Hempen heard the *carumph* of the distant mortar firing an illumination round in his direction. Seconds later the round popped overhead and the flare glared into life as it drifted down under its parachute.

"Desert, Runner One. You're on target. Let me have another."

The rest of the VC were quickly found under the light of the flares. Nine of them had fallen in the failed flanking attempt: three dead, six wounded. A few blood trails were seen disappearing into the trees. Ronson asked Hempen about the condition of the wounded VC, did they need to be med-evaced immediately to live. No, no head wounds, no sucking chest wounds, no guts spilling on the ground. The Marines could patch them up well enough to last the night. Ronson said to sit tight, he'd send a squad out to help carry the prisoners and weapons back to camp.

CHAPTER NINE

Early morning, November 9, 1966

The VC were carrying cloth tubes slung across their bodies. In each tube were a few pounds of rice, a small jar of nuoc mam sauce, one or two captured American field dressings, and not much else. The Marines bandaged their prisoners with the field dressings they took from the tube packs, then tied their arms behind their backs—and as for one whose right arm was shattered and had bones sticking through the flesh, they tied his good arm tightly to his body and fashioned a sling for the other arm from one of the VC packs. They gathered the packs and weapons in one place and the bodies in another and searched the dead and wounded for documents. Hempen let the PFs take the Vietcongs' food. None of the prisoners was carrying ammunition the PFs could use in their M-1 carbines.

The squad from the grunt encampment at the foot of Camp Apache's hill arrived with a corpsman, who checked over the prisoners. Three of them were litter cases, but were pronounced able to travel. The Marines and PFs picked everything up to leave and the squad leader looked at the eleven bodies stacked together. "Leave the bodies there," Hempen said. "They'll be gone in the morning." They started back and Hempen suddenly remembered the supply bearers he had let go through. What made him remember was the gunfire he heard on the flat near the river below Camp Apache.

He held his radio to his head and listened to Webster's excited voice reporting his patrol had just run into a five-man supply run with two armed guards. They killed both guards and four of the bearers—the fifth one dropped his pack and ran before they could drop him. They didn't need help carrying the packs and weapons.

When the other transmissions were over Hempen pushed the speak button on his radio and said, "Road Runner Two, Road Runner Two, this is Runner One. I should of told you they was coming. Sorry 'bout that, 'pano. Over."

"Runner One, Two," Webster said back. "No sweat, buddy. It was more fun this way. Out."

Hempen started to sling his radio back over his shoulder but another voice came up. "Road Runner One, this is Arizona Desert. You will explain that last transmission when you come in. Out." It sounded to Hempen like First Sergeant Graves's voice.

The night felt secure and they weren't in a regular patrol formation, Lewis wasn't on the point. Instead he was walking close enough to Hempen to hear what he said to Webster. "Dumb fuck," he said. "I told Jay Cee he should make me patrol leader. I would'a remembered and called in about the supply run."

"But you didn't, did you?"

"I remembered but you had the radio."

"Bullshit, Billy Boy. If you remembered you would've been all over my case for forgetting."

"I knew you forgot, I just didn't say anything."

"Fuck you, Billy Boy. You thought about it, you'd been

on my ass like stink on shit." It was bad enough Hempen knew he had forgotten something important on the first patrol he ran. It was worse knowing First Sergeant Graves was going to ream him a new asshole for forgetting. No way he was going to take any crap from Billy Boy Lewis about it.

"I didn't forget, you forgot." It hadn't been Lewis's job to remember, it had been Hempen's. Lewis couldn't be accused of having forgotten something he didn't have to remember in the first place. And maybe Jay Cee and Scrappy would let him run the next patrol.

There was no more talking the rest of the way. The only sounds were occasional clanks from the captured weapons and moans from the wounded VC. Lieutenant Burrison and Sergeant Bell were waiting in Captain Ronson's CP with him and Graves. The sides of the tent were down and its interior was lit by three lamps, two kerosene and one propane. The supplies and weapons captured by Webster's patrol were piled in the middle of the room. Webster and his people had already been debriefed and sent off to get some sleep. The six wounded VC were left outside, guarded by the squad that had brought them back. Hempen, Lewis, and Robertson went in with the squad leader. They deposited the weapons and packs on the dirt floor in front of the captain, then sat on the dirt floor themselves.

"Did you get to count the bodies, Jack?" Ronson asked the squad leader.

The sergeant nodded. "Eleven of them. Not counting the WIAs we brought back."

Ronson stared at the CAP Marines for a long moment, then said, "I think you proved a point tonight. Two patrols, six Marines, twelve PFs and you killed fifteen VC and captured six more. Seventeen weapons, a few hundred rounds, and enough supplies to keep a platoon in the field for a month." He shook his head. "You didn't even have an NCO with you. Amazing. I hope my people understand what happened."

"Those're the happiest bunch of bloodthirsty gooks I

ever seen," the Echo Company sergeant said. "When we were getting the shit ready to come back they kept jabbering at each other and laughing and they talked to us in pidgin English about how they hate the Vee Cee, they killed these and wanted to find more to kill."

"Charlie ruled here for a long time," Bell said to him. "You better believe our little people want to kill his ass and win this war. If Charlie ever takes over here again they're dead meat."

"You let the supply run through," Ronson said to Hempen, "and waited for someone else to come through. Why? What made you think there might be more coming?"

"Sometimes the point man on those supply trains carries a small lamp to lead the way down the ridge, sir. When he does he always puts it out before he reaches the bottom. This point man still had his lamp lit when he reached our ambush. I knew something was wrong, like they were decoys. Last month I was with Stilts, that's Corporal Zeitvogel, when we hit a supply train that was followed by a Vee Cee company. I thought this might be like that."

"Tell me all about it."

So Hempen told them everything that happened from the time Mai pointed out the light on the ridge until the relief squad arrived. The supply run had been legitimate, the contents of the packs brought back by Webster's patrol confirmed that. But the Vietcong knew how Papa Niner operated: small patrols and ambushes, less than a squad in each. Charlie followed this supply run with what was probably a platoon. If the supply bearers and their two guards were ambushed, the platoon would flank the ambush and wipe it out. He was willing to sacrifice the seven men in this run to wipe out a CAP patrol. Lewis interrupted Hempen several times to add details or opinions, but Robertson only spoke when questioned directly. He told about hearing the Vee Cee trying to flank the ambush and opening up on them before they were ready to assault.

"That's probably how you managed to break them up as fast as you did," the captain interjected.

All the details of the action took less than ten minutes to tell. All of the details except one.

"Why didn't you tell us about the supply run you let through?" Graves demanded.

Hempen froze. This was the question he dreaded and he didn't have a good answer for it, nothing that could satisfy the first sergeant. "I don't know," he mumbled.

"You don't know. You were the patrol leader. The patrol leader is supposed to report all enemy activity and you didn't report an enemy supply run you saw and let go past you. You didn't do your job as patrol leader, did you?"

The short lance corporal tried not to cringe. He thought he had done well guessing that someone was trailing the supply train and said so. "Besides, we got the supplies anyway," he finished and looked at Lewis. The wiry Marine who had wanted to be the patrol leader glanced at him and looked away. It was too easy for him to imagine himself in Hempen's place.

Ronson held up his hand before Graves could say anything more. "For a first-time patrol leader you did well," he said to Hempen. "That was fast thinking on your part. Next time remember to call in all activity." He swung his head from side to side, pausing to look each man in the eye. "Do we have all the information we need? Good. Top, see to it the prisoners are secured for the rest of the night. You can leave now." He directed that last at Hempen and his men.

The three lost no time leaving the CP tent, Hempen faster than the others. He had seen how the first sergeant looked at him when Ronson was making his last remarks and wanted to get as far away as he could as fast as possible so the senior NCO wouldn't have a chance to do anything to him. Webster, Wells, and Pennell were already asleep when they reached the squad tent. They hung their cartridge belts on the end of their tables, laid their rifles where their hands would land on them if they suddenly woke and rolled off their cots, took off their boots and utilities, lay down, and were asleep in minutes.

* * *

Much had already happened at Camp Apache by the time Hempen woke up. Lieutenant Houng arrived at daybreak to question the prisoners. They confirmed that they were part of a thirty-man platoon following the supply train, but they didn't know—or wouldn't say—if that was going to be the standard procedure. Captain Ronson sent a platoon reinforced with a machine gun squad and a 60mm mortar to Road Runner One's ambush site to see if it could track the survivors. If it couldn't find a trail to follow it was to go as far as the top of the ridgeline before turning around and coming back. A helicopter from Division G-2 had picked up the prisoners. Ronson, the rest of his platoon leaders, and Graves, along with Burrison and Bell, had a strategy meeting to discuss ways of countering the new VC tactics, if it indeed was a new tactic and not a one-time incident. The men who had ambushed the supply train were cleaning their weapons and reloading their magazines. Corporals Zeitvogel and Randall were sitting with them, questioning them about the previous night's activity.

Zeitvogel turned to Hempen when he heard him waking up. "'Bout time you decided to get with the program, Short Round," the tall black Marine said.

"Oh yah," Hempen said and grinned, remembering how he outsmarted the VC who tried to trap his patrol. Then a kaleidoscope of emotions flickered across his face when he thought of First Sergeant Graves's reaction to his forgetting to include the supply train he had let through when he made his first radio reports. But so what, he decided. It was one bodacious successful ambush that killed eleven Charlies and captured six more. Especially bodacious because it was the first patrol he had led himself. Even Captain Ronson said it was a good patrol. The Top could go fuck himself—he probably had a way to fuck Hempen anyway, but this wasn't the time to worry about that, this was a time to brag and get praised. He rolled to his feet and said, "I gotta take a piss," then turned to leave the tent.

"Don't forget to put your pecker back in," Randall called after him.

Hempen flipped his middle finger over his shoulder at the stocky corporal.

"Jay Cee says you learned something from me," Zeitvogel said when Hempen returned from emptying his bladder down one of the six-foot-long metal tubes half buried in the earth. Marines called them "piss tubes," and the half sticking out of the ground resembled a mortar tube, which is why mortars were also called "piss tubes."

"Sure did, Stilts. I didn't fuck up like you did." Pain appeared in Zeitvogel's eyes and Hempen remembered the VC trap that cost them PFC Isidore Perez, who was so badly shot up he was medevaced all the way back to Balboa Naval Hospital in San Diego, and two PFs who were wounded and one more killed. "Sorry, Honcho," he said softly, "it wasn't your fault."

"Want me to hold him while you pound on his head?" Randall asked.

Zeitvogel shook his head. His voice thick, he said, "No way I want to pound on his head. I do that he'll be too short to be in this man's Marine Corps. They'll ship him back to The World and kick his ass out of the Crotch. Then he won't have to go on any more night patrols. It's better punishment to let him stay here."

"Sorry," Hempen said again.

"No sweat, Short Round," Zeitvogel said and swallowed to clear his voice. "Now tell me about last night." He had already heard about it from each of the other five Marines who were on the two patrols; now he wanted to hear from the man who led the patrol he should have taken out himself.

"Billy Boy and Big Red already tell you what happened?" Hempen asked and started rooting through a box set under his ammo crate table. Zeitvogel nodded. "Now you want the 'this ain't no bull' version, right?"

"You got it."

Hempen nodded to himself. He found what he was

looking for in the box, a can of C-ration fruit cocktail he had been saving for a special occasion, and started opening it with his John Wayne can opener. "Well, it was like this," he began slowly. It wasn't long before Lewis and Robertson were yelling and lobbing nonlethal objects at him.

CHAPTER TEN

Afternoon, November 9, 1966

Late in the afternoon every day since Tango Niner was established, a helicopter had flown out to its hill with a cargo of insulated five-gallon containers. The containers held a hot meal prepared by the cooks of whichever battalion Tango Niner happened to be administratively attached to at the time. The helicopter stayed only long enough to drop off the meal. So each day the Marines in Camp Apache wiped out the insides of the containers after eating and handed the previous day's empties to the helicopter crew when the next meal was delivered. "This is a deposit policy I like," one of the Marines had said during their first week in the compound. "Turn in an empty and get a full one for free." Almost every day a few of the Popular Forces would join the Marines for dinner; they would bring along some rice balls and fresh vegetables to stretch the meal out. The hot-meal birds also brought five-gallon cans of drinking water.

The first few days Echo Company was reinforcing Camp Apache, a daily hot meal was also flown out for it. Once it became obvious that Captain Ronson and his men were going to be around for more than a few days, the battalion sent a couple of cooks to set up a field kitchen and fix three meals a day for the company. The Marines of Tango Niner were invited to join Echo Company at its mess. This was good for the Marines of Tango Niner because they had three hot meals a day that were fresher than the single daily one they had had before—at least those meals they were awake for—but made it difficult for them to share their food with the PFs. By the time Houng and his three squad leaders—Collard Green, Willy, and Vinh—showed up at evening chow the day after Hempen's patrol ambushed the VC platoon, the Marines of Tango Niner had worked out a couple of ways of getting the extra food to feed their fellow CAP members.

PFC Big Red Robertson sidestepped through the chow line with a mess kit in each hand. Flanking him were PFCs George "Jesse James" Wells and Willie Pennell. Pennell also held two mess kits. They had their rifles slung over their shoulders. Robertson stopped in front of the first cook, who had a ladle in each hand, one serving salisbury steak with gravy and the other mashed potatoes. The cook dumped the meat, gravy, and potatoes in the larger dish of one aluminum mess kit, the same as he had for Wells, and waited for Pennell to step in front of him.

Robertson made his voice as deep as he could and it rumbled out from somewhere deep in his large chest. "The other one, too."

The cook stared across the food at Robertson. He saw a hard-muscled man of average height who was built like a bull. Sunburn still showed under Robertson's baked bronze. His utility uniform was faded and worn but clean. His rifle was unloaded but six magazines were on his belt along with a bayonet and a commando knife. The cook himself was the same height as Robertson, but a year and a half of tasting and testing his own food without enough exercise to work off the excess calories had added fat to his body and slackened his muscles. His white mess uniform was clean, but darkly stained from being worn too long too often with too little application of bleach. He was un-armed. Unarmed—but this was his mess line; he was in charge here. "Ony one meal per man," the cook said.

"I know that," Robertson said. "My main man's got radio watch. I'm getting chow for him, too."

"Bullshit. You're in that CAP. I know who your radio-man is, he came through this line a few minutes ago," the cook said, sounding exasperated.

Robertson made his voice rumble again. "I didn't say the radioman, I said my main man. How come you think the radioman is down here getting chow? You think we let him go and don't leave anyone on radio watch?"

"When he gets off radio watch he can come and get his own chow," the cook said and shook his head firmly.

Robertson shook his own head more firmly. "Might not be any left when he gets off radio watch. I'll take him his chow now."

The cook started to argue more but before he could Wells interrupted him. "Big Red's main man's my buddy, too," he said with all the juvenile delinquent toughness he could put in his voice. "You tryin' to tell me my buddy ain't gonna get his chow?" His left hand held his already filled mess kit, his right caressed the pistol grip of his rifle.

The cook's eyes flickered to Wells. Beyond him he saw several other Marines who wore bush hats looking at him menacingly. He looked back at Robertson and said, "This is a load of shit and you know it. I'll give you chow for your buddy this time, but next time he comes for his own." The meat, potatoes, and gravy slopped over the sides of the second mess kit.

Robertson moved on and Pennell stepped up to the cook with his two mess kits. He was grinning.

"I suppose your main man's got radio watch, too," the cook sneered.

Pennell shook his head. "He's manning the gun on the main gate," he said. "Yassah, thank you, sah." Pennell grinned more widely. The soft-spoken nineteen-year-old black Marine from South Dakota knew subservient words spoken cheerfully to a white man could annoy—especially when he won his point.

"Shut up," the cook snarled and filled the second mess kit.

"Move it, Fast," Knowles said. He was next in line. "I want my chow." Pennell was ironically called "Fast Talking Man," or "Fast" for short, because he said so little and said it slowly.

That was one tactic the Marines of Tango Niner used to get the extra rations for two of their PFs. They used the other one to get the third and fourth meals they needed.

A few minutes after Robertson and Pennell had each taken an extra ration, Lance Corporal John Hempen reached the food table. No one knew where he had gotten them, but Hempen owned two mess trays of the type used in mess halls—stamped aluminum with six depressions for entree, two vegetables, bread, dessert, and milk glass or coffee cup. He carried one of those mess trays now. The cook blinked once at the unexpected tray, then slopped the meat, potatoes, and gravy across three of the sections. Instead of moving on to the next cook, Hempen stayed in front of the first cook and held it closer to the deep pans holding the food. The cook looked blankly at the tray for a moment, then made a "move along" motion with his ladle. Hempen replied with a "put more on it" jerk of the tray.

"You got enough," the cook said. "Move it."

"I'm a growing boy," Hempen said, "I need more than most men. Gimme more." He held the tray closer to the pans.

The cook looked down at Hempen on the other side of the table. "Move it, mouse," he said.

"I'm not a mouse, I'm a growing boy. I need more food."

"Fuck off, short round. Move." The cook didn't call Hempen by his nickname—mouse and short round are names Marines use for all short men whose names they don't know. The cook looked at Hempen's bush hat. "You're in that CAP, not this company," he said. "You should be glad I'm giving you any food at all." He was still pissed off about having given Robertson and Pennell the extra rations earlier.

Men in the field are served their food in reverse order of rank, privates first, generals last. There's a morale factor at work there; it's supposed to make the men feel their leaders care about them. It also helps keep the leaders honest—if they don't make sure there's enough food to go around, they are the ones who go hungry. The reverse order of rank is why Hempen didn't come through the line with Robertson and Pennell and why Billy Boy Lewis was next to him carrying the other mess tray. It's also why corporals Zeitvogel, McEntire, and Slover—all of whom stood more than six feet tall—were standing behind him and Lewis instead of being in line with him. Tex Randall—who was only five foot ten—was holding the other corporals' place in line with Corporal Ruizique. The three had rifles, borrowed from men in their platoon, slung over their shoulders. Because they had been officially disarmed they risked disciplinary action if they were caught carrying them.

Zeitvogel leaned forward slightly and laid a hand on Hempen's shoulder. His hand rested little higher than his own elbow level and his hand flowed over Hempen's shoulder, covering large parts of his chest, back, and upper arm. He looked down at the cook from half-a-foot higher and said, "This here little bitty Mo-rine's one of my men, and I need him for my basketball team. You gonna stand there with your teeth in your mouth and your bare face hanging out and tell me you ain't going to let him eat enough to grow tall enough to play roundball?"

The cook screwed his face up at Zeitvogel. "You're shitting me, right?"

"No way, my man"—Zeitvogel grinned broadly—"I wouldn't shit you. You're my favorite turd." He leaned over more, so his shoulder hovered over the hand that engulfed Hempen's shoulder. "Now you're just going to give my little 'pano enough chow he can grow up into a full-sized man 'n' quit being the runt of my litter, aren't you?" Hempen smiled a cherubic smile and continued holding his tray out to the cook.

The cook swore to himself, looking at the easy way the tall black corporal rested his right hand on his slung rifle and at the other two big corporals standing with him with their arms folded across their chests. The three corporals all wore the bush hats of the Combined Action Platoon. Scowling, the cook slopped more food on the tray. "This is bullshit," he said. "I'm going to have the first sergeant deal with it."

"I'm a certified war hero, my man," Zeitvogel told the cook, "I got me a Bronze Star. First sergeants don't scare me."

Hempen moved on and Lewis took his place. The cook looked at the tray in his hands and at the three CAP corporals who still stood there. "Now what," he said.

"My fire team leader said I'm too skinny and I need double rations to bulk up," Lewis said innocently and tipped his head back at McEntire. Corporal Dennis McEntire was not Lewis's fire team leader, he was the machine gun team leader. What he was, though, was a huge man who looked taller than the one inch over six feet he actually was. His nickname was Wall. Big Louie Slover decided he should be called Wall because "He's not tall enough to be a Tree and not fat enough to be a Bear."

"Right," the cook said and dumped double portions on the tray without any more argument.

"You are going to tell the Top about this, aren't you," Lewis said as eagerly as before. "I don't like having to eat double rations because it fills me up too much and makes me feel like I'm getting fat. I don't want to get fat. Do you think I should get fat? I mean, would you want to get fat just because your fire team leader thought you were too skinny?"

The cook scowled and pulled his stomach in.

The cooks had close to a hundred and ninety men to

feed, a hundred and ninety men who sidestepped one at a time through the chow line in reverse order of rank from private to captain. Only three men, Captain Ronson and his executive officer and weapons platoon leader, both of whom were first lieutenants, went through the line after Second Lieutenant Burrison. Willy and Vinh ate with Robertson and Pennell when they brought their mess kits up the hill, Houng and Collard Green chowed down with Hempen and Lewis when they arrived with the mess trays. The CAP NCOs and Burrison ate when they got their food.

This is a hell of a way to have to do it when you invite your friends over for dinner, but when someone else changes the rules on you after you've settled in you make what accommodations you can to live with the new system. Burrison and Bell were annoyed that they didn't get to talk business with their PF counterparts over dinner. But they got their business done anyway. It didn't take long.

The three squad leaders had assigned their men to find all of the civilians they knew who had been hired to work on rebuilding Camp Apache and find out if anyone seemed to know anything that could shed light on the two mysterious packages the lieutenant colonel had found in the sideless outhouse. It had taken a half-day for them to locate forty-five of the fifty men who had worked on the compound. Many of those forty-five reported the presence of a few strangers, strangers who had dug the new pit for the four-holer and erected its box and roof. No one seemed to know the names of the strangers, but enough were able to give physical descriptions that matched so that they were able to get a good idea of what they looked like. One of the men who mentioned the strangers said he thought he had seen one of them with Captain Phang, another said he thought some of them worked for Captain Phang, and two others had overheard them talking about how much Captain Phang was paying them to do this work.

"We've got to find those men," Burrison said.

Houng nodded. "We find," he said. "Phang boo-coo numba ten. We get Phang."

One other piece of business concerned Collard Green.

He was to go back to his middle-aged relative by marriage through his mother-in-law and try to convince her to testify against Phang for killing her friend. Collard Green's face twisted as he reluctantly agreed to this assignment and several of the Marines near him involuntarily drew back. His complexion had a constant slight greenish cast to it, making him look chronically dyspeptic. When his face twisted this way he looked like he was about to throw up. That's why the Marines called him Collard Green—that and the fact that none of them could pronounce his name with its three different inflected vowels.

The final piece of business was the night's patrol orders. Webster would take Lewis, Robertson, Collard Green, and five of his men and set an overnight ambush overlooking the cleft the Song Du Ong flowed through. Hempen, Pennell, and Wells would patrol the area east of Camp Apache, from the rice paddies above Hou Dau to the bend in the river where the market hamlet Hou Cau started. Vinh and five of his men would go with them. Echo Company would set two ambushes in the scrub forest west of Camp Apache.

"What is this shit," Lewis mumbled, "how come I don't get to lead a patrol?"

They were getting up to prepare themselves for the night when Swarnes called from the entrance to his radioroom. Ronson wanted Burrison and Bell at his CP toot-sweet and three helicopters were less than five minutes out.

CHAPTER ELEVEN

Late afternoon, November 9, 1966

Captain Phang relaxed in his office at the district headquarters in Phouc Nam city. He held a cigarette French style in his left hand; the cigarette was between his thumb and index finger pointing away from his hand—his palm cupped his chin when he brought the cigarette's end to his mouth. That mouth smiled a tight smirk. He sat at his desk, a highly polished expanse of teak, and gazed lovingly at the exquisite jade carvings he had so artfully arranged at the left front corner of the desk where they could most impress visitors. On the other front corner stood a plaque, a sheet of engraved bronze mounted on an exotic imported wood—black walnut, he had been told. The plaque had been given to him by an American Army adviser and the words on it expressed gratitude for his assistance to the advisers in 1964–65. It wasn't stated on the metal that Phang's assistance had kept the American officers' club well supplied with liquor, food, bartenders, cooks, waiters, and boom-boom girls. And the American officers seemed to be unaware that Phang had shared with his boss, the district chief, in twenty-five percent of the price of the liquor and food and one-half of the wages of the Vietnamese nationals who worked in the club—wages that were handed over to the district chief and his assistants, who then paid the workers. A sterling silver cigarette box sat near an obsidian ashtray right where his left hand would most easily come to rest. A small framed photograph of a smiling woman looked at him from the near right corner of his desk; visitors who did not know would think this woman was Phang's wife, while those who knew better did not know who she was. There were no in and out baskets.

On the wall behind him hung a large framed photograph of Air Marshal Ky, autographed by the premier himself. Framed paintings and citations also hung on the other walls of Phang's office. Richly colored panels of silk were suspended from the ceiling, giving the room the air of a desert princeling's tent. Phang's chair was upholstered in oiled leather, and the visitors' chairs were fine rattan. A divan with a pillow at one end lay along one wall. A folded silk sheet was hidden under the pillow. When a beautiful woman came to request a favor from him he would unfold the sheet onto the divan for her to demonstrate to him the sincerity of her request and the depth of her need. Phang had long since lost count of the number of beautiful women who had convinced him on that couch.

A Chinese man sat across from Phang. He looked as relaxed as the ARVN official. "Well, my friend," he said, "my agent in the labs has reported the test results have been reported as we knew they would be."

"They could have been reported no other way," Phang said and bowed his head slightly, "thanks to your generosity." They talked in the melodious Vietnamese singsong.

The Chinese lifted a hand to wave away the thanks. Gold glittered from his fingers. "Four kilos of heroin are little enough to expend in support of your cause—I should say, our cause. You have been of untold assistance to me in collecting the rents honestly due to me, rather than the parsimonious amounts officially permitted by the Saigon regime. Without your aiding me in collecting half of all the crops harvested by my tenant farmers, as provided in the leases that have been signed in all generations since my family was ceded that land, instead of the niggardly quarter of the primary crop only as the meddling Americans forced your Saigonese to agree to, I would be impoverished today."

Phang's smile deepened the slightest iota. He knew that if this Chinaman only collected the legal rent he would be richer by far than Phang ever hoped to become. Collecting as much as he did, he was wealthy beyond Phang's wildest dreams. The foreign dragon did not understand that Phang helped him collect his usurious rents only because he split ten percent of the charges in excess of the legal ceiling with his district chief. At least Phang thought the Chinese did not understand this.

"At any rate," the Chinese landlord continued, "those meddling Marines who have caused you so much distress are threatening to prevent me from taking that which is due me from the coolie farmers who owe to me their livelihoods and all they claim to own."

"It is good that those meddlers have been placed under house arrest as they have; they have been unable to do anything against either of us since then." Phang picked up the conversation again. "A house girl in the Marine compound has passed information to me that the Marine doan truong, the lieutenant colonel, whom I had informed about the hiding place of the heroin, is about to convene a court-martial for the Marines of Tango Niner. They have already been hamstrung. Soon they will be gone from us forever."

The corrupt Vietnamese official continued smoking and smiling at his companion. The Chinese steepled his fingers before his mouth and looked back inscrutably. They sat this way a while longer, each considering in his own mind the other's value to him and how to prevent the other from getting an unacceptable upper hand in their relationship.

* * *

First Sergeant Graves met the CAP leaders at Echo Company's CP. "Come on," he said. "The Skipper's already at the LZ," and led them to the open place where the helicopters could touch down. Three birds were drawing near by the time they reached it. Two of them flew low; the other was a couple of hundred feet higher. The low-flying choppers went into orbit around Echo Company's camp and Camp Apache. Machine guns were visible on each side of them. The third bird stayed higher until the others had completed two circuits, then came down facing into the billowing plume of smoke released by the green smoke grenade thrown to guide it in. The other two continued circling the camp.

A tall Marine with a craggy face burst off the helicopter before it finished settling to the ground. He was followed closely by another Marine with captain's bars on the collars of his utility shirt.

"I've got bad news and bad news, and some of it's worse for me than for you," the tall Marine said. He was the lieutenant colonel, and he never wasted time on pleasantries when he came to Camp Apache. "The bad news for you," he said to Burrison and Bell, "is the lab report came back positive. Those two packages each held a kilogram of pure heroin. I've referred the matter to Division legal and requested that a court-martial board be convened." He turned to Ronson and Graves. "Your bad news is late this afternoon a battalion ran into something bigger than it can handle by itself and your company is the only operational unit available to assist it. Have your people saddle up. A helicopter squadron will be here at oh seven hundred to lift them out. You will go back with me for a briefing and be returned afterward so you can brief your platoon leaders." The last was directed at Ronson. "That's worse for me"— he turned back to Burrison and Bell—"because it means I have to reactivate you and your NCOs and delay the court-martial I requested earlier today. It also means I have to put someone else in command here. That someone is Captain Hasford"—he indicated the other man who got off the helicopter with him. "Any questions?" There were none. "Captain Ronson, hand command over to your XO and get on my bird. I'm ready to leave now." He turned to Hasford. "Ronson will bring your gear with him when he returns."

The lieutenant colonel gave Burrison and Bell a piercing look, spun on his heel, and strode back to his helicopter. He ducked under its spinning blades and climbed aboard.

"Top, tell Smitty he's got the duty until I get back," Ronson said and followed the lieutenant colonel.

Hasford, who was an intelligence officer with an infantry background, looked at the three Marines standing bewildered in front of him. "Top," he finally said, "get your XO. I didn't expect to be staying here just yet, so I want to meet with all four of you."

When they assembled in Echo Company's CP, the four quickly briefed Hasford on the night's patrol scheme. He thought for a moment, then asked Burrison, "Can you get in touch with Lieutenant Houng in time to change the plans?"

The young lieutenant glanced at his watch. "I think so."

"Do it. We'll draw up new orders that use only Tango Niner personnel." He saw Bell staring at him blank-faced and added, "Don't worry, Sergeant, I don't know this area but you and your people do. I'm not going to make your patrol orders—that's your job. You two get started on drawing up your patrol routes so we can get them out tonight." He turned to Graves. "Return their weapons, Top."

Graves nodded slowly and locked eyes briefly with the CAP leaders. He led them to the company's gunnery sergeant who was holding the weapons and told him to release them. Minutes later the two were on their way back up their hill, grinning. Bell carried two of his fire team leader's M-14s slung over one shoulder, his own and the third on the other shoulder. Burrison stuck his issue .45 in his belt and slung Slover's and McEntire's weapons over his left shoulder while his own rifle dangled in his right hand.

"Man, this feels good," Bell said. "These past few days

are the first time except for liberty and leave I've been unarmed since I hit receiving barracks at Parris Island."

"I know what you mean, Jay Cee," Burrison agreed. "In OCS and the Basic School, they drilled into me how you never let your weapon be out of reach."

"Billy Boy, Short Round," Bell shouted as he and Burrison entered the Camp Apache compound.

In seconds they were surrounded by all their Marines.

"What'd you do, break into an armory?" Randall asked when he saw the rifles they carried.

"Hey, man, they got some kind of special slot machine down there, you drop in a quarter and if bars come up it feeds you M-14s?" Zeitvogel asked.

"Which one is mine?" was all Ruizique wanted to know. He held his close and started talking softly to it when it was handed to him.

While Burrison explained to most of the platoon what was happening, Bell gave Hempen and Lewis instructions. "Take the jeep and go to town, go to Houng's hootch. Bring him and his squad leaders back here most ricky-tick. Go."

They went. With the jeep the trip to Hou Ky took a few short minutes—the way Lewis drove it. He told Hempen it was how he learned to drive with the revenuers on his trail. They found the PF lieutenant, Collard Green, and Willy at Houng's home. Vinh and half of his squad had already left for Hou Dau, where they were to meet Hempen's team.

"You fill these guys in, I'll go get Vinh and his people," Lewis said. "See you back at Camp Apache." He revved the motor, ground gears, and spun his tires racing back the way he came.

"Echo Company's dee-deeing out in the morning," Hempen explained. "Tango Niner is back in business as of now. Get your men and let's go get our new orders for tonight." A grin split his face. Houng and his squad leaders looked like they were trying to outdo him and each other with their smiles.

Because of the last-minute change in plans, Ruizique and Vinh would form up their patrol in Camp Apache. The other PFs who would be patrolling needed to be alerted about the changes. It took Collard Green and Willy twenty minutes to locate all the Popular Forces platoon members who were scheduled to go out and notify them. When all had been informed, Collard Green and Willy rejoined Hempen and Houng and the four walked back to Camp Apache. When they passed from the trees into the open they saw Lewis speeding through the main gate with several passengers bouncing in the back of the jeep. They'll be sore tomorrow, Hempen thought. He rubbed his own backside. There wasn't much cushioning on the jeep's passenger seat. "So will I," he said aloud. The Vietnamese looked at him, wondering what he was talking about, but were so happy to be reunited with their Marines they didn't ask.

Houng recognized Hasford immediately and greeted him warmly in rapid Vietnamese. Hasford was the only American he had met who could speak Vietnamese almost as well as a Saigonese, and the Saigonese could speak the language almost as well as the Vietnamese could. They spoke briefly for a few minutes, the PF lieutenant expressing how glad he was that his friend Trung Si Bell and the others were back at their duties with the platoon, and the Marine captain explaining to him how it was only temporary because of the heroin problem. They switched to English.

"You no worry her-rin," Houng assured Hasford. "Chay Cee not sell her-rin. That be Phang do." He spat into the dirt. "Phang numba fucking ten. We know, we prove."

"Sir," Burrison said, "I hope you don't believe we had anything to do with that heroin. Captain Phang has to be the most corrupt person I've ever encountered and he knows we're fighting him. We know he had it planted on us. Houng and his men are close to locating the people he had do it. All we need is a little more time and we'll be cleared of these absurd charges."

"I hope you are, Lieutenant," Hasford said, "but the heroin was found here and the burden of proof is on you.

Proving such a thing against an official of the government we are defending won't be easy without a smoking gun."

Bell replied by telling Hasford, with much help from Burrison and Randall, about the false indemnity claims Phang was filing, claims that said the Marines of Tango Niner were burning down homes, killing livestock, and injuring and killing people in villages they hadn't even heard of, much less visited.

When he was through Houng picked it up again and told Hasford about his platoon's investigation, what they had done, what they had learned, and what their next steps were. "One day, two day," he concluded. "We very close find men Phang give her-rin, put here."

Hasford listened carefully to everything. He stopped them only to ask an occasional penetrating question. When they were through he said, "I'll do whatever I can to help your investigation, but"—he held up a hand to stop the Marines and PFs from getting carried away with something he wasn't promising—"I won't do anything to impede the legal proceedings. You are innocent until proven guilty, but the wheels of justice must turn."

CHAPTER TWELVE

Early night, November 9, 1966

Now it was time to give out the revised patrol orders. Stilts Zeitvogel's team and Collard Green, along with five of his men, would sit in ambush near the foot of the finger ridge coming down from the mountains, in a place where they could also watch the western rice paddies. Tex Randall and his fire team, plus Willie and half his squad, were to cover the trail leading from the Song Du Ong's gorge.

"Zeke, you take Knowles from the gun team and Athen and Reid from mortars for your team," Burrison told Ruizique, the corporal from the Dominican Republic. "Vinh and five of his men will fill out your patrol. Go out an hour after Tex does and set in on the river a hundred and fifty meters short of his position." A sheet of acetate with lines drawn on it overlaid his tactical map, his fingers tracing the lines as he gave the orders.

"Where's that leave me and the Wall?" Big Louie Slover asked.

"I don't think we'll need your tube or Wall's gun tonight," Hasford said.

"If we do," Bell broke in, "you and Flood can handle the piss tube just fine, and Wall's big enough—he's a one-man gun team all by himself."

The two weapons corporals laughed. They knew they were good, but aside from them and Flood, there were only the two officers, docs Rankin and Trackers, and Swearin' Swarnes to hold the compound after the patrols went out, and that wasn't enough.

"Maybe Captain Ronson will be willing to put a squad up here tonight to help out," Burrison said. Then he turned to Houng. "I want you to take the rest of your platoon and set another ambush a hundred meters east of Stilts's."

"The duc," the PF lieutenant said, "can do." He nodded vigorously. At his home in Hou Ky hamlet he had a PRC-20 radio set to the frequency used by the Marines and he often monitored the radio transmissions of the patrols. He usually had up to ten of the PFs who weren't patrolling with the Marines spend the night with him. If anyone needed help he and the rest of his platoon could act as a reaction force, but he didn't often take out scheduled patrols of his own. Being asked to now pleased him.

"Last night," Hasford said, "a Vee Cee platoon followed a short distance behind a supply train. If Hempen's ambush had opened up on that supply run, that Vee Cee platoon would have been in perfect position to wipe out our friendly forces when they were inspecting the bodies. If this is a new tactic Charlie's using to hurt us so he can get his supplies through, we're going to be ready for him tonight. Zeitvogel, Randall"—he looked both corporals in the eye when he said their names—"if a supply run walks into either of your killing zones tonight, let it go. Get on the horn and notify the next squad down it's coming. And then watch for anyone following it. If the Viet Cong think they can make a trick that already failed against this platoon once work by pulling it again, they're going to be sadly mistaken. Questions?"

As usual, there weren't. The radio call signs were Ballroom and Rumba. Zeitvogel was Rumba One, Randall was Rumba Two, Ruizique Three, and Houng Four. The PFs left to assemble and brief their men, the Marines prepared to move out themselves.

The last rays of the setting sun were flashing over the mountaintops. Lewis shrugged and did as he was told. He was angry again because he hadn't been given the chance to lead a patrol himself, but at least if he wasn't the patrol leader, it was because the patrol leader was his regular fire team leader, the corporal he had followed for two months. Randall followed the wiry automatic rifleman and was trailed by Wells. Pennell brought up the rear.

Echo Company's camp was bustling with activity as its Marines finished readying themselves to be lifted out at first light. Night had fully fallen by the time the CAP patrols left the grunt company behind. Lewis picked his way through the cane fields toward the broad band of trees lining the river where it widened out before swinging on an arc to the northeast, where it bent southeast at Hou Cau hamlet. At the river's widest point there was a ford immediately upstream from a small island. A few derelict hootches were all that remained of the fishing hamlet of Hou Binh, which had once thrived on that small spit of land in the river. The Vietcong had visited the island too many times and taken too many fish from the villagers; and their visits had been followed too many times by the ARVNs looking for the VC, and taking too many of the fish the guerrillas had left. Finally the villagers of Hou Binh gave up and moved away—most of them to Hou Cau, where they continued to fish, while others went farther downriver to live in and fish for the hamlets of other villages.

When the Marines first arrived in Bun Hou, VC traveling down the river in sampans or walking along its south bank frequently used Hou Binh because, as an island, all approaches to it were open and any enemy coming to it could be seen before they got there. The Marines didn't see it that way, though—they saw the river as giving them clear fields of fire at the isolated hamlet. More than a hundred casualties inflicted by CAP ambushes over a three-month period convinced the VC to stay away from Hou Binh, and the island was now thoroughly deserted. Randall's fire team was to meet Willy and his men at the northern end of the ford and watch the island for half an hour before continuing upstream.

Minutes after Randall and his men left the Marine compound by its rear gate, Big Red Robertson left by the north gate and angled left toward the rice paddies that wrapped around Hou Ky. He was followed by Zeitvogel, Webster, and Hempen. Well inside Hou Ky was the home of Houng's brother, Thien, the hamlet chief. Thien's home was a stucco building that had been built by the French. The house was shaped like an L with a thick short leg and a thinner long leg. Thien and his family lived in the short leg and village elders who had lost their families to the war slept in stalls in the longer leg. The building formed two sides of a square that was bounded on its other sides by a low wall. Collard Green and his men were waiting for the Marines, sitting on benches, smoking cigarettes, and talking softly among themselves.

Robertson led the Marines around the west end of the building. At the corner he stopped and watched the unaware PFs. Zeitvogel joined his point man for a moment before scuffing his foot on the ground to warn the militiamen someone was coming—he didn't want to appear too suddenly and risk getting shot. The six small men, none of them wearing a complete uniform, jumped at the sound and spun toward it.

"Man, if we was Charlies you fuckers would be dead now," Zeitvogel said in a voice loud enough to reach the PFs but not loud enough to be heard beyond the square.

"Boo-shee-ich," answered the short Vietnamese they called Pee Wee. "We know you there. We want see how much boo-coo noise you make you snoop poop on us."

"Bullshit yourself, you little runt," Lewis snorted. "You

were watching for us to come the other way around. You couldn't of jumped any higher when Stilts kicked the dirt if we'd opened up on you with AKs."

The banter went on and everyone was grinning in the night. Except Collard Green. As usual, Collard Green looked like he was about to lose his dinner. "He looks like he just realized how nuoc mam tastes" is the way Randall once described the PF squad leader. But he had another reason for not grinning with the others—he knew the tall Marine corporal was right—even if they were in their own hamlet and they beat the Vietcong every time they met them, they should always be alert at night. Collard Green knew he had failed in an important aspect of his job. He would have to be more careful of security in the future.

Then Zeitvogel quieted everyone and organized his patrol. They paralleled the westbound trail.

An hour and a quarter after Randall pointed Lewis out the back gate of Camp Apache, Ruizique tapped Pham on the shoulder and nodded toward the opening in the wire. The PF picked his way through the staggered opening. A few minutes later the ten-man Combined Action Patrol was beyond Echo Company's security perimeter. Their route would lead them to a point on the river west of Hou Binh island; then they would prowl the water's edge until they reached their assigned ambush site.

At about that same time, Houng gave the rest of his men their final inspection, doused the yellow-orange flame of the kerosene lamp in the main room of his house, and, with one word, set his men out to patrol the edge of the paddies toward the place where they would sit in ambush for most of the night.

Three hundred meters to his right, barely visible through a narrow gap in the trees, Tex Randall could make out the sky in the deep vee of the gorge down which the Song Du Ong flowed from the mountain lake that was its birthplace. Seventy-five meters to his front, on the other side of the river's border of trees, the Song Du Ong bubbled across the flatlands to the South China Sea. The corporal looked at the luminous hands of his watch. He had radioed in his latest report when his patrol settled into its ambush, and it was almost time for his next report. Earlier, he had heard Stilts Zeitvogel report his ambush going to ground and a few minutes ago Houng had called in that he was in place. All that was missing was Ruizique. Randall looked at his watch again and wondered where the corporal from the Dominican Republic was—he should have been in place by now.

Jesus Maria Ruizique had enlisted in the United States Marine Corps on the strength of a promise that he would be given a captain's commission in the Army of the Dominican Republic if he attained the rank of corporal within four years. He did, and the entire time he had been in Tango Niner he had complained about being in Vietnam and insisted that all he wanted to do was complete his enlistment and go home to that commission. Ruizique thought the war in Vietnam was an American affair, one that he shouldn't be involved in. "If you Norte Americanos want to fight a war in Asia, that is your business," he said often and loudly. "But you gringos should not make we who are not your countrymen go to fight it, this war that is not ours." The counter argument, "When you enlisted you signed up for anywhere this Mean Green Machine wanted to send you," never stopped him from saying again later that he didn't belong where he was.

Randall hadn't said anything to anyone about it, but he noticed that Ruizique was acting oddly since the VC attempted to overrun Camp Apache. The enemy's last machine gun burst of that battle had given Ruizique's fire team one hundred percent casualties: Lance Corporal Steven Lam, an American of Chinese descent, and PFC Dale Carrilo, a Mexican-American from San Diego, were killed by that burst; PFC William "Kid" Tucker was badly enough broken up by it he had to be sent back to The World to have his wounds tended. A bullet tore through the fleshy part of Ruizique's arm. Since returning from the hospital and discovering he was under house arrest with the rest of the platoon's NCOs, the Latin corporal had become quiet and withdrawn. He didn't say anything about not belonging in Vietnam and he had nothing to say when a patrol made contact—although not saying anything about patrol firefights might be because he wasn't on them and he didn't have any men who could be involved in them. He seemed to be avoiding the other corporals, though they were all in the same situation and needed to work together to clear themselves of the charges. He always seemed to be sitting on the perimeter fingering a machete, or looking out over the countryside as though waiting. Where was he now, when his ten-man patrol should have already set into its ambush?

Where Ruizique and his patrol were was a few hundred meters short of where it was going. The patrol was taking longer than it should have because he wanted to cover both the river and the relatively open scrub on the north side of the band of trees along the river. The patrol route as assigned called for them to walk the river's edge for a quarter of the distance, then move over to the scrub side for the second quarter, the river again, and then the scrub for the final quarter before returning to water's edge to wait for the bad guys to wander into the trap. Ruizique had switched between river and scrub every two hundred meters. The band of trees along the river averaged close to a hundred meters deep—from twenty-five at its narrowest to a hundred and fifty at its broadest. The extra distance they walked ate up more time than had been allowed for.

The soft crackling of static on Randall's radio was silenced and the soft voice of Swearin' Swarnes on the radio at night came over the air. "Rumba Three, Rumba Three, this is Ballroom. Come in, please, over." Two seconds were swept away by the sweep hand of Randall's watch before he heard Ruizique's voice respond, "Ballroom, Rumba Three. Go."

"Three, Ballroom. Have you reached your objective yet? Over."

"That's a negative, Ballroom. I've been going slow and easy. Will reach objective within one zero. Over." Ruizique's voice sounded very flat to Randall. He wondered if anyone else on the radio net noticed.

"You will reach your objective in one zero. Roger, Three. Ballroom out."

That's what Ruizique said, ten more minutes until he was in place. He wouldn't, though. It was closer to a half an hour before Rumba Three was in its ambush site. At least nothing went wrong because of it. The only thing the delay did was give Captain Hasford his first taste of the frustration the platoon leader could feel because of the independent way the Tango Niner fire team leaders ran their patrols. If any of them had known what Hasford was feeling they would have thought, He'll get over it. The three ambushes that were already in place radioed in their next situation reports before all four were settled. "Ballroom, Rumba One. Situation as before, over," Zeitvogel murmured tersely into his radio. "One, roger. Ballroom out," Swarnes replied. Randall and Houng in turn made identical terse reports and got identical replies. Radio traffic was kept at a minimum to maintain silence.

In each ten-man ambush, five men slept while five men watched, three to the front, two to the rear. Every two hours the watchers woke the sleepers and then took their own turn sleeping. Until the moon set.

CHAPTER THIRTEEN

Late night, November 9, 1966

Randall woke instantly at the light touch of Lewis's hand on his shoulder. He waited for his automatic rifleman to say something, but understood to listen to the night sounds when Lewis touched his finger to Randall's lips. Then he heard why Lewis woke him. Or rather he didn't hear it. The night was unnaturally, deadly silent around him, the only sound was the faint gurgling of the river. The insects, night birds, and lizards had stopped their night hunting and courting. Randall shifted his body as quietly as he could until his mouth was near Lewis's ear. "Anything?" he said into it. He felt rather than saw the other man's head shake. Then Lewis took his hand and pointed it to the right front, indicating that as the direction someone was most likely coming from, the direction from where silence had fallen.

Randall listened, breathing through his mouth to eliminate even that amount of noise. After an eternal several seconds he heard a muted snap—the sound of a not-quite-dry twig breaking under a soft-shod foot. The snap sounded like it was less than fifteen feet away, too close to risk making noise by waking the other sleeping members of his patrol. He depressed the speak button on his radio to eliminate the soft fuzz of static coming from it. The silence on their radios would also alert everyone on the net. Randall hoped Pennell and the three PFs who were awake understood well enough to let whoever it was go through, to not fire on them unless discovered. A shadow, dimly seen in the inky darkness under the trees, floated past, looking almost close enough to reach out and touch. A thin slice of starlight shot past a leaf that fluttered in the light night breeze and drew a faint line that disappeared almost as fast as it appeared on a rifle barrel. The shadow moved on and was replaced by another drifting shadow, a shadow made larger than the first by a huge pack. Three more bulky shadows floated almost soundlessly past, followed by a thinner shadow, then no more.

Randall waited for a long moment before releasing the radio's speak button and putting his mouth near Lewis's ear again to say, "Wake everyone." He again felt rather than saw the other man's head movement. The VC supply train was not on the trail, it was walking parallel to it and had almost walked on the ambush. He thought the VC were finally beginning to understand the danger of coming through Bun Hou.

The corporal pushed on his radio's speak button again and said into it, "Rumba Three, this is Two. Six bad guys coming your way. They are not on the trail. I say again, they are not on the trail. They almost stepped on me. Do you understand? Over."

"Two, Three," Ruizique answered immediately. Randall knew he must have been waiting for a transmission ever since he first broke squelch. "Six bad guys almost stepped on you. Gracias. Three out."

The static was cut again and Swearin' Swarnes's voice

said, "Rumba Two, Rumba Three, this is Ballroom. I heard your last. Stand by."

Randall wondered why Swarnes had told them to stand by, what message was coming their way? He didn't have long to wonder. A new voice came over the radio, Hasford's voice. "All Rumbas, this is Ballroom Actual. Full alert. Count off to acknowledge, over."

"One," Zeitvogel answered.

"Two," Randall said softly.

"Three." Ruizique.

"Four." Houng.

All four ambushes had everyone awake.

Randall waited and listened. He waited and listened for anything that would warn of the approach of more men from the west and for the sound of gunfire when the supply run reached Ruizique's killing zone—if the third ambush was in a location the VC could be detected from. Coming on the other side of the trail, the Vietcong might be able to slip by undetected.

Then Ruizique called Camp Apache. "Ballroom, Rumba Three," he said. "I have boo-coo unlit boats on the water, over."

Unlit boats on the water could only be Vietcong infiltrators. Fishermen were allowed to ply the river at night, but their boats were required to carry lit lamps or torches. Any boat seen at night without lights was assumed to be the enemy and was a free target for anyone who saw it.

"Three, Ballroom. How many? Over."

"I see six, make that seven, Ballroom. There are probably more that aren't close enough to spot yet. Over."

"Roger, Three, stand by." Swarnes sounded excited. He came back immediately. "Rumba Two, can you get to the water and take a look? Over."

Randall's throat tightened; he did not want to be crossing the river's fringe of trees when a VC platoon came through, if one was coming. But it wasn't far, only about sixty meters from where his patrol was to the other side of the trees. They could do it in a hurry. "Roger that, Ballroom," he said into his radio. "I am moving. Out."

Then he tapped the men at his sides and said to them, "On your feet, we're going to the river. Pass it down and pass it back." He stood up and waited. An almost inaudible murmur and rustling faded away from him as the order was passed and the men in the ambush rose to their feet. The murmuring increased again in volume until the men on both sides told him, "Everyone's up."

Passing the word down and back wasn't as efficient as the patrol leader going from man to man himself, but it was faster for each man to tell the man on his far side and the men on the ends of the line to repeat the order to the men they received it from, who repeated it to the men they got it from until it got back to the patrol leader.

"Line on me. Pass it, let's go." This time Randall didn't wait for the word to come back to him, he just started walking as fast as he thought he could without sounding like an elephant crashing through the woods. In a moment he was looking through the trees at the Song Du Ong. "Holy shit," he whispered to himself. A line of boats was visible as dim shadows on the river. "Ballroom, Two," he said into the radio. "I see boo-coo boats. Over."

"Two, Three, stand by for light," Swarnes drawled.

"Standing by."

But the river wasn't the only place there was movement. To the north Zeitvogel lay with his unfocused eyes scanning the paddies dimly lit under the stars. A hint of movement on the left flickered in his vision. Without thinking of what he was doing, he pointed his still unfocused eyes to the side of where he thought he saw the movement and waited for it to come again. At night peripheral vision is far superior to direct, and movement is easier to spot than shapes. How to use night vision was a skill Zeitvogel had developed with long practice. He waited and the movement came again. And he saw more flickers behind the first. Ruizique was talking on the radio telling Ballroom about the unlit sampans when Zeitvogel first saw the movement. Randall reached the riverbank and reported more boats when the first fire team leader saw movement again. He waited for a pause in the transmissions before making his own report. "Charlie wants to tango tonight," he finished.

Hasford came on the radio. "How many do you have, One? Over."

"I'm not sure, Actual," Zeitvogel answered. "Vague movement I can see out of the corner of my eye, not people I can count. Over."

"Roger, One," Hasford said. "You and Four keep sharp." At the moment the boats on the river seemed more important. "Two and Three, Two has tactical command. Two, it's in the tube. Stand by to adjust, over."

Randall heard the mortar's *carumph* on the radio almost obliterating Hasford's last words. "Roger, Actual," he said. Then the sound of the mortar reached him through the air. The dimly perceived boats seemed to swerve slightly toward the middle of the river. A shrill whistling from Randall's left told him the mortar round was descending on the final leg of its trajectory. A few shouts came from the boats and they started moving more rapidly in all directions. The flare round popped open with a small explosion and there was a sharp hissing before it ignited. The flare drifted slowly downward on its miniature parachute and cast an eerie blue light over the river, illuminating more than twenty scattering sampans. Each sampan had two or three or four men in it and they all seemed to be so heavily loaded with cargo their gunwales were barely above water.

Randall's thumb smashed down on the speak button of his PRC-6 radio and he screamed "Open fire" into it and at his own men. At two different places along the river a dozen carbines, two full automatic M-14s, and five of the main battle rifles firing semiautomatic opened up at the sampans and their panicking crews.

"Ballroom, Two," Randall said more calmly into the radio, "there are at least twenty sampans out there, just on my side of the center of the river. Rear boat is upstream from me, lead is down from Three. The flare round was on target, put some Hotel Echo with proximity fuses out here. Those boats are scattering fast. Over."

"Two, what direction are they scattering in? Over."

Swarnes was back on the radio and he sounded very much in control.

"Upstream, downstream, and to both banks. They're spreading out fast. Fire for effect now or it'll be too late, over."

"Fire in the tube, Two. Stand by to direct. Do you want more light? Over."

"Put out some HE. Give me another light in about thirty seconds. Over."

"Roger. Hotel Echo on its way."

Half of the twenty-four boats the Vietcong were using to try to ferry supplies down the Song Du Ong were headed for the south bank of the river. Four were trying to make their way back upstream and an equal number were attempting to flee downstream. The rest were heading for the north bank, and one of them was pointed straight at Randall. The muscular corporal put his radio down for a moment and sighted his rifle on the man poling it in the front. He squeezed the trigger and immediately locked his sights on the second, rear, poler. He didn't see the first one flip backward into the water. He blew the second poler out of the boat and dropped his aiming point to the water in front of the prow. He cranked off five quick rounds and saw the overloaded fifteen-foot craft shudder under the impact of the heavy bullets slamming into and through its wooden bow below the waterline. The sampan stopped its forward movement and started drifting downstream, its front slowly dipping deeper into the water.

Six high explosive antipersonnel mortar rounds arced down in rapid succession. Their proximity fuses set them off before they reached the surface of the river, and they spewed shrapnel out and down in cones of death. But the boats were too widely spread over too large a part of the river and only three of them were rocked by the flying chunks of jagged metal. A second flare popped open overhead, lighting up the night like a fragment of sun turned loose.

Randall quickly scanned the scene on the river. He decided nothing could be done about the boats speeding to the west, but the others were another matter. "Ballroom, Two," he said into his radio's mouthpiece, "a dozen are headed for the south shore on a two-hundred-meter front. Its west anchor is on me. Drop some Hotel Echo over the water near the shore. Do you understand? Over."

"That's an affirmative, Two," Swarnes said back. "Hotel Echo on its way to the south edge of the Song. Over."

"Tell the big boys at the foot of the hill there's four more boats coming down. If they meet them at the ford in about twenty minutes they can party hearty, over."

"Roger that, Two," Swarnes said. He sounded excited. "I'll pass the word."

Then Randall turned his attention to the two sampans that were beaching themselves between his patrol and Ruizique's—one other was drifting aimlessly in the water, its crew either dead or dying. Seven VC were scrambling ashore between the two CAP positions. He thought fast: there was no safe way for either of the units to advance toward the Vietcong, no way they could move without running too great a risk of getting shot down by the other. "Billy Boy, Jesse James, Fast, fire on the boats across the river," he shouted to his Marines. The he ordered the PFs, "Willy, you see Vee Cee?" and pointed to where the two boats crews were landing on their side of the river.

"Me see," Willy shouted back over the bedlam of the three Marines firing their heavy rifles at the opposite shore and the mortar rounds exploding among the sampans trying to reach dry ground there.

"Fay epp stay down, fire on them. Okay?"

"We do," Willy answered, then gave rapid-fire instructions to his men. The six carbines started firing to the east.

"Three, Two," Randall said into his radio. He instructed Ruizique to have his Marines shoot across the river and to have his PFs catch the Charlies in a crossfire. The M-1 and M-2 carbines the Popular Forces were armed with were much lighter weapons than the Marines' M-14s. Randall thought the lightweight, low-powered bullets wouldn't be likely to get all the way through the hundred and fifty meters of trees between the two ambush sites, but the 7.62mm rounds the Marines used would.

Another flare popped above the river and Randall looked to the west to see if it was worthwhile sending any mortar rounds after the sampans going in that direction. "Oh, shit!" he shouted. Out of the corner of his eye he spotted bodies illuminated by the flare moving toward him through the trees. "Everybody turn around," he shouted. "This way!" And opened up on the VC platoon that was gathering to assault his ambush from its flank.

There was instant confusion on both sides. The Vietcong massing on the flank were caught by surprise by the sudden light from the flare and Randall's fire. Only a few returned the fire right away. The other Marines and the PFs of the CAP patrol had forgotten about the possible covering platoons. But the Americans and their allies got organized first.

Within seconds the men of Rumba Two were turned around and blazing at the flickering figures visible through the trees. Randall picked up his radio again and said into it, "Ballroom, Two. Charlie's trying to flank me. Give me a spotter up fifty from my position, over."

Swarnes's reply was spoken slowly and measured. "Two, do we know where you're at? Over."

The question made Randall smile grimly. Under normal circumstances the corporals who ran Tango Niner's patrols put their heads together after getting their orders and re-arranged their times, routes, and ambush sites according to their own knowledge of the area and likely paths of enemy movement. But tonight, with four patrols out in ambushes in support of each other, they were all within fifteen meters of where the lines drawn on a map overlay said they were supposed to be. "That's affirmative, Ballroom," he answered. "I am sixty meters left of my original map location, over."

"Wait one, Two."

Randall looked up in time to see a black-clad soldier

with his rifle extended charging at one of the PFs. He shouted a warning and rapid-fired three rounds at the running man. The third round was a tracer, which told him he was down to one round in his twenty-round magazine. With one fluid motion, he knocked the empty out of the rifle's magazine well with his left hand, pulled a full one from its pouch on his belt with the other, and slammed it into the well. He had time to pick out another target and put two rounds into it before Swarnes came back on the radio.

"It's in the tube, Two," Swarnes said, "stand by to adjust."

There were screams all around Randall as the firefight rose to a fever pitch. Some screams were men yelling directions at each other, telling them where to shoot; some were curses or taunts at the enemy; some were screams of the wounded and the dying. AK-47s clanged and stuttered in the trees in front of him, and carbines, nearly drowned out by the louder booming of M-14s, chattered at his sides.

"Two, this is Three, should I move forward? Over," Ruizique wanted to know.

"Stay put, Three. There's too much shit flying around up here for you to make it," Randall radioed back. Then the spotter round hit earth and erupted behind the VC. "Ballroom, down twenty-five, fire for effect," Randall shouted into the radio.

"Rumba Two, Ballroom. Are you sure? Over." Twenty-five meters was a very fine adjustment for a mortar to make near the limit of its range. Most mortarmen wouldn't want to try it. But Big Louie Slover was on the mortar and the Marines of Tango Niner had total confidence in his abilities with the big tube. He said he could make his piss tube do things it wasn't designed to do and they believed him.

"I'm positive, Ballroom. Down twenty-five, fire for effect." If the mortar rounds weren't brought in closer to his own position, close enough for some fragments to fall in among his men and maybe wound some, they wouldn't hit the enemy and the VC would simply close in and out-number them three to one in hand-to-hand combat.

Slover must have been ready to make exactly the ad-justment Randall had requested because within seconds high explosive rounds started exploding on top of the VC. The screaming on that side increased and a new sound was added—the sound of bodies crashing through the brush, trying to run away from the death-dealing explosives.

"Up fifty, Ballroom," Randall transmitted, "up fifty." A second barrage of six rounds crashed into the trees close to him before the next ones fell farther away. Then the firing stopped. "Cease fire," Randall ordered his men and the mortar. The rounds that were already in flight completed their arcs, crashed down, and exploded. And then there was silence. Randall breathed deeply a few times, held his breath, and listened. The only sounds he could hear were the rushing of blood in his temples, the gurgling of the river, and the raspy breathing of some of his men.

"Billy Boy, check the troops," Randall ordered. On the radio he said, "Give me a candle twenty-five meters up from my location," and waited for Lewis's report on friendly casualties and for the illumination round so they could look for Vietcong bodies. Both came at the same time.

"Everybody's cool." Lewis laughed his relief. "Nobody got hurt."

"Bull-fucking-shit," Randall said, "I wasted three of them my-own-damn-self."

"I mean us, Honcho."

"Everybody, on line. Let's sweep through. Watch for anyone playing possum." He stood up and looked to both sides before sweeping his arms forward and walking to-ward the VCs' former position. Eight bodies were found where the rounds had fallen. Ruizique now moved Rumba Three forward and joined forces with Randall and his peo-ple. They swept the area between the two ambush sites and found four more bodies. They estimated somewhere be-tween six and ten others had been killed on the water.

More mortar-round flares showed several boats drifting down the river with the current; a few others might have been sunk.

In the meantime another drama was unfolding two kilometers to the north along the edge of the rice paddies.

CHAPTER FOURTEEN

At the same time, a couple of kilometers away

The flickering movement in the paddies stopped at the sound of the mortar firing its first illumination round. Zeit-vogel waited patiently for several minutes for it to start again. In the dark of night you don't see things by looking directly at them; you see with peripheral vision, out of the corners of your eyes. Look directly at something, and the gray shadow it is at night blends in with the gray shadows of everything else under the moon and the stars. Zeitvogel unfocused his eyes and let them rove from side to side, looking for any hint of movement or mass in the paddies. There was nothing to be seen under the stars. After a while, with the sounds of the fight on the river booming distantly to his rear, he curved his fingers and thumbs into tight tubes and held them in front of his eyes like binoculars. The small peepholes he looked through limited the breadth of his field of vision and brought everything into sharper focus. Details and shapes can be seen at night using this technique, but only if you already know where to look. Zeitvogel didn't know exactly where to look, but he had a good idea. So he looked and thought he saw a few darker lumps scattered on what should have been a smooth surface broken by the flat lines of paddy dikes, but he couldn't be positive that he actually saw them—or of what they were.

On another night the tall black Marine might wait and watch longer and then ask for an illumination round so he could see what was out there. If it was VC, his people would have light to see them, to aim their weapons—to waste them. If it was no one, he would move. But tonight the mortar was busy on the river, lighting up and pounding on a flotilla of sampans that Randall and Ruizique had ambushed. The mortar might be busy on the river for a long time and Zeitvogel didn't want to disrupt it from what it was doing to give him a candle where there might not be a target. He had to know what, if anything, was out there, so he got together with Hempen and Collard Green.

"I think someone's out there," he said. "I'm going to recon it. Swap blades with me, little bro." He held his bayonet hilt first to Hempen. The short Marine hesitated a second before taking it and handing over his own K-bar. The legendary Marine killing knife with a seven-inch blade looked like a penknife in Zeitvogel's huge hand. "I want Pee Wee to go with me," he said to Collard Green. "Two of us on a recon. Blades only, no rifles. Okay?" The Popular Forces squad leader nodded and went to get the tiny Vietnamese the Marines called Pee Wee. "Anybody got a sidearm?" Zeitvogel asked himself. He didn't say it aloud because he knew no one in his patrol did. The next time he had a chance, he resolved, he'd get one for himself. Maybe a Dan Wesson .357 magnum like the one Jay Cee Bell carried on his belt.

Collard Green crawled back with Pee Wee.

"A real Mutt and Jeff act," Hempen whispered.

Zeitvogel grinned. Yah, Mutt and Jeff. The six-foot-five Marine teamed up with a PF who topped the scale somewhere short of four-foot-ten. Yah, Mutt and Jeff. Quickly he explained to his diminutive partner what they were going to do and got a nod of understanding in return. "You're in charge until I get back. Make sure nobody wastes us when we come back in," he said to Hempen and handed him his rifle, radio, and bush hat. He gestured with the hand that held the K-bar and he and Pee Wee slipped into the first paddy.

The Northwest Monsoon was late. There had been heavy rains in the mountains but not yet on the flatlands, so the paddies weren't yet full of water. Only enough to make them uncomfortable to go through. They crawled low enough to be below the tops of the dikes. Pee Wee, on hands and knees, was wet to mid-thigh and to above his elbows. Zeitvogel, having to crawl much lower, was wet to his groin and his shoulders—he was barely able to keep the front of his shirt above water. They huddled at the next dike while the Marine eased his head up until his eyes were above it and he scanned the next paddy and the ones beyond it. From where he was, all he could see was starlight glimmering on the water of the next paddy and the dike on its other side. He flattened his body next to the dike and rolled over it in a fluid motion. Pee Wee did the same. An observer watching the right place at the right time in the right manner would have seen the dike top seem to buckle upward briefly in two places and flatten out immediately, but unless he had night vision equipment he wouldn't have known the significance of the buckling.

They crossed four more paddies the same way and when they rolled into the sixth paddy Zeitvogel came face-to-face with the one flaw in their method of movement. When he peered over the top of a dike it was impossible to see what was directly on the opposite side of it until he rolled to the other side. When he rolled into the sixth paddy he came down a foot away from a Vietcong soldier squatting low with his back against the dike wall and his head hanging between his knees. His rifle was held loosely in his hands, barely above the water. As surprised as he was to stumble on an enemy soldier, the other was caught so unprepared that Zeitvogel had more time than he needed to cup his left hand over the man's mouth and slit his throat with the K-bar that had never left his right hand. He grabbed the body and rifle before either could splash into the paddy's water and eased the one down before laying the other on the dike top where he could find it on the way back.

As soon as Pee Wee saw what was happening he looked around and saw a second VC squatting against the dike wall with his head between his knees a few feet away. The tiny man reached the other Cong before he could react and slashed upward with his knife, impaling him through the bottom of his jaw, slamming the mouth shut before a cry could escape, bursting through the bottom of his cranial cavity and killing him before he understood he was dying.

The huge American and the very small Vietnamese looked at each other and breathed deeply. Slowly they looked around the paddy, but they were alone with the two corpses. Zeitvogel pointed to the side of the paddy. They crawled to it and he looked over the top. Two more Vietcong squatted in the water against the south dike, their heads between their knees. They backtracked to the other side of the dike and looked over it. Two more VC were in it, waiting like the other four. Zeitvogel leaned close to his companion and mimed with his face and hands that they would check one paddy deeper before turning to the safety of the rest of the patrol. Pee Wee nodded.

The clatter of distant small arms fire to the south increased when they reached the dike separating them from the next paddy. Zeitvogel raised himself up and all he could see was the starlight on the water and the opposite dike. Cautiously he raised himself higher and slid forward on his chest to look at the other side of the dike he leaned against. The back of the shoulders and neck of another VC were directly below him. He looked to his left and saw Pee Wee hanging over another. There seemed to be two VC to a paddy. The PF waved his knife in a small arc and the Marine returned the gesture. He looked down at the hunched figure below him, considering his angle of attack.

Then he reversed the knife in his hand like an ice pick, slapped his hand onto the back of the man's head, and plunged the knife into the top of his shoulder, behind the collarbone and in front of the shoulder blade. He pushed the head into the water and twisted the knife, pulling it out and ramming it back in several times looking for the heart or aorta. The dead man thrashed weakly a few times and then settled softly into the water. A few feet away Pee Wee had dispatched his man and was already holding his rifle. Zeitvogel groped in the water in front of his victim to retrieve his weapon and slithered back into his own paddy. They crossed back, picked up the first two VCs' rifles, and, staying low, left the paddies as quickly as they could.

The firefight along the river reached a crescendo while Zeitvogel and Pee Wee retraced their path through the paddies. The Marine hadn't intended to go back the same way they had gone out and didn't like doing it, but with the VC in the paddies the way they were he didn't want to take the chance of rolling into one with enemy soldiers on its far side. He gathered his men as the last mortar rounds were falling among the Vietcong fleeing from their fight with Randall.

Zeitvogel had his Marines kneel by his sides facing the paddies so they could keep watch and the PFs squatted low, facing him from the front. "We got Charlie out there and I don't know how many." He described how he and Pee Wee had found the VC situated, two men in a paddy. He outlined a plan of action to them and waited until the messages coming over the radio made it clear the fight along the river was over. Then he called in his own situation report and outlined his plan to the CAP's leaders. Hasford gave him a go-ahead and Houng acknowledged he understood his ambush's role in the operation. "Let's go," he said and rose to his feet. He scanned the paddies with unfocused eyes once more and swore. He saw movement again out of the corner of his eyes. If the dead men hadn't been discovered yet, they would be soon. "Move it," he urged, and the ten-man combined patrol hurried to the west.

A hundred meters away they angled into the paddies—hunched low, they walked on a dike until the last man in the column was four paddies deep. They broke into two-man teams and turned parallel to the trees edging the paddies on the south and moved out slowly, two men on a dike. Fifty meters along they slowed even more and stopped. With no signals being passed, they all slipped into the paddies and got into fighting positions. Men who often fight at night and live to tell the tale usually develop a sort of sixth sense that tells them when there is activity nearby. Most of the men in Tango Niner had that sixth sense. Small noises, almost indistinguishable from normal background noises; nearly imperceptible flicks of movement; touches of alien aromas wafting on the air—all add up to tell the successful night fighter's heightened sense that someone who doesn't belong is there.

The VC had discovered the bodies and were searching for intruders in the paddies between them and the tree lines bordering them.

Zeitvogel held his radio's mouthpiece close to his lips and murmured, "They found the ones we wasted. Gimme some light." He didn't bother with call signs because he knew Swearin' Swarnes would recognize his voice and the fewer words he had to say out loud, the less chance a sharp-eared VC would hear him.

Houng didn't use the radio when he heard Zeitvogel's transmission; he just brought his men to their feet and rushed west, to close the gap between the two ambush patrols. Running softly, they covered fifty meters before a shrill whistling in the sky announced the arrival of the mortar round. Houng ran forward a few more meters before signaling his men to hit the deck. They barely got down before the flare fizzed to life.

The paddies looked empty.

"I know they're here," Zeitvogel murmured into his radio. "Pop in a few Willy Peter rounds." That'll wake them up, he thought. White phosphorus, a chemical that burned like the sands of hell when exposed to oxygen, was a terribly feared weapon. Water couldn't put it out because it would catalyze with the oxygen in water and burn as easily as with the oxygen in air. Only napalm, B-52 Arclight strikes, and the Vulcan gatling guns fired from C-47s, specially modified DC-3s called Puff the Magic Dragon, were more fearsome weapons.

The request for immediate Willy Peter was denied. The chemical couldn't be relied on to burst evenly in all directions and Hasford wanted to drop a high explosive round first to be certain of the aim. Zeitvogel had once seen a Willy Peter hand grenade spew all of its burning chemical a hundred feet in one direction, so it was easy for him to agree. "Fire one Hotel Echo spotter," he replied.

There was a distant *carumph* followed seconds later by the keening whistle of the round falling to earth. It exploded two paddies up and one to the right of Zeitvogel. He was glad his request for the Willy Peter had been turned down in favor of the HE. "On my azimuth," he said, "up fifty, left fifty." That much displacement would put the impacts far enough away to allow a safe margin in case any of the rounds decided to do something odd. He hoped. It might also chase the VC toward the tree line—straight into fire from Houng's squad, and a withering crossfire from Zeitvogel's.

BOOM BOOM BOOM BOOM, howled the distant mortar, and they waited in the paddies and the bordering tree line.

KA-*BOOM* KA-*BOOM* KA-*BOOM*, the rounds exploded in the paddies, masking the sound of more high explosive rounds being fired from Camp Apache. The three white phosphorus rounds spumed flowers of red-, yellow-, and white-hot glowing chemical embers in all directions. A few fronds arced out farther than others but all within expected norms. The fourth round was another flare.

Screams came from near the explosions and were followed by screams from men who thought more chemical death would rain down on them. The flare burst to life and exposed ten figures running toward the trees.

"They're here," Zeitvogel said excitedly into his radio.

"The Willy Peter has them up and running. Send me some Hotel Echo. Hold your fire, Four, hold your fire until everyone has a target."

"Rozh-ah, One," Houng replied.

BOOM BOOM BOOM, the mortar coughed. The scything antipersonnel high explosive rounds would keep coming until Zeitvogel called a cease-fire. The sound of the next three rounds being fired reached the paddies almost simultaneously with the arrival of the last three rounds. Six running bodies disappeared in the explosions. Other VC jumped up from where they were hiding and dashed about aimlessly, not knowing in what direction lay safety.

"Fire!" Zeitvogel bellowed. He didn't need to use the radio to tell Houng and his men to open up. Bullets from nineteen rifles and 40mm grenades from the M-79 slammed into the darting VC, sent them careening, crashing, flopping, flying, falling.

Low moans keened from the disturbed waters of the paddies, moans of the wounded and the terrified.

KA-*BOOM* KA-*BOOM* KA-*BOOM*, the next three rounds geysered water, mud, muck, flesh, blood, and bones into the air. *BOOM BOOM BOOM*. Three more mortar rounds were fired from the hill. Some of the moaning, screaming voices were stilled as some of the wounded died. Other voices took up the chorus as more casualties were created.

An unpanicked voice rose above the others, a disciplined voice shouting for calm, calling for order—an officer trying to forge his battered forces back into a cohesive fighting unit.

"One, this Four," Houng called on his radio, "him say get ready charge to you. Him say them close to you, mortah no can fire, me no can fire, ovah."

"Outstanding, Four," Zeitvogel said. "They try to come my way they been had."

The Vietcong officer shouted his orders, paused, and then blew his whistle. Twenty VC arose and charged the combined Marine-PF position. In the glare from the rapidly falling flare they were easy targets for the Marines and

Popular Forces, who had them from two sides. One of them turned this way and that, waved a pistol in the air, shouted orders, dodged all bullets flying his way. Not all of his men were that lucky—there were fewer than twenty of them left standing when three more mortar rounds landed behind them and knocked down more. The officer was nowhere to be seen under the new flare glaring down on the paddies. The few survivors saw they were alone without leadership and most of them dropped down. The couple who tried to run were gunned down before they covered ten feet.

"Cease fire!" Zeitvogel shouted. "Cease fire." He used the radio to include the mortar in his order.

"Rumba One, Ballroom. Stand by, three more big bangs are on their way. Out." Again they waited in the paddies and they waited in the tree line.

"Any casualties? Anyone hurt?" Zeitvogel asked while they waited.

KA-*BOOM* KA-*BOOM* KA-*BOOM*, the last of the mortar rounds erupted in the paddies, stilling more of the moaning and screaming voices.

The reports came back to Zeitvogel: none of the Marines or PFs of Tango Niner had been hurt. The VC, even in their final, fatal charge, had not fired a shot.

"Four, tell them to put down their weapons and stand up with their hands on their heads. If they do they won't get hurt. If they don't we'll kill them. Over."

"Rozh-ah, One." Hung's voice rose in a singsong that carried clearly across the paddies. He waited and when no one stood up he repeated his orders. Seconds passed and when no more rounds from the mortar crashed into the paddies and the mortar remained silent two men rose with their hands on their heads. Two more stood like the first two and a fifth struggled erect with one hand on his head, his other arm hung shattered at his side.

"Collard Green, gather them together, tie their hands behind their backs," Zeitvogel ordered. He waited until the PFs reached the VC before calling for another illumination round. Under the brilliant but unsteady light of flares he and Houng directed a search of the paddies. They found two more Vietcong soldiers alive but too badly wounded to respond to the original surrender order. Nearly forty dead were bobbing in the paddy water. A length of cord was tied around each corpse's ankle and jerked from a safe distance before the bodies were searched. At dawn when a helicopter touched down to take away the six prisoners—one of the two badly wounded died before it arrived—it found Zeitvogel standing with his arms folded over his chest. He was facing the mountains in the west. He turned from the mountains long enough to load the prisoners, then looked at them again. "Charlie's over there, little 'pano," he said to Houng. "He's over there in numbers and he's planning something. I wish I knew what it was."

A third firefight broke out while Rumbas One and Four were searching the paddies. A platoon from Echo Company had been dispatched to the Song Du Ong near Hou Binh island. It caught the original supply train Randall had let by, the one that had slipped past Ruizique after the discovery of the sampans on the river. That platoon also caught the four boats that had fled downstream.

Two Navy river patrol boats were dispatched to round up all the drifting sampans that hadn't been sunk.

CHAPTER FIFTEEN

November 10, 1966. The Marine Corps Birthday

Low-lying clouds lumbered in during the short hours before dawn and left a ground-hugging mist behind. The ground fog was dense enough that Echo Company had to fire the hand-held flares called red star clusters to direct the helicopters in to pick them up. The first wave of choppers whipped enough higher air into the mist that the second wave saw an inverted bowl of white air on its approach and could see the ground through it when it hovered over the bowl. The third and fourth waves had it easier, and by then the early morning sun was starting to burn the mist off.

Captain Ronson left on the first wave. "Some way to celebrate a birthday," he muttered. Before boarding his helicopter, he said farewell to the CAP Tango Niner leaders. He looked in the direction of the fog- and cloud-hidden western mountains and shook his head. "Someone once told me CAPs were candy duty," he said to Captain Hasford. "Whoever it was never heard of a night like last night. Or the night before my company came in here." He looked at the other captain. "How many Charlies did we get last night, sixty, sixty-five? He's probably going to want revenge and will try to make life very hard on whoever's here." He shook his head. "Captain Hasford, good luck"—he held out his hand to be shaken—"I think I'm going to have it easier than you will over the next couple of weeks." That would be very tough. The operation he had been briefed on the night before was very bloody; the battalion whose aid his company was going to was getting pretty badly chopped up. They couldn't do much more than try to hold on against the reinforced regiment they were facing until sufficient reinforcements showed up. All one company could do was keep that battalion from being totally destroyed.

Hasford wished Ronson good luck and good hunting.

The grunt captain turned to Burrison and said only, "Whichever way it goes, let's hope justice is done," and ignored the lieutenant's outstretched hand. Then he looked at Bell and shook his head sadly before ducking under the whirling blades of his helicopter. "Happy birthday to you, too," Bell said softly, glaring at the captain's back as he climbed onto the bird. The three left behind turned their backs on the downwash of the helicopter as it took off. In ten more minutes Echo Company was gone, leaving its cooks behind to watch over the tents and other equipment and gear the company couldn't take into combat. And something else.

The mist, thinned out by the powerful rotorwash of the waves of helicopters and burnt by the sun, cleared enough to see across most of Echo Company's former bivouac. Off to one side, sitting on the folded canvas of the squad tents, was a group of seven very uncertain-looking Marines.

"You may as well go and introduce yourself, Sergeant Bell," Hasford said. He had decided not to call anyone in the platoon by his nickname until he knew all of them. "Bring them topside and we'll get them assigned."

"Aye-aye, Captain," Bell said. He took a deep breath

before starting toward the strangers. The seven new men were unknown quantities and they'd be replacing some very good Marines. But Tango Niner had been through this before, when Ruizique and his fire team replaced Lanani's.

"I don't know how long I'm going to be here," Bell heard Hasford saying as the two officers walked toward the hill, "but I may as well look the part for as long as I am. Where do I get one of those bush hats?"

Bell tipped his own camouflage bush hat forward so it almost covered his eyes and marched to the seven waiting Marines. May as well introduce myself right, he thought, so they don't think this is some kind of candy-assed outfit where all they have to do is sit around and circle jerk. He drew himself to his full height, stood arms akimbo before the seven uncertainly lounging Marines and started talking slowly. "My name is Sergeant Jay Cee Bell. That's sergeant as in two stripes more than any of you has. Stand up!" he snapped the last two words.

Six of the seven jerked. This wasn't the way they expected a sergeant to talk in the field. Slowly all seven rose to their feet and stood, not quite at attention, in a clumsy row. They looked nervous, all except the one who hadn't jerked when Bell snapped at them. That one's lips twisted in the beginnings of a smile.

"As I was saying," Bell said and started pacing, "my name is Sergeant Jay Cee Bell. It's an easy name to remember. That's Jay Cee as in Jesus Christ, which is who I am around here, and Bell, as in what I am going to ring of yours if you don't shape up right." He stopped pacing and glared at each of the seven. "See that?" he shouted and his arm shot out to point at the hill on which the Marine compound sat. "On top of that hill is Camp Apache. We call it Camp Apache because we live here and we are deeper in Indian Country than any other Marine unit in Eye Corps." He started pacing again, not looking at any of them. "When the Marines of Tango Niner arrived here back in June a Vietcong company owned Bun Hou village. We came here to tango. Charlie wasn't ready to tango so we killed him," he said without emotion. "Then the Big Charlie in the Sky sent in another company of his boys"—he paused for dramatic effect—"and we killed that one even faster than we killed the first company." He suddenly spun face-to-face with the Marine who was fighting off a smile. "You hear somebody saying something funny, boy?"

"No, Sergeant," the Marine managed to say without his smile getting larger and without laughing.

"Then why do you have that shit-eating grin on your face?"

"I don't have a shit-eating grin on my face, Sergeant." His mouth twisted more while he tried to control it. "It's just that you remind me of somebody," he blurted.

"And just who do I remind you of?" Bell asked. His face was so close now that each word expelled puffs of breath into the other's face.

"My drill instructor."

Bell blinked and backed off an inch or two. "Spell 'you,'" he said softly.

"Y-O-U, Sergeant."

"You're sure it's not spelled E-W-E?"

"Positive. Only DIs spell 'you' E-W-E."

"You remember that." Marine recruits in boot camp always address their drill instructors in the third person, never as "you." The first time a recruit speaks to his drill instructor he learns that. "A ewe is a female sheep, you whale turd. Do I look like a female sheep to you, maggot?" the DI demands. Calling a drill instructor "you" is a mistake that is never repeated.

"What's your name, fuckface?" Bell demanded of the Marine, who was now openly smiling.

"PFC Wayne F. Mazzucco."

"Mazzucco, huh. Sounds dago. Are you a dago?"

"No, Sergeant Bell, I'm not a dago. I'm a nice Italian boy from South Philadelphia." Now he was grinning broadly.

"You still think this is funny, don't you."

"No, Sergeant." His voice cracked as though he was going to laugh.

"South Philadelphia, huh?"

Mazzucco nodded; he didn't trust his voice.

"One of my fire team leaders is from Philadelphia. North Philadelphia. I think I'll give your ass to him. Corporal Zeitvogel. He'll straighten your shit out most ricky-tick, or you'll die trying."

"I think I'll like being in Stilts's fire team."

"We call Corporal Zeitvogel 'Stilts' because he's so tall normal men need to use stilts to look him in the . . . how did you know his name is Stilts?"

"I went through boot camp with Swearin' Swarnes. In the past few days he's told me all about everyone in Tango Niner."

Bell bent forward at the hips and put a conspiratorial arm around Mazzucco's shoulder and cleared his throat. "You say you heard all about everybody here from Swearin' Swarnes. And you went through boot camp with that same Swearin' Swarnes. Then you know that you should not believe you know everything about everyone here," he said in a friendly voice. "As a matter of fact, since you heard it from Swearin' Swarnes you should believe that you don't know anything at all." He cleared his throat again, stepped back from Mazzucco, and looked at the others. "All right," he said to them, "who the fuck are the rest of you?"

They were: Lance Corporal Herbert B. Kobos, machine gunner; Lance Corporal Jack D. Willard, who had been a fire team leader in Echo Company; PFC Lawrence R. Dodd, rifleman; PFC Terry A. Graham, mortarman; PFC Gene Thomas Neissi, rifleman; and PFC Larry W. Vandersteit, assistant machine gunner. None of them was particularly happy about the new duty assignments. They all wanted out of the grunts, but the time they had spent at Camp Apache showed them action was more constant there than in an operational battalion, which meant to them they stood a better chance of getting killed in Tango Niner than they did going on operations with Echo Company. And where the hell did this Sergeant Bell get off acting like he was in a chicken-shit garrison back in The World?

* * *

Hasford looked at Burrison, Bell, Houng, the corporals, and the PF squad leaders. He didn't need a mirror to tell him he looked as red-eyed as they did. No one in Tango Niner had gotten more than two or three hours' sleep the night before and their haggard faces and slumped bodies all showed it. Houng and his squad leaders, Hasford knew, had to go out and track down the strangers who had helped rebuild Camp Apache after the VC overrun attempt. He, Burrison, Bell, and the patrol leaders had to analyze what had happened last night. The seven new men had to be integrated into the platoon. He also knew all the patrol leaders had made their after-action reports into his tape recorder. The rest of it would have to wait.

"I'm calling for six hours' rack time," Hasford said. "Mr. Burrison, Sergeant Bell, Swarnes, and I will rotate on radio watch. Sergeant Bell, I want you to set up a perimeter watch rotation. Use the new men, but make sure you always pair one of them off with an experienced man. Lieutenant Houng, you and your men get some sleep, too, before you do anything else."

These were orders everybody appreciated even though they knew they would make this a good time for Charlie to hit. But they also thought Charlie was too busted up after last night to try it. Besides, Charlie still wasn't bright enough to understand that in Bun Hou the Marines and PFs held a bigger advantage at night than they did during the day, that the first few hours after sunup was when Tango Niner was most vulnerable.

In the early afternoon the officers and NCOs gathered together to work everything out over a C-ration meal. Burrison wondered how he happened to get Ham and Limas again, then shrugged and lit a heat tab in the bent can with holes cut in its sides that he used as a field stove and put his open Ham and Limas can on it to heat. The first thing they did was assign the new men. Kobos, Vandersteit, and Graham were easy—the first two came from Echo Company's machine gun section, and Graham was from the battalion's mortar platoon. If Pennell stayed in the rifle squad, then McEntire needed two men in his gun team and Slover needed one mortarman.

"I've already decided to give Mazzucco to Stilts," Bell said. "They're home boys and Mazzucco is a wiseass. Stilts'll straighten his ass out in a hurry."

The tall black corporal grinned with a mouth that looked like it had too many teeth.

"What about the others; wasn't Willard a fire team leader?" asked Hasford.

The sergeant nodded. It could cause a morale problem that might become a discipline problem if he was assigned as automatic rifleman in one of the fire teams. "Willard carried his squad's blooker before he was given a team. He can do the same with us. I'll make Malahini Zeke's ARman." He looked at Ruizique for confirmation and the Dominican nodded. "It's a sort of bust for both of them, but I think I can talk them both out of that and it'll work out for the best." At that time, the T/O—Table of Organization—for a rifle squad said corporals were fire team leaders and the automatic rifleman and grenadier were lance corporals with the grenadier being the senior lance corporal, the one next in line for promotion to fire team leader and corporal. But promotions in rank for infantry companies seldom kept up with promotions in job, so most fire team leaders were lance corporals and most ARmen were PFCs. So the way it normally worked was that the grenadier was either the junior lance corporal, next in line to become a fire team leader without getting a promotion in rank, or the senior PFC, next in line for promotion to lance corporal, but not necessarily to fire team leader.

"If I transfer Pennell from Tex's team to Zeke's, then none of the corporals except for the Wall will have more than one new man to break in," Bell concluded.

"Makes sense to me," Hasford said. "Comments?"

Zeitvogel grinned—he liked the idea of having a "home boy" in his team. Randall grimaced—he didn't really want any new men. Ruizique nodded—Pennell, the soft-spoken black PFC from South Dakota, was someone he knew would do a good job in his fire team.

McEntire laughed. "'Break in' is right. Those newbies do a job for me or I break them."

"Any bros in this bunch?" Slover asked.

Bell nodded. "Willard and Graham. You get Graham."

"Hot damn," the big corporal said, slapping a massive thigh. "It's been so long since we got any black replacements in this platoon, I was starting to think Stokeley Carmichael and all like that had the bros back in The World so fucked up none of them had enough balls to enlist in this man's Marine Corps."

"Tex, you get a junior flip by the name of Dodd," Bell said since his assignments were approved, "and, Zeke, you get someone called Neissi." Now to get everybody together.

Meanwhile, the cooks looked at each other and wondered what they were supposed to do with the turkeys and cake and other fixings that had been delivered to them in cold boxes the day before. Today, November 10th, was the Marine Corps Birthday and it was traditional to feed a huge turkey dinner with all the fixings to every Marine possible, including the men in the field on combat operations. The cooks had enough turkey, stuffing, sweet potatoes, cranberry sauce, vegetables, ice cream, and, of course, Birthday cake, to stuff every man in Echo Company and Tango Niner and have plenty left over to feed company. Finally, the chief cook, a corporal, shook his head and said, "No point in letting it go to waste. Let's get busy and start fixing the birthday dinner." But they weren't given time to do the job. They left the cake behind, though.

CHAPTER SIXTEEN

The same time, another place

Nguyen Thi Chinh stood bowed respectfully in front of the massive teak desk. He had pleaded his case and must now wait for a decision. While he knew that all he requested would not be granted, certainly he would be given the boon of some part of it.

"You do not need to kowtow to me, elder," Captain Phang said. He was at ease in his leather chair behind the desk. His fingers played with a swagger stick that had been given to him by a U.S. Air Force chief master sergeant. "Stand up straight."

Chinh straightened, but did not come fully erect. A lifetime of working in his rice paddies and kitchen garden had permanently stooped his shoulders. That same lifetime's working in the glaring sun and relentless heat of the tropics had dried and wrinkled his skin so his face looked more like a carved mahogany mask than a living countenance.

Betel nut stained his lips and the stumps of teeth rotted away by too many years of chewing and sucking on sugarcane. To western eyes Nguyen Thi Chinh looked like a very old man, one who should have already retired. He was fifty-one years old.

"I wish to understand thoroughly your problem," Phang said. "Taxes and rent leave too little of your crops for you to properly feed and clothe your family, is that what you are saying?"

Yes, Nguyen Thi Chinh nodded.

"You wish me to enforce Saigon's rent cap, to not let the landlord take more than a quarter of your principal crop for rent?" Phang rested his swagger stick alongside his nose. "But the landlord is an honorable man. He says he must have more than Saigon tells him he is allowed to. He needs it in order to feed and clothe his family. If I force him to reduce the rents to what Saigon allows, then who will feed and clothe his children?"

Chinh's stooped back slumped more. He could understand the landlord's problems, but what about his own? "Some relief, Captain. Some small relief so my children's stomachs do not growl when they lie down to sleep at night."

The swagger stick now lay on the desk and Phang's fingers beat a tattoo on it. He gazed unwaveringly at Chinh, apparently deep in thought. "You are a man of potent virility, are you not, one with many children?" he asked at length. Chinh nodded. Phang seemed to lose himself once more in thought. "You have a daughter, do you not?" he asked abruptly, sitting up and taking his swagger stick in hand again. "A daughter by the name of Yen? She is, I believe, sixteen years old."

Chinh's expressionless face stiffened. "Yes." Yen was the last child borne by his second wife.

"Have her come to me at five o'clock. Let her plead your case for you. Let sixteen-year-old Yen explain to me how she and her many brothers and sisters ache with hunger when they lie down to sleep." He tapped his desk sharply with the end of his swagger stick, put it back down, and turned his attention to a small, neat stack of papers that lay by his right hand.

Nguyen Thi Chinh hesitated, waiting for Phang to say more, wanting to say something himself. Wanting to tell the assistant district chief that no, he would not prostitute his daughter. In his deepest thoughts he killed this officious bureaucrat. He turned and shuffled from the office.

Nguyen Thi Chinh returned to Phang's office at the appointed hour. Nguyen Van Yen, his sixteen-year-old daughter, was with him. The girl stood in such a way that she seemed to huddle behind her father.

Yes, this is the one, Phang thought, looking beyond Chinh at the girl. I have seen her before in the village. Her perfect oval face is unpocked and her complexion is clear and smooth. She took care to brush her hair before coming to me, and it shines like the darkest teak. The unmarried youths of the village must lust after her, they all must want to take this one's body for themselves before they are drafted into the army or into the Vietcong. Yes, what I can see is beautiful, and the fit of her tunic suggests that what I cannot yet see, that slender body, is as beautiful.

"You must return to your village, Thi Chinh," Phang said out loud.

"But what of my daughter?" asked Chinh. He did not want to believe he was handing his daughter over to Phang. "She has never been this far from home before. If she has to walk alone it will be night long before she arrives and she might get lost, or be kidnapped by bandits."

Phang's gaze flicked to the man. "I will have her returned to you after she convinces me of the truth of your need. She will not have to walk home at night. You must leave now." He looked back to the girl, savoring the look of her delicate face.

"How will I know of your decision if I am not here when you are through interviewing my daughter?"

"I will send it with her. Leave us, return to your village. One of my men will take you partway in a truck."

Nguyen Thi Chinh stooped lower and bowed. He looked

silently at his virgin daughter, the otherwise impassive mask of his face tinged with grief. One hand fluttered over her shoulder but didn't touch. He bowed again to Phang, hung his head, and left without speaking or looking at his daughter again.

Phang sat at his desk staring at the girl standing mute at the other side of his office. His relaxed posture disguised the internal tension that wracked him. Outside a vehicle coughed before its engine turned over and roared to life. Phang waited until he heard it drive away before he spoke.

"Co Yen, do not be frightened. I do not intend to hurt you or punish you," he said and rose from his chair. He walked to the front of his desk and sat on it. "You should place your trust in me. Come closer."

The girl edged closer but stopped out of arm's reach.

"Your father is a good man. You know that, don't you?"

She nodded.

"He tells me that when you go to bed your stomach growls because you have not had enough to eat. I know this is true because your father is a good man and good men do not lie. Now tell me, Co Yen, why do you not have enough to eat."

"It is because," the girl said slowly, fumbling for her words, hoping that maybe Phang was only going to talk with her, do no more than talk, "my father has ten children living with him whom he must feed. He also has my mother's aged parents to feed, and a brother who lost a leg fighting the Vietcong. He is not a rich man, the paddies and garden he has are only enough to care for his family, and the rent and taxes he pays take so much that when it gets near harvest time most of the food we have left from the last harvest is gone and we have to eat little in order for the food we have to last. Our ribs show."

"Do your stomachs become hollow?"

Yen nodded.

"Unbutton your tunic from the bottom, let me see."

The girl swallowed and grew faint for a few seconds. Phang was going to do what she hoped he wouldn't. With trembling fingers she undid the buttons from the bottom of her tunic to just below her breasts and held it open.

Phang looked greedily. Yen's stomach was not hollow, it was flat and smooth. His hands hungered to touch it. "Remove your tunic. Let me see your ribs that show."

Her face flushed. "I cannot," she stammered. "No man has seen me without my tunic or shirt since I . . ." She couldn't say, since she had reached puberty.

"Turn your back to me. I will look at the ribs of your back."

The girl's entire body trembled as she turned around and opened the rest of the buttons. Her shoulders quivered as she lowered the tunic from them, trying to keep her breasts covered.

"Take it all the way off." When the garment was hanging from her hand he stood away from the desk, took a step forward, and removed it from her grasp. He carelessly tossed it into a corner and lowered his hip to the desk. He saw skin stretched tautly over a perfect wedge-shaped back. Her ribs were visible but not prominent; they were the ribs of a well-formed woman, not the ribs of a malnourished child. "Turn around."

Yen swayed as she turned, wishing she would faint, wishing she were somewhere else.

Phang's eyes devoured her breasts, too full to be conical, too young to be round. They will reach their fullness in another year or two, he thought. Then in a few years more, after too many infants have suckled them like rutting piglets at their dam's teats, they will wither and droop, emptied of their vitality. But for now they are beautiful. For now, for me. "Remove your pants," he said with a voice thickened with lust.

Yen swayed again and staggered to catch her balance. She wanted to scream, she wanted to run, but she could do neither. She was not concerned with the shame of being shirtless on the streets of the district capital—she knew if she ran she would not live long enough to feel that shame. Phang would kill her if she did not comply with his wishes —she knew that because she knew of others who had crossed him and died for it. Her concern was with what would happen to her family if she did not do as he wished.

She untied the cord that held up her loose black peasant pants and let them fall, crumpled around her ankles.

"Step out of them and come to me," he said huskily.

Almost blind with dizziness the girl did as she was told. She did not stop until she felt his hands on her body, fondling her breasts, rubbing over her stomach and thighs and back, squeezing her buttocks. His mouth was hard and wet on hers, crushing her lips against her teeth. She stood unresponsive, her mind trying to find another place to be. Like an automaton she let him lead her to the divan at the side of the room and stood motionless while he spread the sheet he kept folded under the pillow. She allowed him to lay her down and arrange her legs to admit him where no one had been before. While he was unbuckling his belt and removing his trousers her mind finally found the otherwhereness she had been seeking. She did not feel him enter her or the ripping of her hymen. Later, when a leering soldier drove her home to her village, she felt the stickiness on the inside of her thighs, the wetness in the crotch of her pants. She bore a message for her father: Captain Phang would see to it that the landlord lowered the rent. Phang did not tell her by how much but it would only be a marginal reduction. After all, even though Co Yen had not resisted him, she only lay immobile under him and he had had to do all the work himself.

Co Yen also did not know that after she left him, Phang cut a one-foot square from the sheet she had lain on and set it aside to dry before adding it to his collection of other such squares.

CHAPTER SEVENTEEN

Night, November 10, 1966

Lieutenant Houng and his squad leaders were unhappy.

It wasn't the fact that they had been up all night killing Vietcong and had consequently gotten very little sleep afterward. No, killing all those VC without suffering any casualties of their own left them feeling flushed with pride and accomplishment.

Nor was it the fact that even though Vinh had learned the name of one of the strangers who had been hired to help rebuild Camp Apache he hadn't found out where the man lived. "One man stranger, him name Nguyen Minh," Vinh had proudly reported on trudging into Camp Apache after an afternoon of questioning men he had brought in to help. No, getting the man's name had been the hard part. Now that they knew who they were looking for, finding him would be easy.

It wasn't even the fact that, after having been up all night, hardly getting any sleep, then going out to track down people they didn't know, they were going to have to be up most of tonight trying to pick another fight with Charlie that had them unhappy. Hell, they were up most of the night almost every night looking for the enemy anyway.

It didn't even bother them all that much that tonight they'd be patrolling with Marines they didn't know, Marines just transferred from Echo Company—the same Echo Company whose men had gone to lengths to demonstrate they didn't trust the PFs. After all, the Marine corporals of Papa Niner would be running the patrols and the new men would be learning how a Combined Action Platoon actually functioned.

What made them unhappy was something that had absolutely nothing to do with going on night patrols, getting into firefights, and going out during the day trying to locate people who might know something about the heroin that had been found attached to the inside of Camp Apache's new four-holer.

Helicopters had come in during the day and lifted out everything Echo Company left behind. Including the cooks. The daily hot meal flown into Camp Apache had been suspended while the cooks were there to feed Echo Company. Someone forgot to start them again now that the cooks had left. Houng, Collard Green, Vinh, and Willy arrived in time to eat evening chow with the Marines. What made them so unhappy was the evening chow was C rations.

Oh, the Marines tried to make it less painful for the PFs; they didn't make them pick their meals blindly. They let them have the good stuff: the Beans and Franks, the Spaghetti and Meatballs, the Turkey Loaf, the Beefsteak. But come on, fella, C rations are C rations. Nobody who has a choice will willingly eat C rations. Houng and his squad leaders could have gone home for dinner and had something appetizing, something like rice with greens and fish heads smothered in nuoc mam sauce. But it was too late for them to go home for dinner. All they could do was grimace and try to be gracious dinner guests. So what if the food they were given to eat looked so strange and tasted so bland it couldn't possibly have any nutrient value. They wouldn't come back for dinner again until they knew hot meals were being flown in again, that's all.

All that notwithstanding, they did enjoy the Birthday cake and the small ceremony the Marines made around it. The Marines grumbled that the cooks should have left a couple of turkeys—even if they didn't have stoves or ovens, they would have found a way to roast them.

The officers talked about the previous night's actions. What the enemy had done was too complex for it to be a new standard operation, not unless they were planning a new major operation to the east and needed a rapid buildup. The seven-man decoy supply train seemed to be exactly that, a decoy to tip the hand of a CAP patrol or ambush so the platoon following it could flank it and wipe it out. Charlie did that two nights in a row, and even though it didn't work either time he might try it again. But for them to do it two nights in a row as a diversion for a sampan convoy on the river while two platoons tried to sneak across the paddies to the north was asking too much of the Vietcong resources. Unless they were massing for a big push somewhere and already had their plans laid to repeat last night's tactic several times.

"I seriously doubt we'll encounter anything like that again tonight," Captain Hasford said. "What I'm more concerned with is the possibility of the suspected VC company in Bun Anh making some sort of reprisal on Bun Hou. Captain Phang's corruption just might be what's keeping them in business there, as you believe, Sergeant Bell. You people have already messed with him there, and they might want to keep Tango Niner so busy here we don't have time to visit Anh Dien or any of the other hamlets there. Also, Charlie might decide to hurt us by making a raid on Hou Toung or Hou Cau. You haven't run many patrols to the east recently, have you?"

Burrison and Bell glanced at each other and shook their heads.

"Most of the action since I've been here has been supply runs and reinforcement infiltrations going from west to east," the young lieutenant said. "Patrolling east of Hou Dau hasn't been productive."

Hasford nodded. "I'm sure Charlie knows your recent patrols have been more west than east. I want to reverse the pattern for a few days and see what happens."

Nobody argued, though some of them felt like it. They knew the action was between Hou Ky and the ridge. On the other hand, the captain might be right about the VCs wanting to try something in Bun Hou's eastern hamlets. And anyone coming through and making it as far as Hou Dau hill or the sharp bend in the river west of Hou Cau might think he was home free and get careless. Careless enough to die before he could react to getting killed.

"There's one other change I want to make because of all the unfriendly activity around here recently," Hasford continued. "I want a full eleven-man fay epp squad to go on each patrol. Fifteen men pack a hell of a lot more fire power than ten and I don't want to lose any men because we didn't have enough there when the shooting started."

The normal patrol sequence was totally disrupted when the Vietcong attempted to overrun Camp Apache, so they started it all over again. Every night three patrols went out. One was out all night. It would leave some time between an hour before and a half-hour after sunset and come in at dawn or a little later. The all-nighter would sit in an ambush for at least half of the night. The second patrol would leave after dark and come back before light. Its average time out was six hours, though that time could vary by an hour or so in either direction. This patrol would lie in one or more impromptu ambushes of a half-hour or longer when- and wherever its leader thought advisable. The third patrol would slip through the wire an hour or two before midnight and stay out half the night.

Assigned routes were drawn up for each of the patrols and given to the patrol leaders before evening chow, but they were rarely followed. After getting their orders for the night the three patrol leaders got together over their own copy of the 1:10,000 topographical map of their area and decided what they'd actually do. Lieutenant Burrison and

Sergeant Bell drew the routes, but they understood that they didn't have the intimate knowledge of the land the three corporals who led the patrols did, so they turned a blind eye to their orders' being changed.

Basically what Zeitvogel, Randall, and Ruizique did was divide the area to be patrolled into three segments based on the assigned routes. The leader of the all-nighter would place his ambush somewhere near where it was supposed to be, but if heavy brush blocked the front of the ambush site, he'd move to where the brush was thinner, where he'd have a better chance of catching someone. He made sure Big Louie Slover knew where he'd actually be in case he needed to call in mortar fire. If one patrol leader wanted to patrol along the border between his segment and an adjoining one he'd pick a time window and say something like "I'm going to sweep through here some time between oh one hundred and oh two hundred" to the leader of the patrol in the next segment. The patrols didn't want to bump into each other unexpectedly at night. If one of them had an idea of a good site for an ambush at a particular time, he'd tell the others, and before they went out all three knew what the others had planned for the night's activities—as far as they could decide in advance.

It was a difficult choice, but everyone agreed Ruizique's patrol had had the easiest time the night before. Not by much, but by enough to justify giving him the all-night patrol. Willy and his squad were to join the Marines in Camp Apache a half hour before sundown. They would patrol the thinly wooded area between the paddies and the bulldozed road between the Marines' hill and Hou Dau hill, then swing north of the hill and check out the sugarcane fields east of Hou Dau before prowling through Hou Toung and setting up in a tree line in the paddies northeast of that hamlet. Hou Toung was a small hamlet in the northeast corner of Bun Hou village and was the only one completely surrounded by paddies.

Ruizique was very intense in preparing his men for the patrol. Not only did he inspect the Marines for properly painted camouflage and loose gear, he also inspected the

PFs when they arrived. The man who received his closest inspection was PFC Thomas Neissi. He supervised Neissi while he painted his face, arms, and hands, and followed him every step of the way when he stuffed his canteen inside a woolen sock, removed the sling from his rifle, taped down the front keeper, tied off his bayonet scabbard, taped his dog tags together, tucked the chin strap of his brand-new bush hat inside it, emptied his pockets of all coins and other objects that could go clink in the dark, and removed his wristwatch and high school class ring.

"How long have you been in Vee Cee Land," the corporal asked when his new man was ready.

"About four months." Neissi was eighteen years old, but four months of combat had given him old man's eyes and an old man's set to his jaw.

"Zap many?"

Neissi shrugged. "I donno. I've been in boo-coo fire-fights, but I never seen a man drop in my sights."

"You scared about going out tonight?"

The young Marine nodded. He hadn't gone on many night patrols and was always nervous about it when he did. After all, the night belonged to Charlie, didn't it?

Ruizique slapped his new man on the shoulder. "Don't sweat it," he said. "In this unit we kick ass and don't even bother to take names."

Webster and Pennell stared at their fire team leader. In all the time they had known him, he had talked about how he didn't belong in this gringo's war and only wanted to get out of the Marine Corps so he could go home to the Dominican Republic for his captain's commission. He fought well once the shooting started, but he was known to not cover the area he was supposed to and sometimes argued against his assignments. Now he was talking tougher than Zeitvogel and Randall combined. They wondered why.

Ruizique's arm still hurt from the machine gun bullet he had taken at the end of the attempted overrun. His Latin pride was hurt along with his arm when he was shot by an enemy who had already been defeated. He took that wound personally and wanted revenge. And nobody knew that but him.

It was time. The fifteen men in the patrol with the radio call sign Rampart Three left Camp Apache through the main gate and the barbed wire closed behind them.

The selection between Ruizique and Randall had been difficult, but Randall's patrol was the one hit from the flank by the trailing VC platoon. So Randall's second fire team and Vinh's PF squad were given a 2130 to 0400 patrol. Randall didn't like his assignment at all: zigzag back and forth between the river and the trail down the ridge west of Hou Ky. Of course the westernmost edge of the patrol route was only a kilometer west of Camp Apache, but with all the men of the three PF rifle squads patrolling, Houng didn't have enough left for a reaction unit. So the only help available if Rampart Two ran into more than it could handle was Big Louie Slover's 81mm mortar. Oh well, Randall thought, after last night Charlie probably isn't going to try to pull anything on us—I hope.

Randall inspected his men for noise and reflective surfaces as Ruizique had, but not as closely. PFC Lawrence R. Dodd, his new man, received the closest attention. Dodd didn't reflect light and the only noise he made was the thumping of his boots on the wooden pallet floor of the tent when he hopped. Dodd's face was blank, but it was a blankness that Randall interpreted as meaning "I don't care about anything."

"Are you okay?" Randall asked.

"Yah." Dodd's voice carried a tone that sounded like "As if anybody cares."

"Do you know where you are?"

"More or less," Dodd said, sounding like he meant "Does it matter?"

"You scared?"

"Nah," but it sounded more like "Do you care?"

"Nervous?"

"Nope," which seemed to mean "It doesn't matter."

"You gonna be all right?"

"Yah," or he could have said, "Can anything else go wrong?"

Randall tried to blank the concern from his own face. He hoped Dodd was okay and would be all right. "Tomorrow we'll start showing you around," he said, "so you'll know what the places you go to at night look like during the day. That's one thing that gives us the edge on Charlie around here."

"All right," or, "This place, that place. They're all the same."

Randall led his men into the night a half hour before they were to leave to meet Vinh and his squad at the square in Hou Ky. They needed the time to get their full night vision. Their first stop after picking up the PFs would be overlooking Hou Binh island. That would also be the last place they went before coming back in. If they didn't run into something else that would cancel all plans.

It was generally agreed that since Stilts Zeitvogel and Pee Wee had crawled through the half-flooded paddies and killed four Vietcong with their knives, their night had been the hardest. So tonight Zeitvogel was given the short patrol. They were to slip out the back gate a half hour after Randall's patrol and meet Collard Green and his squad where the main trail leading south from Hou Dau crossed the bulldozed roadway that wound around the south side of that hamlet's hill. They were then to proceed through the light forest between there and Hou Cau and spend a couple of hours skulking through that marketplace hamlet on the riverfront and the woods behind and downstream from it before calling it an early night—at about two in the morning.

By now it was a clear routine: the patrol leader inspected his men for light and sound giveaways and paid closest attention to his newest man, PFC Wayne F. Mazzucco.

"Home boy," Zeitvogel snorted, looking from his great height down at Mazzucco. "I don't give a good goddamn where you from, you still ain't tall enough to be on my basketball team." It was painfully true. Mazzucco was, like Big Red Robertson, the statistically average five foot eleven. Add in Hempen's five foot four and Zeitvogel's own six foot five, divide by four, and they didn't average that statistical average. "They need to spot me Wilt Chamberlain, Bill Russell, and Tom Gola, I'm gonna field me a roundball team can take on and beat a girls' high school team with this crew. Shee-it!"

"Come on, Stilts," Mazzucco said. A broad grin split his classic Italian face. His white teeth almost dazzled in his sun-darkened face and contrasted sharply with his glossy, coal-black hair. "Take the four of us and add Swearin' Swarnes, we can beat the pants off the Lakers. We get the ball to old Short Round and he dribbles right between their legs and get it to you upcourt for a lay-up before they even realize we've got possession." Swarnes had told Mazzucco about Zeitvogel's obsession with having men in his fire team who were tall enough to play basketball on a high level. Swarnes meant it as a pun when he said "high level."

"Bullshit." Zeitvogel couldn't think of anything else to say. This was the first time one of his men had claimed he could play well despite the fact that only the fire team leader was over six feet tall.

"Come on, Stilts," Mazzucco joked, bouncing his hands like he was dribbling a basketball from one to the other. "Bet I can get it past you in here without fouling." He shuffled his feet, shifting his weight from side to side, then bolted toward Zeitvogel and rolled around one side of him between the cots. He finished by darting to the far end of the tent and jumping for a lay-up. "We've got schoolyards in South Philadelphia, too."

"Yah, you got schoolyards in South Philadelphia, home boy," Zeitvogel said. "And you all hang around them singing, hoping some producer comes around to make you the next Fabian." He was smiling with approval when he said that; approval at the move Mazzucco had put on him and how none of his gear made any noise when he did. "Now if you think you got such fancy footwork, let's get to work and see what kind of moves you can put on Charlie."

Hasford was right. If any Vietcong came through Bun Hou that night they managed to avoid the Marines and Popular Forces who were waiting and looking for them. As it turned out, it was a good thing they had an easy night. The next morning brought other difficulties to the officers and NCOs of Tango Niner.

CHAPTER EIGHTEEN

November 11, 1966

The first thing in the morning, Swearin' Swarnes did something unusual. It wasn't the first thing in the morning military style, not 5:00 or 6:00 A.M. It was a few minutes after 0800 and it was the first thing in the morning for Swarnes because he hadn't had time to brush his teeth or shave yet—it was his every other day to shave. Sergeant Bell had just woken him up to take radio watch again—he was allowed to sleep until eight because of the shift he had had in the middle of the night. At some point on this early morning radio watch he would brush his teeth, shave, and eat his morning chow.

The unusual thing that he did was, he took pencil firmly in hand and stuck his tongue firmly in the corner of his mouth and he wrote. It wasn't a letter or anything like that that he wrote. What it was, was he copied on paper a confidential coded radio message for Captain Hasford. This was unusual because he had never before had to copy down a confidential coded radio message. For that matter, Tango Niner had never before received a confidential coded radio message regardless of who was on radio watch.

Captain Hasford accepted the sheet of paper after Swarnes repeated its code groups to the sender, then retired to a secluded corner of the compound with his code book to decode it. When he was through with the decoding he read through the message twice and then summoned Lieutenant Burrison and Sergeant Bell.

"You're going to Da Nang," Hasford told them. "You and your corporals. For a pre-court-martial conference with your appointed defense counsel."

"I thought this whole thing was on hold," Burrison said.

"So did I. But this is a bureaucracy. Once things are set in motion, I guess they're hard to stop." Hasford took a deep breath and let it out almost in a sigh. "This must be another reason I'm here—so there'll be someone on hand to be in command when you and your corporals get called back to be hung." He looked at his watch, then looked down at the sheet of paper and read from it. "You're leaving in half an hour. Wear helmets if you've got 'em, carry regulation soft covers—no bush hats"—he glanced momentarily at their heads—"take shaving kits, changes of skivvies and socks, and khaki uniforms." The captain looked back up. "That's it. Get your corporals ready."

The reactions were varied.

Zeitvogel set his face somewhere between a sneer and a scowl. There were drugs where he came from, drugs he always stayed away from because he saw what they did to the dope heads. He found the idea that anyone could suspect him of drug dealing offensive.

Randall's feelings were mixed. He had a healthy fear of the military justice system; he knew the military establishment didn't want anyone alleged to be a criminal to be in uniform and that court-martials seldom acquitted anyone brought before them. On the other hand, going back to Da Nang would give him a chance to see beautiful Bobbie Harder again.

Ruizique turned surly and broody. He did not want to leave Bun Hou, not now, not until the end of his enlistment. There were no Vietcong inside the Da Nang base, none for him to kill. Who knew how many VC would pass through Bun Hou in his absence, VC who would escape his wrath? No, the Dominican did not want to leave, he wanted to stay where he was and kill more enemy soldiers.

Slover was pissed off and stomped around the weapons section tent slamming things about. He had never messed with drugs, that was for losers. Burglary had been his bag. Stealing from businesses and from people's homes had kept him in money. Hell, the only strong-arm he indulged in was to keep his gang and the punks in line. He had been caught only once for something he did. The judge gave him a choice of fourteen to twenty months in the slammer or an enlistment in the Marines. He figured he'd learn more as a Marine than as a con. And now he faced boo-coo years' hard time for something he didn't do? He was pissed, and nobody who knew him wanted to get in his way when Big Louie Slover was pissed.

McEntire tried to put a happy face on the whole proceedings. "Hey, look at it this way," he said to the other corporals, "we'll pull some liberty in Da Nang town, get drunk, and find some boom-boom girls to ream our pipes for us. Man, that sounds good to me. I haven't gotten my rocks off since San Diego."

"Wall," one of the others said back, "you're so damn big you lay on a boom-boom girl she's gonna get squashed like a pancake and it'll be like humping a rubber dolly you forgot to blow up."

"Blowing!" McEntire exclaimed. "That's it. I'll find one to play the skin flute on me." He got himself up, but failed to raise anyone else's spirits.

Hurry up and wait is the most common thing in the military. Especially for Marines in Vietnam who were waiting for a helicopter to go from here to there because the Marines never had enough choppers to go around. They had a half hour to get whatever they were taking with them ready

and be at the white painted circle of earth in the northwest
corner of Camp Apache. The helicopter took another forty-
five minutes to get there. Enough time for Zeitvogel to
become more deeply offended, Randall to get more anxious, Ruizique to become surlier, Slover to get angrier, and
McEntire to become hornier.

Bell and Burrison tried to stare each other down. Both
won. Or lost, depending on how you look at it. Neither
broke eye contact until Hasford joined them. All the intelligence captain could do was shrug and say, "I don't know
any more than you do."

The tadpole-shaped UH-34 helicopter finally arrived. It
took off again, sluggishly because of the weight of its
four-man crew and seven passengers. A greeting party was
waiting when it landed on one of the Da Nang helicopter
runways, a stern-looking captain from the Provost Marshal's Office, four MPs, an MP panel truck, and two MP
jeeps. The four MPs held twelve-gauge riot shotguns at the
ready and looked very willing to use them.

The MP captain spoke briefly to Burrison, who paled as
much as he could through the deep sun-baked tan of his
face, then the young lieutenant turned back to his NCOs.

"We're under arrest. Put your weapons and ammunition
in the back of that jeep"—he pointed—"and get in the
back of the truck." He turned to board the other jeep.

"Mr. Burrison," Bell stopped him, "where are they taking us?"

"We'll find out when we get there."

Where they went to wasn't a brig, but it might as well
have been: a small quonset hut unused since the earliest
days of the Marine presence at Da Nang, alone in a corner
of the sprawling base. The NCOs were herded into it and
its doors were locked. Two MPs were posted as guards
outside the quonset hut. Burrison was taken to a transient
officers' quarters, where he was installed in a room. The
door was locked behind him and a guard posted outside it.
The Marine Corps was taking the heroin smuggling charge
very seriously.

* * *

As soon as Lieutenant Houng learned about his good friend Jay Cee Bell and the others being ordered to Da Nang for pre-court-martial proceedings, he assembled his platoon to issue new orders to them. The Popular Forces of Combined Action Platoon Tango Niner would immediately intensify their search for Nguyen Minh and the other elusive strangers who had worked on the four-holer at Camp Apache. All regular patrol operations were suspended until one of the men who had planted the heroin was found and persuaded to testify. The patrols were very important; catching and killing the Vietcong was very important. But it was more important to the PFs to get their Marines cleared and returned to them. Houng waited until his men had dispersed in four-man teams before going to Camp Apache to inform Captain Hasford that he wouldn't have any PFs to work with until their new mission was completed.

"You're kidding me," Hasford said. "You can't do this —you can't abandon the patrols while you conduct your search."

"Maybe it is true, what you say, that I can't do it," Houng replied, "but I have done it. Jay Cee is a friend of mine and he is a good man. I know he is not a heroin smuggler, I know the others aren't either. Captain Phang had that heroin planted and I know who he had do it. If we do not patrol until we find them, we will find them quickly. If we do patrol while we search, it will take much longer and we might not find the guilty persons until it is too late."

"But you are being paid by your government to keep the Vietcong out of your village. If you stop patrolling you are not doing what you are being paid to do, you are in violation of your contract."

Houng cocked an eye at the American. "Captain, do you know how much we are paid in the Popular Forces? Do you realize that when we take the food from the Vietcong we kill, we do that because if we don't we cannot feed our families; our pay is too low to support them?"

"If you are not patrolling, the VC will be able to come into Bun Hou and no one will be here to stop them."

"No, they will not know right away that we are not patrolling. If they are able to slip a few supply runs or a few reinforcements through Bun Hou they will simply think they are being lucky. It will be several days before they realize they are getting through because we have no patrols out. And by then we should have found those for whom we are looking. I am going now to help my men find the wrongdoers."

Hasford stopped him. "What will you do if you are ordered by your GVN superiors to cease what you are doing and resume patrolling?"

Houng looked at Hasford for a long moment before answering. "How will my superiors learn the patrols are not being run, will you tell them? Who would you report this to, Captain Phang? You will not do this thing. Phang is the criminal who steals from the people and supports others who steal from them. He is the evil man who brought about the false charges against my friends. When I get the information I need, Phang will fall."

Hasford considered his options and immediately realized he had almost none. As soon as he could arrange for helicopter transportation to Chu Lai he would go to that southern Eye Corps air base and make a report to the lieutenant colonel, who was now there. Until the PFs returned he would put an eight-man listening post/ambush out every night to screen Camp Apache from the mountains, but none of the aggressive patrolling they had been doing. But how long would it be before the PFs came back?

The next day he flew to Chu Lai. The lieutenant colonel exploded when he heard what the PFs were doing. After roaring his displeasure he roared with laughter.

"I have to believe them," the lieutenant colonel said when he got himself back under control. "If it wasn't for the heroin we found I would refuse to believe those people are involved in anything illicit. I hope they find the people they're looking for in a hurry and everything can return to normal with Tango Niner and you can get back to your own job at S-2. Now get your ass back to Camp Apache until this business straightens itself out."

The PFs found Nguyen Minh and one of his comrades on the second day of their search.

CHAPTER NINETEEN

November 12, 1966

"How soon do I get base liberty, sir," was the first thing Tex Randall asked Second Lieutenant Craig, the court-appointed counsel for the NCOs. Now that he was at Da Nang, all he could think of was getting to see Bobbie Harder. "There's someone I want to see."

"Base liberty," Craig repeated. "Corporal Randall, don't you understand? You're under arrest. That quonset hut may not be a brig, but you are in the brig. You don't pull liberty." He thought for a moment, then said, "Maybe we can arrange for you to have visitors, but liberty is out of the question."

Randall lunged forward without leaving his chair. "In the brig! Why am I in the brig? I didn't do anything."

It was the middle of the afternoon and all six Tango Niner NCOs were together in the office set aside for their defense counsel. Bell sighed, closed his eyes, and sank deeper in his seat. Ruizique gritted his teeth. The others didn't do anything.

"You didn't do anything, you say? You are charged with smuggling heroin, a felony," the lieutenant said, reading from papers he held in his hand. "If found guilty you face several years' hard labor at Leavenworth and a Bad Conduct discharge. You're going up on these charges and you will be found guilty, make no mistake about that. It's only a matter of what your punishment is." He shuffled the papers and paused to skim over one of them before continuing. "If we do this right we can probably, on appeal, get your sentences reduced to not more than one year hard time and have the bad paper reduced to Undesirable. Unless"—he looked them all in the eye—"one of you is willing to take the fall for everybody."

Bell opened his eyes and spoke. His words were very slow and deliberate. "Get one thing straight, Mr. Craig. We are innocent and you had best believe that."

Craig tapped his desk with the papers in his hand. "Then how do you explain two kilograms of pure heroin being found in your possession?"

"It wasn't found in our possession," Bell said patiently. "It was found attached to the inside of our shithouse. Somebody put it there and that somebody wasn't us."

"If it wasn't you, then it was someone else in your platoon," Craig said just as patiently. "Who do you want to burn?" It was obvious he thought they were guilty as charged and, while trying to get them something less then the maximum sentence, he wasn't going to do much more than go through the motions of defending them. "Listen, you're all intelligent men," he continued. He seemed bored with the whole proceeding. "You wouldn't be Marine NCOs if you weren't—so you understand the concept of an example. I'll explain this to you once and I don't intend to repeat myself. The Army is starting to have a drug problem down south. We don't have a drug problem up here yet, and the Marine Corps intends to keep things that way. The Marine Corps intends to establish right up front that drugs won't be tolerated. What that means is someone is going to hang for it. No drug problem can get established unless the NCOs allow it to. The best way to drive that home is to hang some NCOs for drug abuse. It's simple: two kilos of heroin were found in your compound. You are the NCOs, nothing can happen there without your being involved—or at least nothing can happen in your compound without your knowing about it. You're going to hang. Cut, sealed, and delivered. Make no mistake about it, you are going to be the example that prevents the Marines in Eye Corps from developing a drug problem."

Bell stood abruptly, fire in his eyes, and the others rose with him. "I want different counsel," he said. "If our own attorney is going along with this charade instead of listening to what we have to say, we'll be lucky if they don't put us up against a wall and shoot us. Call the guards and tell them to take us back to our brig."

Craig looked dumbfounded at the sergeant. "You sound like you actually believe you're not guilty."

"Lieutenant," Bell said, losing his patience, "I sound like I believe it because it's true."

"If you didn't do it, then who did?"

"You wouldn't believe me if I told you."

"Try me."

Bell did. They all did. Sometimes Craig had to stop them because all six were trying to talk at the same time. When they finished the lieutenant looked less certain of their guilt but didn't necessarily believe what they said was the truth. Of course none of them knew Houng had suspended patrols until his men found the guilty parties. That knowledge wouldn't have convinced Craig of his clients' innocence, but it might have convinced him they might be less guilty than he thought.

"That's a tough one," the lieutenant said, shaking his head when they were finished. "Unless your Lieutenant Houng can come up with the witnesses, the court-martial board won't believe a word of it. I have to think over what you said." He stood up in dismissal and asked, "Do any of you have any questions or other comments at this time?"

"Yessir," Randall said. "How do I get visitors?"

* * *

Burrison, since he was an officer, was going to be tried separately from his men. His defender was Captain Powell, an officer with an attitude very similar to Craig's. "Lieutenant," he started, "if we do this right we can make out that Sergeant Bell was the ringleader and you didn't know anything about it. Then all that'll happen to you is you'll get a letter of reprimand in your file. Of course you'll have to forget about a career in the Marine Corps, but that's better than hard time and bad paper."

"Bullshit, sir," Burrison said heatedly. "Sergeant Bell isn't any kind of ringleader and neither I nor my men had anything to do with that heroin. I don't care where it was found, none of us put it there."

"Lieutenant," the captain said, sounding bored with the whole business, "there's no defense you or those NCOs can give that a court-martial board hasn't heard before. If you're going up on charges like this, you're going to be found guilty. Period. The only questions are degree of guilt and severity of sentence. It's my job to get you off as lightly as possible."

"You sound like a goddamn Philadelphia lawyer," Burrison shouted.

"I am," the captain said drolly. "I was prelaw at Temple University in Philadelphia before I got my commission, and when I was stationed at the Navy yard there I was working part-time on a law degree at the University of Pennsylvania. And I've been accepted for admittance to the law school at the American University in D.C. when I report there for my next duty. Now what we have to do here," he said, returning to the main subject, "is work up a defense that makes you look guilty of being dumb and incompetent instead of being a drug smuggler."

"But I'm not," Burrison said, his voice cracking, "and neither are any of my men."

Powell looked expressionlessly at Burrison for a moment. Then he said, "You don't seem to understand the situation, Lieutenant, so I'll spell it out for you. Do you understand what ticket-punching is?" He didn't wait for an answer. No matter how dumb the young officer was acting, he had to know what "ticket-punching" was. "The prosecutor is a captain who was a first lieutenant when he arrived in-country. He served as XO of a line company, but never commanded a platoon in combat. He was promoted to captain after he got reassigned to staff and is now too short to have a crack at commanding a company before he rotates back to CONUS. He's missing important points for promotion. Maybe he'll get another tour over here and get a command then, and maybe he won't. If he can't get his ticket punched with a combat command, then he has to do something else to score some points. Burning a brown bar for smuggling drugs will be a nice coup for him. The judge is a major who's never had a combat command and won't —unless he manages to come back as a lieutenant colonel and gets a battalion. These men need to get their tickets punched so they can go higher on the promotion list. You're the punch."

"But I didn't do anything and neither did any of my people," Burrison repeated. "Or aren't you listening to anything I say?"

"All right"—Powell shrugged and glanced at his watch —"I don't have anything better to do for the next five minutes, so we'll play it dumb. If you aren't guilty, who is?"

So Burrison told him. When he finished the captain drummed his fingers on his desk for a few moments, lost in thought. "Maybe I was wrong," he said at last. "Maybe there is a defense a court-martial board hasn't heard before —I have certainly never heard this one. It might work. Do you have, oh, I don't know, say five or six hundred dollars?"

"I—I think so. Why?" Burrison was confused by the sudden change of subject.

"For the witnesses." Powell leaned forward with his arms on his desk and clasped his hands in the middle of it. "Listen, this is a novel defense. Blame it on an official of the government whose country we are defending, a man who is not under our jurisdiction and can't be prosecuted by us, a man who thereby needn't worry about prosecution. For five or six hundred dollars we can probably get two or three Vietnamese nationals to testify they saw Phang give the heroin to one of his agents with instructions to plant it on you." He shook his head and looked at the ceiling; the whole scenario was unfolding in his mind and he was getting excited about it. "Hell, if your NCOs can raise some money the same Vietnamese nationals could testify for them, too." He sat up and slapped his desk. "That's it," he shouted gleefully, "that's how we can get all of you off the hook!"

Burrison stared slackjawed at the captain. He couldn't believe what he was hearing. The man didn't believe a word of what he said, but was plotting to do through perjury exactly what Burrison and his people wanted to do legitimately.

"I have friends here at Da Nang," Burrison said lamely. "How can I get to see them?"

On the second day of the intense search Long, Butter Bar, Pheet, and Hien went to the hamlet named Duc Nhuan. Duc Nhuan was the second largest hamlet in the district and, since it was more centrally located than the district capital, most of its residents thought it should be the district capital. Six thousand people lived in Duc Nhuan, more than lived in all the hamlets of Bun Hou combined. It was almost a town and had a farmers' market that was open three days a week, unlike the one-day-a-week marketplace in Hou Cau that included farmers, fishermen, artisans, and everyone else. Duc Nhuan also had regular stores and shops and boasted a restaurant that had tables under a large roof overhang—it would have been a sidewalk cafe if there had been sidewalks in Duc Nhuan.

The walk from Bun Hou to Duc Nhuan was long and dusty and the Tango Niner PFs decided to rest at the sidewalk cafe and drink a beer or two before wandering around looking for their men. They had only been there long enough to place their order before a raucous laugh at a nearby table attracted Butter Bar's attention. The laugh sounded somehow familiar and he turned to see who it was. He saw two men engaged in hearty conversation. Both were wearing loose-fitting black peasant pants, but one was wearing a pastel pink shirt and the other had on a gaudy aloha shirt. An army fatigue hat sat on the back of the aloha shirt's head and a similar hat sat on the table near the other's elbow. Each had a half-empty quart bottle of Tiger beer in his hand and two empties lay on their sides on the table.

Butter Bar nudged Pheet and said in a low voice, "Do you know them? They look familiar to me."

Pheet looked intently at the two men and nodded. "What do you think?" Butter Bar asked Long and Hien. Long didn't recognize the two men but Hien thought he did. They looked like two of the strangers who had worked on rebuilding Camp Apache. The PFs drank their beer, talked quietly among themselves, and tried not to be too obvious about listening to the others. The two were becoming drunker and louder as they emptied the bottles they were holding and started a third round. Their tongues loosened and they started boasting to each other about their acquaintance with the assistant district chief, each trying to make out that he was in tighter with Captain Phang than the other. Then one used his companion's name, Nguyen Minh, and the PFs knew. Now it was only a matter of waiting for the best time to kidnap the two men. Eventually Nguyen Minh and his friend had enough to drink and staggered off.

The PFs knocked off the last of their beers and discreetly followed. They made their move on the outskirts of Duc Nhuan. They hailed their quarry as jolly fellows well met and suddenly six seemingly happy drunks linked arms and unsteadily weaved their way into a copse of trees. The laughter and joyful voices were silenced by two low-pitched but sharp thuds, followed by two duller and louder thuds as Phang's men were knocked on their heads and fell down. Rapidly, the PFs trussed and gagged the prisoners. Then they slowly became crestfallen as it dawned on them that the walk back to Bun Hou would be much longer carrying the two unconscious men.

* * *

"You will tell me when and where Captain Phang gave you the heroin," Houng said. His voice was cold and emotionless. "You will tell me who else was present when Phang gave you the heroin. You will tell me what instructions Phang gave you with the heroin. You will tell me how much Phang paid you to carry out his instructions. And you will tell me when and how you planted the heroin in the Marine compound."

Nguyen Minh and Lanh Thi Dang looked at the floor of the small storage bunker—small enough to be cramped even with only three people in it—they were being questioned in and didn't answer.

"After you tell me these things you will go to the American base at Da Nang and you will tell these same things to the American Marine authorities," Houng said.

Nguyen Minh and Lanh Thi Dang continued looking at the dirt floor and remained silent.

"You will tell me these things and you will not lie to me because I know the answers and I will know you are lying. You do not want to face the consequences of lying to me."

"If you know all these things there is no reason for us to tell you," one of the bound men said.

"Ah, but there is," Houng said, holding his face close to the other's. "If I tell the Marine authorities what you did they will simply think I am trying to protect my friends and they will not believe me. But if you tell them what you did, they will believe you."

Silence.

"Do you fear the wrath of Captain Phang?" Houng asked and rocked back on his heels.

"If we talk to you Captain Phang will kill us."

Houng leaned close again and breathed into both their faces. "You should not fear Phang," he said. "You should fear me. Phang does not have you. I do."

"I will not talk to you, I do not want Captain Phang to kill me. You will not kill me."

"What you say is partly true," Houng said, staying close. "After you talk to me, if Phang catches you he will kill you. That is true. It is also true that I do not want to kill you, because if I kill you then you will not be able to tell the American Marines what you have done and so save my friends. But if you do not talk, then I have no reason to keep you alive. If you chose to keep silent about what you did, then I will kill you to prevent your ever doing such treachery again." He rocked back. "What is your choice?"

Silence.

Houng sighed deeply, as though the silence of the prisoners hurt him to his heart because of what that silence was about to make him do. "Then you will die," he said. "When your souls return to this earth, do not blame me. I gave you a chance and you chose to die." A small bag lay on the ground by Houng's heels. He opened it and took several candles from it. He placed the candles in niches around the small bunker room and lit them. Before leaving, he loosely taped gauze over the mouths of Nguyen Minh and Lanh Thi Dang to prevent them from being able to blow out the candles and said, "Your death will be slow. If you change your minds while you still have breath to talk, there will be someone nearby who will hear your cries." A heavy curtain closed behind him, cutting off circulation, preventing fresh air from entering the tiny bunker.

Nguyen Minh and Lanh Thi Dang stared wide-eyed at the burning candles. Their wrists and elbows were tied behind their backs and their ankles and knees were also bound. A short length of rope ran from their ankles to their wrists, so they couldn't uncurl from the fetal position they were sitting in. They knew at the most they would be able to douse only a few of the candles. How long would it be before the flames ate all of the oxygen in the small room and they suffocated?

Nguyen Minh struggled with his bonds, but the harder he fought, the deeper the cords dug into his flesh. In his heart he knew Houng wouldn't let them die—or so he hoped. He breathed deeply and told Lanh Thi Dang he knew Houng would not let them die this way. And he watched the wavering candles. Dang did not reply. The air slowly became heavy in the room and the candles began to flicker out one by one. Minh gasped for breath, still not believing Houng would let him die and struggled once more against the cords that bound him. His face grew red, then turned blue. His back arched and his body spasmed in its struggle for oxygen before he collapsed into unconsciousness.

Lanh Thi Dang breathed slowly and shallowly the whole time Nguyen struggled and talked. He did not struggle and he did not talk. He watched the candles and he waited impassively. Sooner or later Minh would pass out, then he would call for help. He did not want to die and this madman PF lieutenant would kill him, there was no doubt in Lanh Thi Dang's mind about that. After he told all he knew to whoever he had to tell it to he would leave Quang Tin province forever and go where Phang would never find him to extract revenge. But Nguyen Minh might still manage to find him. Nguyen Minh was a favorite of Phang's and would stop at nothing to aid his leader, it had been he who had most wanted to plant the heroin in the American Marines compound.

Lanh Thi Dang watched Nguyen Minh struggle, become spastic, and collapse. He waited longer to be certain Nguyen Minh wasn't faking, he waited until he was afraid, he, too, would lose consciousness. Lanh Thi Dang waited until Nguyen Minh's eyes bulged in their sockets and his anal sphincter loosened. He waited until he himself had only one breath remaining and then he called for help.

The heavy curtain over the entrance to the bunker was thrown open immediately and the two prisoners were pulled out of it into the fresh air. Lanh Thi Dang recovered quickly. Anyone familiar with cardiopulmonary resuscitation could have revived Nguyen Minh in a matter of moments—but neither Houng nor any of his men had ever heard of cardiopulmonary resuscitation.

As soon as Lanh Thi Dang regained his breath he told Houng everything he knew about the heroin. He agreed to go to the American Marines and tell them everything he knew. He asked one thing in return—that Houng would request of the Americans that they not turn him over to

Captain Phang or to Phang's district chief. Houng guaranteed it. Lanh Thi Dang walked somberly to Camp Apache, where he repeated what he knew to the huge American introduced to him as Dai uy Hasford. He knew Dai uy Hasford would keep his promise not to turn him over to Phang or the district chief—Dai uy Hasford had to be an honorable man, no American who spoke Vietnamese so fluently could be anything other than honorable. He prepared himself to go to Da Nang.

But by then the evening chow bird had already come and gone and it was too late to go to Da Nang that day.

CHAPTER TWENTY

About that same time, but a different place

The windows of the room in which Captain Phang sat were tightly shuttered against the night. Two flickering candles pooled their light, one on each end of the table he sat at. Light reflected dimly from the room's thatch walls while shadows gathered in its corners and under the cross-beam of the roof. Phang sat close to the table, his forearms crossed on its rough-hewn top. Two men wearing black peasant pajamas sat on rickety chairs across the table from him. A well-worn sheet of paper, starting to split at its folds, lay between them. A map was hand-drawn on the paper.

"It looks very simple, Dai uy," said the man with the scar that ran from the bridge of his nose down past the corner of his mouth to his jowl. "But how do we know it will work?"

"There is a thieu ta a major of yours who has done

business with me in the past," Phang said. They were careful to avoid using names, not even calling each other by name. Who knew? Even the walls might have ears. "You know him, you have talked to him within the past day or you would not be here now. If you do not wish to believe what I say will work, you can ask him. He will tell you when I make a promise it is kept."

The scar-faced man nodded and pursed his lips as he studied the map.

"Tell me again how much is there," said the man who had bandoleers crossing his chest.

"Right now there is nothing," Phang said, curling the corners of his mouth in the beginning of a smile. He was not going to be caught in a game of words. "But tomorrow at this time there will be cases containing one hundred of the American M-16 rifles, which the Americans claim are superior to both their own M-14 rifles and your AK-47s. They are surely superior to the M-1 carbines the Americans have given to us in the past."

"Rifles are of no use without ammunition for them," said the man with the scarred face.

Phang tilted his head in an of-course-not manner. "There will also be two cases of 5.56mm ammunition for those rifles, ten thousand rounds. In addition to the rifles and bullets for them there will also be cases containing three hundred American hand grenades."

The eyes of the man with the crossed bandoleers lit up at the mention of the hand grenades. The Chinese hand grenades his men normally used were unreliable; often they did not go off, and sometimes they exploded while still in the hand of the man who had cocked them before they could be thrown. Not only were the American hand grenades far more reliable, they were more powerful and no harder to carry than the Chinese ones.

Phang's nostrils flared; he knew he had his audience hooked on what he was telling them. "In addition to that there will be ten M-79 40mm grenade launchers and four hundred rounds for them." He settled back on his chair, leaving only one hand resting easily on the table. "All of these things will be there by this time tomorrow night and they will be there for two days." He gave his visitors a moment to absorb all he had told them, then added, "The weapons are so new they will still be coated with Cosmoline."

The man with the scar nodded after a moment. "What about guards? Such an armory will have to be guarded."

"There will be no more than five guards."

"We will have to kill them. You understand that, don't you?"

"Of course you have to kill them. There might be suspicion if the guards are not killed—suspicion that could shift to me. Kill them."

"You are willing to have your own men killed?" asked the one with bandoleers crossing his chest, suddenly suspicious.

"In this case I am. I have employees who do not appear on any roster anywhere. Five of these employees recently proved themselves untrustworthy, perhaps enemies of mine. They stole something from me. They must be punished for that theft, and as an example to others who might think of stealing from me in the future." He knew that only two of the four kilos of heroin had been found.

"How good are these men as soldiers, how many of my men might they kill before they themselves die?"

"They are not soldiers. They do not normally have rifles. I will give them rifles to use for this duty. The rifles will be old carbines. They will kill none of your men unless your men become involved in hand-to-hand combat with them and one of them is lucky. Two of the carbines will have broken firing pins, one will have an essential piece missing from its trigger housing group and will be unable to fire. One has a blockage in its barrel and will explode when fired. The fifth man will be given faulty ammunition that will not fire."

"How will you explain to your superiors that only five men were on guard?"

"I will tell them I assigned a small guard so your attention would not be attracted."

All three men tried not to laugh at this joke.

"How much do you want for this?" Scarface asked.

"Ten thousand dollars in American greenbacks. Half in advance and the balance after you have verified that you indeed have everything I have promised."

The two men dressed in black pajamas thought about the weapons and ammunition and studied Phang for a long moment before one of them asked, "What is to prevent us from killing you now and taking what will be there tomorrow without having to pay you?"

Phang smiled openly at that question. "The shipment has not yet been delivered. The guards have not yet been assigned and armed. If you kill me now, the shipment might be diverted or it might be delayed. When it comes here, if it comes here, someone else will be responsible for its security. That someone else will assign more than five men to guard it and they will be armed with weapons that will work. If you kill me, you risk not getting those arms and ammunition, or getting it only at great cost in lives to you." He let them ponder his words for a short moment, then said, "And if you do not kill me now, then I will be alive to do more business with you in the future."

The two men gazed at the map again for a long moment. Finally one said, "A courier will deliver five thousand dollars in American greenbacks to you tomorrow afternoon."

"As soon as I have it I will assign the guards. I will not arm them until after the shipment arrives. They will not have the opportunity to discover their weapons are worthless until it is too late."

Three men sat after sundown in a guard shack from whose warped plywood walls the paint was flaking. The shack stood next to the padlocked entrance of a masonry building in the district capital. The three men played cards by the light of a kerosene lamp and grumbled. They played cards to pass the time and they grumbled because they had, at the last minute, been given this petty job to do. They had planned to go out and get drunk on Tiger beer that night; they did not want to spend it sitting in a musty guard shack. There were only three men because Captain Phang had not been able to locate Nguyen Minh and Lanh Thi Dang. The three men did not know what was behind the padlocked door and they didn't care. Whatever it was, it could not be of importance. If it had been, there would have been more than three men guarding it. They cared more that they were not being paid extra for the inconvenience of having to sit by it all night.

After two or three hours one of the men, Do, yawned and stretched. He stood up and announced, "I am going to sleep."

"We will wake you later to take a watch," one of the others told him.

Do grunted and picked up a cloth to go outside and find a piece of ground so he could lie down and sleep. The other two returned to their cards.

In another hour one of them, Tan, yawned for the third time in less than ten minutes and Duong, the third man, said, "You sleep. When I need to sleep I will wake you to watch for a time."

Tan yawned, nodded his thanks, gathered his ground cloth, and went outside to find a place to lie down on it. The place he found was around the corner of the masonry building which held whatever it was they were guarding.

Duong, the lone man still awake, though not watching well, shuffled the cards and tried to remember how to lay them out for a one-handed game an American had once taught him, a game called solitaire. In due time his head nodded over the cards and lay on his arms. He fell asleep. The fuel in the lamp burned down and it went out.

After the moon set, thirty men, dressed in black pajamas with red armbands, carrying an assortment of AK-47 and SKS and French and Japanese rifles, flitted through the night toward the guard shack in front of the building. Fifty other men, unarmed, waited in the darkness behind them. The thirty men advanced, unopposed and silent, until one of them tripped over something on the ground. He spun around and discovered a man sleeping on a spread cloth. Before Do could wake enough to realize what had stirred him, the man who tripped over him pulled out a knife and slit his throat.

Five men cautiously approached the guard shack and huddled next to it. One of them peered into the open door. In the darkness of the room he made out a darker shadow that looked like a man slumped over, sleeping with his head on a small table. The looker signed to his companions and padded silently to the sleeping shadow. The others followed him into the shack and spread out around its sides, feeling for sleeping men. They found only the one man, Duong, asleep at the table. The first man in dispatched him quickly with a knife stroke that briefly pinned one kidney and lung to his heart, then twisted a large hole in the organs to ease the flowing of blood from the corpse.

Another five-man team rushed the padlocked door and thrust an iron bar through the lock's hasp. Two strong men twisted the iron bar until the hasp snapped. They eased the door open and, using hand signals only, called for the fifty men who were waiting in the shadows. The fifty men hurried forward and filtered into the building. Their leader carried a masked flashlight to direct their work. In short minutes the fifty laborers were back outside carrying the cases which held two hundred M-16s with ten thousand rounds, three hundred M-26 hand grenades, ten M-79 grenade launchers, and four hundred 40mm grenades for them. The eighty men of the raiding party melted into the night without a shot being fired.

Around the side of the building Tan woke from a light sleep when the padlock hasp snapped. He crawled to the corner and poked his head around it. He shrank back when he saw many men moving to and fro in front of the building. Minutes later the shadow men were all leaving. Tan put his rifle into his shoulder and and pointed it at the back of the last man to leave. He would fire one shot and run as soon as that warning shot had been fired—then someone else would come and deal with the raiders. He pulled the trigger and heard a dull *chunk* as the hammer fell forward onto the bolt, but his rifle didn't fire. He swore and moved along the front of the building, where he found Do with his throat grinning at the stars. Tan took his late friend's rifle and tried to fire a warning shot with it. When he pulled the trigger nothing happened, he didn't even hear the hammer fall forward. He found Duong dead inside the guard shack. The bullet in the chamber of Duong's rifle made a small pop when its insufficient powder charge was ignited by its primer.

Tan squatted down with this third useless rifle dangling from his hands and thought. It didn't take him long to realize his loyalty was being betrayed by his leader, the man to whom he gave his allegiance. He understood Phang wanted him dead the way Do and Duong were dead. Tan removed the magazine of faulty ammunition from the carbine in his hands and retrieved what he hoped was good ammunition from Do's rifle. Then, he, too, melted into the night.

CHAPTER TWENTY-ONE

November 13, 1966

On the third day of their incarceration at Da Nang two of the Tango Niner Marines had company.

"I don't believe this, Burrie," Ensign Lily said. "I flat do not believe it." The young officer shook his head. "The job your 'supply sergeant' did was so good I can't believe this has happened."

"What?" Burrison asked. The two were sitting on folding chairs at a card table in an otherwise empty briefing room in a building adjacent to the provost marshal's office. An MP lance corporal stood outside the door looking in through its window. His right hand was on his .45 holster.

"I can't believe the Marine Corps would do something like this." Lily ignored Burrison's question. "There you were out in Indian Country running around like some kind of John-goddamn-Wayne hero, probably doing all kinds of things you'd get medals for in a regular line outfit, and they busted you? I don't believe the Marines would do that on such a chicken charge. I can't believe they'd let the Air Force do it either."

"What are you talking about?" Burrison couldn't figure out what his friend thought he had been arrested for.

"This is a goddamn shame. You should be getting decorated and promoted for what you've been doing out there and instead they've busted you for grand theft auto."

Burrison's jaw dropped and he stared bug-eyed at his friend. He fish-mouthed for a moment before he gained enough control of his voice to be able to ask, "What grand theft auto? What are you talking about?"

Now it was Lily's turn to be confused. "Your jeep. That was the biggest news you could imagine around here for about two weeks. I thought it had blown over and the Air Force thought it wound up in a chop shop. That is what you're here for, isn't it?"

Burrison shook his head. "What does my jeep have to do with anything?"

"That's a relief," Lily said, finally realizing his friend hadn't been arrested for stealing an Air Force jeep. He had supplied the Marines with gasoline for the jeep, and if they were arrested for stealing it, he might find himself facing charges as an accessory after the fact.

A few weeks earlier Burrison had insisted to Sergeant Bell that Tango Niner needed a jeep. CAP Tango Niner was not authorized to have a vehicle, but Bell saw a number of advantages to the platoon having one. So he and Corporal Zeitvogel visited Da Nang and stole an Air Force jeep. A cousin of Corporal Big Louie Slover's was stationed at Da Nang with a Seabee unit and, in exchange for battle souvenirs, took care of painting the Air Force jeep navy blue and provided them with counterfeit registration for it. Burrison did not know the jeep was stolen. He didn't understand how Bell had gotten it, but accepted Bell's explanation that he, as a Marine sergeant, had the authority to requisition it. Lily, a drinking buddy of Burrison's from when they were both in San Francisco waiting to be shipped to Vietnam, had traded them a fifty-five-gallon drum of gasoline for four captured AK-47 assault rifles. Unlike Burrison, Lily understood that Bell had acquired the jeep through what the Marines referred to as a "midnight requisition." The civilian term for midnight requisition is grand theft.

"What happened, what did you do that they arrested you for?" Lily asked, calmer now that he knew he wasn't in any jeopardy. "Why on earth are you being court-martialed?" He couldn't imagine the clean-cut, bright-eyed, bushy-tailed, apple-cheeked Marine lieutenant actually doing something he could be court-martialed for—well, at any rate, Burrison had been apple-cheeked before the tropical sun baked the skin of his face bronze.

"I didn't do anything, dammit," Barrison said. "Someone planted two kilos of heroin in Camp Apache and tipped off the lieutenant colonel where it was. My NCOs and I are charged with drug smuggling."

Lily blinked a few times. Burrison a drug smuggler? It didn't seem possible, this kid couldn't be involved with something like that, not Burrison. "Who could have planted it, and why would anyone do something like that?"

"That's the hell of it. I know who did it and why, but I can't prove it." Then he told his friend Lily all about Tango Niner's problems with Captain Phang and how they knew he was behind the heroin.

When he was through Lily said, "You're right, you can't prove it. I've never heard of an Arvin official going as far as you say this one has gone, but I know some of them are corrupt enough I wouldn't put anything past them. What can I do?"

Burrison thought for a moment. He hadn't expected help from his friend, only sympathy and commiseration. "Do you think you could get in touch with Lieutenant Houng and find out from him what he's learned?"

"Can I find him at Camp Apache?"

Burrison nodded.

"Consider it done, buddy."

They talked about other things for a while longer, then

the guard knocked on the door and opened it. "Excuse me, sirs," the guard said, "time's up." Lily left and Burrison was taken back to his locked and guarded room in the transient officers' quarters.

At about that same time in a different but identical room with an identical door window with an MP PFC standing guard outside it in the same building, Corporal Tex Randall sat in an identical folding chair at an identical card table across from a equally identical folding chair. That's where the similarity stopped. Because the person in the other chair was a woman. Not just any woman, she was a beautiful American woman; she was darkly tanned by the tropical sun and her rich auburn hair cascaded onto her shoulders. Her full lips were a delicate red, and long lashes surrounded the dark eyes under her finely arched eyebrows. The white sundress she wore made her look like the angel of every man's dreams, an apparition any Marine in I Corps would kill for.

"Tex," Bobbie Harder exclaimed after they embraced and kissed briefly under the attentive gaze of the MP on the other side of the door, "what happened? This doesn't have anything to do with the jeep, does it?" While he hadn't helped steal the jeep, Randall had been in on the planning. Bobbie knew all about the incident and his role in the theft.

"No"—he shook his head—"no, not the jeep. It's much worse than that."

She gazed into his hollow eyes and her own filled with worry. "What happened?"

"Do you remember our problems with Captain Phang?"

"Phang!" She spat the word like it was something foul she had to get out of her mouth before it poisoned her. "How could I forget that beast?" Bobbie was a civilian employee of the Department of Defense working as a clerk for the Marines at Da Nang. She had been captivated by Randall's boyish tough-guy act and had gotten information for him that the Marines of Tango Niner gave to Houng and his PFs to use to track down details of Phang's corruption so they could have him removed from office.

"He's trying to burn us, and it looks like he's going to succeed." Then he told her about the heroin.

Bobbie interrupted occasionally with an expression of disgust at Phang or sympathy for Randall and the other Marines. "Do you think your Lieutenant Houng will find the people who did it?" she asked when he was finished.

"I hope so," he said. "If he can't it's hard time and bad paper for all of us."

"Hard time and bad paper?"

"A long sentence in the brig at hard labor and probably a Bad Conduct discharge." His voice cracked on the last words and he swore under his breath.

"That's terrible," she exclaimed. "He can't be allowed to get away with this. Even if Houng can't find the men who did it, we have to prove Phang is out to get you, get something to discredit him." She shook her head vigorously, making her hair fly out. "There's no real evidence you men were smuggling drugs . . ."

"They found two kilos of heroin inside the compound," he interrupted.

"So what? That doesn't prove anything. Nobody saw any of you with it and they didn't find your fingerprints on anything, did they?"

"Of course not."

"That means they can't prove any of you did it. All that proves is someone did it, and from what you say there were a lot of people who were inside your compound in the days before it was found and any of them could have hidden it there. Right?"

"I guess so."

"I know somebody I can go to with the information I gave you last month," she said. "I can put that information together with some more and go to this person and tell him about everyone refusing to talk to your Popular Forces and I bet we get some action." She said it all very decisively. In another minute she stood up, kissed him quickly, and turned to the guard, who seemed very interested in what he was watching through the door's window. "Let me out," she demanded.

The guard did. He stood watching her march away in an extremely feminine manner and wondered how this dope-dealing corporal ever managed to get such a fine-looking woman for himself. It must be the money, he thought. There's a lot of money in dope—until you get caught and wind up spending the rest of your life in the lockup.

Ensign Lily looked for his friend Lieutenant Reeves, the helicopter pilot who had flown him and the fifty-five-gallon drum of gasoline out to Camp Apache a few weeks earlier. It was the afternoon of the third day of the Marines' arrest and preparations for their court-martials before Reeves had a break from flight missions and Lily could find him. Lily explained the situation to Reeves.

The helicopter pilot shook his head and said, "Lily, sometimes I just don't know about you, young son. You make bar-crawling friends with a jarhead second louie and this here salt-sea sailor winds up flying all over the deepest parts of Indian Country helping you deliver contraband and pick up souvenirs . . ."

"Delivering fifty-five gallons of gasoline to a Marine unit in the field isn't exactly contraband. Besides, you got an AK, too," Lily reminded him.

"And now you want me to shag ass out there again to help your compano haul his ass out of some shit," Reeves said, ignoring Lily. "What's in it for me if I fly you out there on a run this time?"

"No souvenirs for this flight, good buddy. I'm taking this trip out of pure friendship."

"Uh-huh," Reeves said. He didn't believe any junior Navy officer would do a favor for an equally junior Marine officer purely out of friendship. There had to be something to be gotten out of it and he wanted his share.

"Really, I'm doing this as a favor for the guy. He's being framed and I want to help spring him."

"Uh-huh. Then what?"

Lily leaned forward and spoke in a confidential voice as though he were giving out a secret. "Look at it this way, good buddy," he said and wrapped an arm around Reeves's shoulders, "my buddy Burrie and his boys are out deep in Indian Country doing some serious ass-kicking. They've got a straight line on coming up with boo-coo heavy-duty souvenirs, know what I mean? If they're in the slams, we have to rely on our own resources to get anything. But if we help them get out of this, then we have a direct pipeline into the most heavy-duty supply of enemy arms and equipment you can imagine. I can see it now"—he let go of Reeves and looked upward, spreading his hands as though indicating a huge billboard in the sky—"we'll be entrepreneurs. Lily and Reeves, the VC and NVA War Surplus Store."

Reeves looked as though he, too, could see the billboard. "Reeves and Lily," he said.

"You got it, partner." Lily grabbed the lieutenant's hand in both of his and shook it vigorously. "How soon can you get that whirlybird of yours warmed up?"

"Couple a days," Reeves answered, staring into his glass.

"What?" Lily squawked. "A couple of days is too long. Burrie's going to be hung in a couple of days. Why can't you wind up your bird right now?"

"It's broke," Reeves mumbled into his drink.

Lily blinked at him and worked his jaw once or twice. "What do you mean 'It's broke'? What's wrong with it?"

"How the hell do I know?" Reeves twisted his shoulders. "I'm not a mechanic, I'm a driver. All I know is it's broke; it won't fly."

"Why not?"

Reeves shrugged. "We took some fire coming back from our last mission. It's lucky I was able to get it all the way in."

"Oh, shit," Lily whispered and sagged in his chair. "If we can't get out to Camp Apache most ricky-tick, it's just liable to be the end of the Lily and Reeves VC and NVA War Surplus Company before it even opens shop."

"Reeves and Lily."

"Reeves and Lily."

"What about the other helicopters in your squadron?"

"They're all busy; no way I can get to any of them." Reeves looked glum for a moment before adding almost inaudibly, "Besides, the other pilots in my squadron don't like the way I drive. They're all afraid I'll break their birds."

They sat slumped over the table for a few minutes, sipping their drinks. Then Reeves bolted upright and said with animation, "Hey, I just remembered. The Army, they're having a major problem with pilferage in Saigon and Cam Ranh Bay. Most of that shit's going straight into the black market, but they think the Marines are taking some of it in midnight requisitions. They sent an accounting team to Eye Corps to inventory Marine supplies to see if any of their stuff is here. The accounting team's got its own Huey and it's stuck here in Da Nang for at least a week." His eyes grew bright. "They aren't going to need that Huey for a few days; maybe I can borrow it."

It wasn't until after evening chow that Reeves was able to round up his copilot and crew chief and talk the army pilot into looking the other way while he went out for a little joy ride. It was almost sundown by the time they touched down at Camp Apache. All of this was on the third day of the Marines' arrest in Da Nang, the second full day of the PFs' search. It was the day Long and others captured Nguyen Minh and Lanh Thi Dang, the same day Nguyen Minh died because he didn't believe Houng would kill him, the day Lanh Thi Dang told all he knew about the heroin.

CHAPTER TWENTY-TWO

That evening, back at Camp Apache

Captain Hasford knew about Billy Boy Lewis's uncanny night-fighting abilities. He had heard of the informal patrol the lance corporal from the Bronx had taken out on the afternoon of the night the VC had attempted to overrun Camp Apache, a patrol that had wiped out a seven-man VC squad and captured its mortar. He knew that Lewis was generally respected by the other Marines of Tango Niner. So he made Lewis patrol leader of the screening listening post he sent out one kilometer to the west of Camp Apache a little before dark on the third night of no patrols. Lewis took with him Wells and the new man, Dodd, from his own fire team and Corporal Ruizique's three men. This meant two of the six men in the patrol were new to CAP operations and weren't well known to Lewis. It also meant Tim Webster, who was senior to Lewis as a lance corporal, was under him. But Hasford felt that couldn't be helped. Anyway, Houng was probably right and there wouldn't be any problems.

Then he divided the perimeter into thirds and assigned Lance Corporals Hempen, Athen, and Flood to them. Hempen had Robertson and Mazzucco from his own fire team along with Willard, the new grenadier, to guard the eastern third. Two out of Hempen's four men were new, but in many ways he was the most mature of the platoon's lance corporals and would be most able to handle that situation. Athen and the machine gun team held watch over the southwestern segment. Like Hempen, Athen had two new men to deal with, but the two men had been in the same machine gun team in Echo Company, so there shouldn't be any particular problems on that account. And Houng was agreeable to putting one of his squad leaders with each of the Marine teams. The PF lieutenant himself took full responsibility for guarding their prisoner overnight. Flood and the other two mortarmen along with Doc Tracker held down the rest of the perimeter and Hasford himself along with Doc Rankin would rotate radio watch with Swarnes.

Less than fifteen minutes after Lewis led his people out, as the sun was dipping down to kiss the tops of the mountains in the west, an unexpected helicopter appeared in the east. When it was close enough for the Marines remaining on the hill to see that it was Army green rather than Marine olive green, Swarnes received a call over the radio.

"Apache, this is Flyboy. I don't see your man in the black flak jacket. Is it all right for me to come down? Over." Big Louis Slover normally guided helicopters onto the helipad at Camp Apache, and he did it dressed the way he normally dressed when he was inside the compound—shirtless. The previous time Reeves had flown into the Marine compound he objected to coming down so close to a half-dressed man who could get injured by the debris kicked up by his bird's downwash. Burrison had answered him, "Think of it this way, the man's wearing a black flak jacket."

"Roger yours, Flyboy," Swarnes replied. "Earth base Apache standing by for your touchdown." Then he ran outside the tent to Captain Hasford and said, "Sir, we got fucking company. I think this is some dumbass swabbie friend of Lieutenant Burrison's who came to visit a month ago."

Hasford nodded. He wondered what was going on, why a friend of Burrison's was paying an unannounced evening visit. Was Lanh Thi Dang lying about the heroin and was Lieutenant Burrison really a smuggler? Was this a pickup to take the heroin on the next leg of its journey? But surely, if Burrison really was a smuggler, he would have gotten word to his contacts by now so they wouldn't come here intending to do more business. He waited. The helicopter was hovering for its landing now. He'd know what it was about soon enough. If the people in the helicopter were smugglers, there was liable to be trouble. If there was, whose side would the men be on?

"What the fuck's that?" Big Red Robertson said, squinting at the approaching helicopter.

Hempen peered at it. It was unlike any other helicopter he had ever seen: its body was small and a slender boom pointed up and back from it; its front was paneled with large sheets of Plexiglas, even at the pilot's feet; instead of wheels it had sledlike skids; doors were open on both sides; and machine guns on flexible mounts sprouted from them. "I think it's one of them Huey-birds like the Army uses," he finally said.

Robertson turned his head and looked down at Hempen. "Huey-bird? What the fuck's an Army bird coming out here for? They ain't even in Eye Corps."

Hempen shrugged. "I dunno."

The chopper landed and a man in Navy officer's khakis jumped off and ducked under the whirling blades. "You must be Captain Hasford," he said. "My old buddy Burrie told me about you, said you're a good head. I'm Ensign Lily." He held his hand out to shake. Behind him the helicopter's rotor blades slowed to an idle.

Hasford took the hand, said, "Yes, I am," and thought, Head? Isn't that a drug term?

"I saw Burrie in Da Nang," Lily continued. Two men in

flight suits, the pilot and copilot, descended from the helicopter. The crew chief sat in the side door with a hand on his machine gun.

Lily's obvious nervousness made Hasford more edgy. Was this ensign—if he really was a Navy officer—going to ask him to join in the drug trade?

"Burrie told me all about what's coming down here." Lily kept talking. Hasford wished he could look around to see what the others were doing without tipping his hand. "So I made a trip to find out if his fay epps have had any luck in tracking down the gooks who planted that shit in the shithouse." He looked around, his gaze extending far into the floodplain around the hill. "Man, it sure gives me the willies, being so far out here in Indian Country." He shivered. "I don't know how you can stand it."

Hasford didn't realize he was holding his breath until he let it all out with a whoosh. He took a deep breath to calm himself, feeling relieved about knowing why Lily seemed so nervous, and said, "As a matter of fact, they brought someone in an hour ago."

"Hot damn," Lily exclaimed. "How sure are they he did it? Is he willing to testify? Where is he? I can take him back to Da Nang now and hand his ass over. We'll get Burrie and his boys out of the brig most ricky-tick and back where he belongs."

That's as far as they got before the shit hit the fan.

Lieutenant Houng's prediction that it would take the Vietcong a few days to realize Combined Action Platoon Tango Niner didn't have any patrols out was a bit optimistic. The first night the VC sent four squad-size patrols through Bun Hou looking for the CAP patrols. They were followed closely by two platoons that hoped to capitalize on any contacts. The first night, the VC simply chalked up the lack of contact to coincidence. There were nights, after all, when the Americans and their lackeys, the so-called Popular Forces, didn't catch any of the supply runs or reinforcement units that infiltrated through the village. On the second night of no patrols the VC sent six squads through, again followed by two platoons to capitalize on contacts. Not encountering a Tango Niner patrol two nights in a row when they had that many men out looking for them seemed too much of a coincidence. So on the day of the third night they used the remnants of their intelligence network in Bun Hou to find out if there was anything unusual happening that they should know about. It took only a couple of hours for them to find out why they had failed to make contact for two nights running when they were trying to. Then the Vietcong leaders made plans to capitalize on the fact that the PFs weren't patrolling and Camp Apache was guarded by only twenty-one Marines. Two platoons, about fifty men, were dispatched to take care of it. They came from the east and were in position by dusk. The navy helicopter was a bonus they found too tempting to resist. They moved northward to where they had a better view of the hilltop landing pad. Charlie wanted to tango.

The first indication Hasford and the Navy officers had of trouble was Hempen's voice shouting, "Incoming," from the east side of the compound.

"This way," Hasford shouted, pushing and shoving the sailors into the nearest trench. Over his words, they heard the distant boom of a B-40 rocket.

"What?" It was a sound the Navy officers had never heard before. The rocket-propelled grenade hit the hilltop and exploded thirty-five meters from the helipad, showering thrown-up dirt onto the back of the bird and into the trench. Hasford tried to hustle his visitors along the trench to the safety of a bunker.

"Wait a minute, I got to get in the air," Reeves shouted, struggling to get away from the Marine officer. When the shooting starts an infantryman's first instinct is to get down, to find protective cover from the incoming fire. A pilot's first instinct is to go up, to fly above the fire where he can come back down on top of it and have the advantage. Reeves's copilot joined the struggle and they knocked Hasford to the bottom of the trench. Lily fell under Hasford. The two Navy fliers vaulted out of the trench and sprinted to their waiting bird. A second B-40 rocket hit the hilltop closer to the helicopter before they reached it. Dirt clods and shrapnel ricocheted off the chopper's rear and sides. The crew chief was trying to turn around to bring his machine gun to bear on the rocket launcher that was shooting at him, but the helicopter was not in the right position for him to see the tree line two hundred meters northeast of the hill where the Vietcong were firing from. A third rocket hit closer while Reeves was speeding his rotors up to take off; it peppered the skin of the bird with metal fragments and punctured it in many places. Then they were off the ground and climbing.

Hempen had been scanning the area he and his four men were to cover for the night when he saw the flash of the first rocket-propelled grenade being fired from the north east and shouted the warning. All around the perimeter Marines and PFs dove for the cover of trenches and bunkers. Some of them huddled low. Others, realizing they weren't under a heavy barrage, poked their heads out looking for targets, thinking the few rounds coming in might be cover for an assault. The only ones who saw anything were a few on the east and north sides of the hill who could see the flashes of the RPG being fired.

West of the hill, Lewis had stopped his patrol when he heard the helicopter coming in from a landing at Camp Apache. He wondered why it was there and decided to wait in place for a few minutes in case he was called back in. The helicopter feathered down and the radio was silent, so Lewis signaled Wells to move out. Wells was a down-home good old boy from rural Indiana, the same as Lewis was a down-home good old boy from the Bronx. The two were fast friends and Lewis was teaching Wells how to be the same kind of night fighter he himself was. They were trying to work up the nerve to tell the other Marines they were cousins and had been born and spent their early childhoods in East Left Armpit, Arkansas, and shouldn't be thought of as Yankees despite having enlisted from north of the Mason-Dixon line. Wells had only gone about twenty-five meters when the first B-40 round went off in Camp Apache.

Lewis waited a few seconds to make sure he wasn't interrupting anyone's important message, then called Camp Apache on his radio. "Home Plate, this is Outfield, over."

"Outfield, Home Plate, go," Swarnes said back immediately.

"What's happening, Home Plate? Over."

There was a brief pause and Lewis imagined Swarnes holding his handset in front of his face, staring at the earphone and wondering what kind of stupid question that was. "Outfield," Swarnes drawled, "as anyone can plainly hear, we are taking incoming. Any other dumbass questions? Over."

Lewis smiled in the nightfall darkness under the trees; he had been right about Swarnes thinking he had asked a dumb question. "I can tell that much, Home Plate," he said, drawling even slower than Swarnes had. "Where is it coming from and do you need a relief pitcher? Over."

"Outfield, so far it seems to be coming from the northeast," Swarnes slowed his speaking cadence more. "Now you just warm up that reliever and tell him to stand by. Do you understand? Over."

"Roger that, Home Plate." It was becoming a contest to see which of them could talk more slowly. "Heat up the bullpen but don't send the ace closer in yet, over."

"Outfield, you just hang in there. Home Plate out," Swarnes said and won the slow-talk contest by being the last one to speak.

Lewis shivered when he thought about the incoming coming from the eastern side of the hill. When the VC tried to overrun Camp Apache they started the assault with diversionary fire from the east—then the main assault had come from the west. He huddled his men together for a moment to tell them what was happening, then pointed Wells back toward the hill. They stopped and waited at the edge of the trees where they could watch the now silent hill.

* * *

When the fourth B-40 rocket hit on the helipad, Reeves's bird was already a hundred feet above it and starting to circle to the north and east. Along with his copilot and crew chief, he scanned the dark ground, looking for the source of the fire. The crew chief was the first to spot the green tracer rounds from automatic weapons climbing at them. He shouted and his throat mike transmitted his words to the pilot. Reeves banked sharply and pulled away from the fire, letting the petty officer manning the machine gun have a clear view of the source of the upcoming tracers, and the helicopter's gun rained its .30-caliber bullets, every fifth round an orange tracer, down on the Vietcong position.

The men on the hill watched the dance of the scattered green tracers and steady stream of orange as they passed each other in the darkening sky. Then the helicopter banked again and flew away. "Apache, this is Flyboy," Reeves radioed back. "You tell my buddy down there I'll be back for him tomorrow before the sun reaches the yardarm. Flyboy out." He turned the controls over to his copilot for the flight back to Da Nang and spent the trip wondering what he'd have to promise the maintenance chief to keep him from reporting the damage the bird had suffered on its unauthorized flight. And what on earth was he going to tell the Army pilot he'd borrowed it from?

Hasford grinned at Lily when they reached the CP and Swarnes relayed Reeves's message. "I guess this means you get to find out what war is like firsthand, sailor," he said to the suddenly pale ensign.

"I'm a POL officer," Lily croaked. He worked at the fuel depot at Da Nang; POL means Petroleum, Oil, Lubricants. "I don't know anything about being a grunt."

"I'll bet you learn fast. Here, take this." Hasford handed him a captured AK-47. "This is the muzzle, it's the end the bullets come out of—keep it pointed at the enemy. This is the trigger, don't touch it unless you want to shoot and the muzzle is pointed at the enemy. Now stay close to me." He looked at the uncertain way Lily was holding the assault rifle and added, "Remember, whatever else you do, keep the muzzle pointed away from me."

Hasford reached for the field phone to check with the perimeter positions while Swarnes filled him in on his conversation with Lewis. "Good," the captain said. "Get him on the horn again and find out where he is." In another minute he knew that the only fire anyone had seen had come from two hundred meters off the northeast corner of the hill. The fire had come from approximately a squad, there was no telling how many more enemy soldiers there might be hidden in the darkness.

"Billy Boy's in the trees west of us," Swarnes said.

"He said that in the clear?"

"Nah. What he said was, 'It's like I'm on Catalina and you're in L.A.'" Swarnes shook his head in admiration and said, "Billy Boy's real good at coming up with code. No way them dumbass gooks out there gonna know what the fuck he's talking about, he says something like that, they got a fucking radio they're listening on."

Hasford nodded. All they could do now was wait and see what Charlie did next. It was a half hour before Charlie did anything, long enough for some men to ease back from the tension of the earlier brief attack, long enough for others to become so tightly strung they were nearing the breaking point.

Graham, one of the new men, was one of the tightly strung ones. He had always had good ears, but four months of combat operations, ambushes, and perimeter duty had sharpened them to almost unnatural acuteness. He poked Doc Tracker on the shoulder. "I heard something, out there," he said and pointed. "It sounded like somebody falling down."

"I didn't hear anything," Tracker said. "Where?"

"Right out there. Sounded like maybe a hundred and fifty meters."

Tracker peered at the shadow next to him. The corpsman was a Kiowa Indian, born and raised on the reservation. He had grown up hunting and could move at night with the best of the night fighters and could hear things that few other men, white or black, could and he hadn't heard anything. "Are you sure?"

The shadow nodded.

Tracker reached for the field phone and reported the noise. He had to accept what Graham said; his own hearing hadn't completely returned from when he had been deafened by the satchel charge that had gone off too close to him when the VC were inside Camp Apache's wire.

Swarnes rogered Tracker's report and, at Hasford's order, contacted Flood and told him and Reid to go to their mortar pit and fire an illumination round where Graham said he heard something. In less than a minute the mortar *carumph*ed.

"Jesus Christ," Tracker swore when the flare popped overhead. On the hillside below he saw irregularities on the ground between the outer and middle banks of concertina wire—irregularities that hadn't been there before the sun went down. "Charlie's inside the outer wire," he whispered into his field phone. "He's camouflaged and trying to hide by laying down," and pointed out the camouflaged soldiers to Graham.

"How goddamn many are there?" Swarnes asked.

"I'm not sure. Could be twenty, could be more."

"Stand by," Swarnes told Tracker, then alerted the rest of the positions around the perimeter. While he radioed this information to Lewis, Hasford talked to Flood and instructed him to fire a second flare just over the inside of the outer wire in front of Tracker's position, then drop a high explosive spotter round at the same place. "Let the flare out there now almost burn out before you fire," he said. "Time it so the next flare pops and the spotter hits at the same time this flare goes out." Then he asked Tracker if he had heard his instructions to the mortar and told him, "Stand by for me to join you."

In five positions around the wire men probed the night with their eyes and ears and hunched lower in their fighting positions. They double- and triple-checked their weapons, making sure magazines were firmly seated, rounds were in the chambers, safeties off, spare magazines in easy reach, hand grenades ready at hand.

"In the tube," Flood said on the field phone after a few seconds. The mortar *carumphe*d twice as Hasford dropped into the trench next to Tracker and Graham. Lily was with him.

"Give me the phone," he said and immediately contacted the mortar pit. The first flare hit the ground seventy-five meters outside the wire and sputtered out. Night returned for an instant, then the second flare lit the north side of the hill like day and the spotter round hit, spouting a geyser of earth into the sky and toppling two of the camouflaged Vietcong who had risen as soon as the first flare went out. "Left twenty-five, fire three," the captain directed the mortar. Near him Graham started firing wildly at two dozen VC who were now charging toward the wire under the direction of their officers' and sergeants' whistles, firing from the hip and screaming as they came. "Slow fire," Hasford told him, "pick your targets." Tracker had been through this before, he was aiming his shots, and a soldier clad in brown camouflage with fake dirt clods attached to uniform backs fell each time he pulled the trigger.

Three mortar rounds exploded behind the right flank of the VC and knocked a half-dozen more of them off their feet. "Left twenty-five, fire three," Hasford instructed Flood, "then pop another flare.'

The VC reached the inner bank of wire and four of them threw themselves on it to act as human bridges for the others to clamber over, despite the telling fire from Flood and Graham—none of the other perimeter positions were in good positions to bring fire on the VC platoon trying to break in. Hasford raised his .45 and carefully fired at the nearest Vietcong. The heavy, slow-moving bullet slammed into the man and sent a shudder through his body before he collapsed to the ground like a pile of rags.

"I told you how to use that piece," Hasford said to Lily. "Pick someone out and blow him away." The ensign clumsily put the captured assault rifle to his shoulder and tried to decide which of the howling attackers to fire at.

Then Hasford returned to the phone. "Right twenty-five, fire three," he said right before the last three rounds he ordered hit. "Left twenty-five, fire three," he said calmly after those three were fired. He didn't call for the mortar to fire closer to the inner wire because then he would be risking wounding the men with him. But if the VC tried to cross the inner wire he'd have to call the mortar in almost on his own position in order to break off their attack. The second salvo of three mortar rounds erupted between the outer and middle banks of wire. One of the human bridges jerked violently as shrapnel tore into his body and threw the man who was running across him into the rows of spiked wire—both VC hung up in the wire writhed wildly for a moment as their life's blood drained from them, then hung limply. A second human bridge screamed in agony at the impact of burning metal ripping his flesh, then whimpered while his comrades pounded over him.

"It won't shoot anymore," Lily said to Hasford. He had pointed his AK-47 at a charging Cong and held the trigger down until the magazine emptied.

"Reload it."

"You didn't tell me how," Lily said, feeling sheepish. Now that he was actually in a fight and had returned fire at the enemy it didn't seem as bad as he had thought it would be. The Marine officer snatched the Communist weapon from the sailor's hands, flipped the empty magazine out of it, yanked a magazine from the belt hanging around Lily's shoulders, slammed it into the magazine well, and jacked a round into the chamber. "That's how you do it," he snapped. "Do it yourself the next time." Lily was too embarrassed to say he hadn't seen how Hasford reloaded the piece.

The next two three-round salvos hit in the wire, raising a wall of flying earth and screaming metal behind the VC —screaming metal that rent the air and slashed into living flesh, turning it into dead meat. Whistles shrilled again and voices shouted new commands. Only eight VC had made it to the inner wire, which they were frantically trying to breach. At the new whistles and shouted orders they spun and tried to get away. Fire from Tracker's and Graham's M-14s, Lily's AK, and Hasford's .45 followed them. A final salvo of mortar rounds burst in front of them and then none were left standing.

CHAPTER TWENTY-THREE

Same time, same place

Lewis received Swarnes's message about the Vietcong in the wire and told his men what was happening. Then he formed them into a sort of semicircle with himself, Wells, Dodd, and Neissi facing the north. He set Pennell facing into the woods and Webster covered their rear to the south. He had no way of knowing whether there were more VC in the area and if they were on the move and would come through where he was. They listened to the fight on the hill and waited. The only indications they had of how it was going were good—the distinctive cracks of AK-47s became fewer and there weren't as many Vietnamese voices screaming taunts and war cries on the north side of the hill. Then the shooting stopped and all they heard was silence and the distant barking of a disturbed dog in one of the hamlets.

After a moment he called Swarnes. "Home Plate, Out-field. What's happening? Over."

"Wait One, Outfield, I'll let you know as soon as I do."

Lewis took a deep breath and eased slightly. "Hang loose," he whispered to his men. They waited longer.

Finally Swarnes's voice came back over the radio. "Outfield, Home Plate. We killed the little fuckers. Stand by."

Lewis smiled at Swarnes's saying "we killed." All the firing had been from one place on the perimeter, so unless Hasford had moved his command post—including Swarnes and his radios—there, the radioman hadn't been involved in the kill. He passed the word the assault had been repulsed and they waited again. But not for long.

Suddenly something told Lewis they weren't alone. He slowly swiveled his head, listening carefully and searching out of the corners of his eyes. Then he caught it—a flicker of movement in the open between the woods and the hill. He concentrated his search there but couldn't see anything more or hear any sounds of the passage of men. "Home Plate, Outfield," he murmured into his radio. "I do believe you have company to the Frisco side of my location. Do you understand? Over."

"Roger, Outfield. Stand by." Swarnes's voice was easy but serious. Lewis knew his message had been understood. Using hand gestures he alerted his men to the threat ahead of them across the open ground at an angle to the left of the hill on their right.

"Stand by for the light, Outfield," Swarnes said a moment later. The mortar *carumph*ed on the hill and seconds later there was a second, smaller explosion above the cleared ground. The small explosion of the mortar popping open was followed immediately by a fizzing as the flare ignited. It blinked and burst into a glaring blue light that lit the land below like a tiny sun floating earthward under its parachute.

Lewis didn't see anything out of place. Sticking to the shadows cast by tree trunks and branches, he stood up to get a better look. He still didn't see anything.

A new voice came over the radio, Hasford's. "Looks clear from here, Outfield. Do you see anything? Over."

"Negatory that, Home Plate, but I don't care. They must be camouflaged. Drop some Hotel Echo on their asses, over."

"Wait one," came the deadpan reply. Lewis wondered what the captain was thinking. Hasford didn't know him very well, didn't understand how good he was at knowing when someone was there. The other Marines of Tango Niner, and the PFs as well, trusted him without reservation when he said an enemy was near or the coast was clear. But this intelligence officer, unlike the men who had patrolled with and fought alongside him, hadn't seen him in action, didn't know in his guts that this self-proclaimed white lightning runner from the Bronx was always right in this regard. "Outfield, can you direct? Over," Hasford's voice came again.

"I'll try, over."

"Stand by for one spotter and another light."

The mortar fired twice in rapid succession. The first round was a high explosive round that exploded halfway between the trees and the hill, the second a flare to replace the first one, which had now almost burnt out.

"Home Plate, bring it closer to you, over," Lewis said when he didn't see any reaction to the explosion.

"Roger. Stand by." The mortar coughed again. The rocket-shaped round whistled through its arc and crashed to the ground, sending a spout of earth and grass upward halfway between where the first spotter hit and the hill.

"I think I saw movement, Home Plate," Lewis said. He wasn't certain, but it seemed that the low grass rippled in an unnatural manner twenty meters away from the explosive impact.

"Roger, Outfield," Hasford replied. "I saw it, too." From his vantage on the hill the captain had a better view of the plain.

At Hasford's phoned order, Flood and Reid dropped three more rounds down the mortar's tube. The first round hit near the point where Hasford thought he had seen movement, the second exploded a few meters from where Lewis thought he had—they hadn't seen the same thing. Whistles shrilled right after the third round hit. The VC commander knew the other half of his raiding party was wiped out before the second unit could get in position. Now that his second unit was discovered and under fire while it was still out of position, he decided to cut his losses and bug out. One, two dozen brown-camouflaged soldiers jumped to their feet and ran for the cover of the trees.

"I can get 'em, Home Plate. Okay?" Lewis dropped into a prone firing position.

"Take 'em, Outfield," was Hasford's immediate answer. Then he ordered the mortar to follow the VC with more rounds.

As one, the roar of six M-14s, two firing on automatic, shattered the night. Bodies in the mass of running Cong jerked to a stop, shuddered, stumbled, pitched to the ground. "Turkey shoot!" Lewis screamed.

"Buffalo Bill gotta feed the railroad," Wells shouted. His laugh pierced the air, causing some of the VC to run even faster than the mortar shrapnel and bullets flying through them did—panicked them, made them flee this demon from beyond the grave. They knew no living person could laugh that way when killing.

Lewis looked to his sides. He knew how Webster, Wells, and Pennell were doing, he wanted to check on the new men. Dodd and Neissi were prone, rifles held firm in their shoulders, their fire slow and deliberate as they picked their targets. They'll do, Lewis thought, they'll do.

The mortar rounds walked toward the trees as fast as Flood could adjust his aim and Reid could drop them down the tube. Slover and Athen, acting as a two-man mortar squad, could have fired two more rounds in the same time, but every round hit its mark. Big Louie Slover was proud of being the best mortarman in the Seventh Marines before he transferred to the Combined Action Program, and he made sure his men became as good as they could with the tube. Between the mortar and the withering crossfire from

Lewis's patrol, only half of the enemy soldiers who had started the flight from the open made it to the relative safety of the woods.

Lewis put his rifle down for a second, balled his fists in front of his face, and twisted. When they came away the left side of his mustache jutted up and forward, the right end curled in a musketeer flourish. He grabbed his rifle and leaped to his feet. "Let's go get 'em," he shouted. The six Marines ran on line, pursuing the crashing noises the VC made fleeing west through the woods. The lance corporal could taste how badly he wanted to wipe out the last of the VC who had attacked his platoon—he ignored Hasford's voice on the radio, the voice that was ordering him to return to the compound.

The Marines were running to kill, but the Vietcong were running to live. In the world of the preyed and the preyed upon, all can tell you those who flee for their lives usually outrun those who chase to kill. The cheetah dashing after his dinner seldom catches the first dik-dik he pursues. The rabbit whose life ends under the claws of a lynx has usually evaded predators many times before. The VC steadily increased the distance between them and their pursuers and eventually Lewis brought his patrol to a halt.

Lewis panted heavily and swore, "Shit. The fuckers got away. Let's go back." He heaved a few times to regain his breath, then answered the calls on his radio. After the first few minutes Swarnes had taken over calling so Hasford could direct his Marines in checking out the bodies in the north wire. "We lost them, Home Plate," he said. "We're coming in."

Later Hasford said to Lewis, "Lance Corporal, when you didn't return to base when I told you to, you disobeyed a direct order. Do you realize what the maximum penalty is for disobeying a direct order in the face of the enemy?"

Lewis shrugged. "I didn't disobey your orders, sir. I didn't hear them. We were in hot pursuit of the enemy. I kept chasing them, trying to catch them and kill 'em."

"The maximum penalty is death by firing squad," Hasford said, ignoring Lewis's answer. "By not coming back you risked being shot either way. Do you understand that? They might have had a blocking force out there for you to run into."

"There wasn't nobody out there but the ones we was chasing," Lewis mumbled.

"There might have been. You have no way of knowing they didn't."

"I know they didn't. If they did I would've known." He didn't look at the captain, he looked at the ground.

"You couldn't have known that."

"Sir," Webster interrupted. Hasford looked at the other lance corporal and nodded for him to speak. "I was out there with Billy Boy, my life depended on his judgment. He said there wasn't anyone else there. I believed him then and I'll believe him the next time he says it."

Hasford stared at Webster for a moment, then turned back to Lewis. "Nonetheless, I ordered you to return to base and you didn't."

Lewis shrugged again. "All I can say, sir, is we was in hot pursuit of the enemy and I didn't hear your order on the radio."

The captain looked at Lewis for a long moment. "You got away with it this time. Don't let it happen again."

They found more than thirty bodies in the north wire and the grass to the west. Four other wounded VC were captured, but one of them died from his wounds before daybreak. Otherwise the rest of the night was quiet. Two helicopters arrived in the morning. One was a Marine medevac bird flying some wounded Marines from a firefight—it stopped to pick up the prisoners and took them to Da Nang. The other was a Navy helicopter flown by Lieutenant Reeves. He picked up Ensign Lily, who was still flushed with excitement from the earlier firefight. That bird took Hasford, Houng, and Lanh Thi Dang to Chu Lai.

Hasford left Hempen in charge of the Marines in the compound. Webster, Flood, and Athen didn't mind, but Lewis was pissed off.

CHAPTER TWENTY-FOUR

November 14, 1966

"Chu Lai! What the fuck do you mean, Chu Lai,"
Reeves shouted. He didn't shout because he had to shout to
be heard over the roar of his bird's turbines and rotors,
even though he had to shout to be heard over them. He
shouted because he was outraged at the idea of going to
Chu Lai. "Bullshit a whole bunch of Chu Lais. Ain't no
way I'm going to Chu Lai. No way." He shook his head
and steered a course to Da Nang.

"No, man," Lily held his mouth close to Reeves's earphone and shouted, "we got to go to Chu Lai." When Reeves
ignored him he pulled the pilot's earphone away and shouted
into his ear, "Chu Lai, we got to go to Chu Lai."

Reeves flinched from the voice booming in his ear and the
helicopter pitched to the left, out of control for a few seconds
until he managed to stabilize it again. He twisted to face Lily
and shouted, "Don't do that! No loud noises, they upset me."

Lily looked at him blankly and wondered: No loud noises? Then what are you doing flying a helicopter? He said out loud, "Chu Lai, we gotta go to Chu Lai."

Reeves shook his head violently. "No way," he shouted. "I'm driving this sucker and I say we're going to Da Nang."

Lily pulled the earphone away again. "We go to Da Nang without going to Chu Lai first we can forget about the Lily and Reeves VC and NVA War Surplus Company."

Reeves hunched his shoulders when he felt the earphone being moved and managed to keep the chopper under control. "Take it," he said to his copilot. He loosened his grip on the collective and the cyclic until he felt that the copilot had them in control, then turned to Lily. "Let's go back," he shouted and unplugged his headset and unstrapped from his seat. Lily had to back out of the cockpit rapidly to keep from being knocked over by the pilot, who pushed him toward a recess in the back of the cabin. "What do you mean, we can forget about the Reeves and Lily VC and NVA War Surplus Company if we don't go to Chu Lai first?" he shouted when they reached it. The roaring of the turbines and rotors wasn't as loud there.

"Just what I said. We have to take the evidence to Burrie's lieutenant colonel first, the one who ordered the court-martial. He's the only one who can call it off." He sensed that he had Reeves on the defensive now and if he pushed he could win his point. "If we don't get to him before it starts it can't be stopped and we lose out on the Lily and Reeves VC and NVA War Surplus Company."

"Reeves and Lily."

"Not if we don't go to Chu Lai first."

"Shit," Reeves swore and looked around the cabin as though he could find help against Lily's arguments somewhere in it. He looked at the ensign again. "Do you know what they're doing at Chu Lai? Do you have any idea what's happening there?"

Lily looked puzzled. "Yah. Same as Da Nang. They're fighting a shooting war."

Reeves shook his head. "On base at Da Nang once in a while we get a few mortar rounds or a sniper or something—

sort of like a quiet night in Harlem. They've got serious fighting at Chu Lai. Chu Lai is worse than the worst Detroit riots."

"Sounds like a picnic."

Reeves's eyes bugged. He couldn't believe Lily meant that.

The ensign grinned. "Man, you weren't ashore with me last night. Chu Lai can't be that bad—and I'm still in one piece."

"You saying we gotta go to Chu Lai?"

"We gotta go to Chu Lai."

Reeves shook his head and turned slowly toward the cockpit. In another moment the Navy helicopter banked right and headed to the southern Eye Corps Marine base. Despite the misgivings of the Navy lieutenant the rest of the flight was uneventful. They received clearance to come in over the barrier islands that were slowly turning the mouth of the Ben Van River into a delta and land at the Ky Ha airfield. They checked in at Operations and were told where they could catch a ride to the First Marine Division headquarters. A half hour later Lily and Reeves were left cooling their heels outside an office while Hasford, Houng, and Lanh Thi Dang went inside to meet with the lieutenant colonel.

The lieutenant colonel's face had a hard edge to it but was expressionless as he stared at Phang's agent. "Do you believe him?" he asked Hasford.

"Yessir, it doesn't seem the kind of thing he'd lie about. I talked to him in Vietnamese, what he told me has verisimilitude, the ring of truth."

"I want my own interpreter to question him. You understand, don't you."

It wasn't a question so much as an order. Nonetheless, Hasford nodded and said, "Yessir. I'd expect you to." He knew it was no slight on him, simply that the more people who heard Dang and believed him, the more likely it was he was telling the truth. No one doubted the seriousness or ramifications of what he was admitting to.

The lieutenant colonel spoke into the telephone on his desk and shortly a Vietnamese Marine officer joined them.

The introductions were brief. The lieutenant colonel had first met Major Hoang Thanh Chuyen, who was then a lieutenant, during an earlier tour when he was an adviser with the Vietnamese Marines. The major was a native of Quang Ngai province and was now, at the lieutenant colonel's request, on temporary duty with the staff of the First Marine Division, assisting with the division's intelligence operations and advising on civic action programs.

"Some Marines were caught smuggling heroin," the lieutenant colonel said to the Vietnamese Marine. "This man says they aren't smugglers, that they didn't have anything to do with the drugs found in their possession. I'm not sure whether to believe him and I'd like your opinion. Talk to him." Major Chuyen was unaware of the pending Tango Niner court-martial and the lieutenant colonel considered him an impartial judge.

Chuyen looked at the lieutenant colonel. He suspected there was much he wasn't being told and wondered why it was being kept from him. Confident there was good reason for his not knowing certain things, he started his questioning. He didn't have much to go on, so his interrogation started slowly, but as Lanh Thi Dang's story unfolded, the questioning became easier and a clear story emerged. It went something like this:

"My name is Lanh Thi Dang and I work for Captain Phang, who is an assistant district chief. Captain Phang is a very good man to work for because the hours are usually not long and the pay is good. I only have to work when he has something he wants me to do, which is not every day and does not always take more than a few hours to do. He and the district chief report to Saigon that they have a full battalion of Regional Forces, twenty platoons of Popular Forces, and two full companies of the Army of the Republic of Vietnam under their command. In fact they have but two-and-a-half companies of RFs, fifteen PF platoons, and, as far as I know, no ARVN troops. Each month they receive enough money to pay the wages of all those soldiers which, of course, is more than they have men to pay. They pocket the difference, except for those monies they use to pay their special agents, of whom I am one. I am paid the wages of an ARVN sergeant. That is better than it sounds, as I do not have to pay taxes on that money. From time to time Captain Phang has jobs which he needs help with, jobs that make more money for him. When I help with one of those jobs he pays me extra money. This extra money is sometimes one thousand piasters, often more. Once he paid me six thousand piasters, enough for me to support my family for two or three months, for work that took me only two days. Captain Phang is a generous man.

"A few weeks ago Captain Phang called for me and three or four other men to meet with him to discuss a special job, a job that was not going to make money for him. For this job, one which took long hours each day for a week, he paid each of us ten thousand piasters. This job had to do with the Americans.

"Captain Phang is a very ambitious man in addition to being generous. He wishes to be wealthy and is generous to those who help him in his ambition. There is a small group of American Marines located in a remote village of the district. Even though the village is remote, these American Marines have been interfering with Captain Phang's ambitions of wealth and they have somewhat cut down his income in recent months. More recently they have threatened to remove him from office or kill him—he wasn't very clear about exactly what they threatened him with. The camp of these American Marines had just come under attack by the Vietcong and needed to be rebuilt and have its defenses improved. We were given four kilograms of heroin to hide in the American encampment in a place where the American authorities would find it and arrest these American Marines. We did this." He barked a short laugh. "The American Marines even paid each of us a hundred piasters a day to work for them.

"No, I do not hate the Americans. They are arrogant, but some of them seem to be decent people. In a way I like the Americans. They are very different from us. To the Americans, excess is normal. What we see as normal, they see as poverty. They have so much and guard it so carelessly it is easy to steal from them. If they did not want us to steal from them they would do a better job of guarding the excess that they have, is that not true? And what they throw away is riches almost beyond belief to be thrown away. I have family and friends who have made complete houses from C-ration cartons and empty cans the Americans have discarded as though they were without value. I know whole families who are completely clothed with garments the Americans cast off because they say they are too worn to be of further worth. The Americans are blind to their riches.

"Because the Americans have so much that is worthwhile to me and my family and friends and put it where we can take it, I was somewhat reluctant to hurt any of them. But Captain Phang pays me far more than I can get from the Americans, so I did his bidding.

"The Americans have some strange habits. To void their bowels they do not go to the riverbank or to a canal that leads to the river and squat so the water will take their droppings away the way people without rice paddies do. Nor do they squat over buckets that can be emptied into the paddies to enrich them to help the rice grow better. Instead, they make something that looks like a bed, except it is not long enough for a man to lie on comfortably and it is made of some foreign soft wood and has sides that come all the way down to the ground. Then they cut four holes in this bed that is not a bed and place it over a hole in the ground. They sit on the bed and balance themselves over the holes so they are not in danger of falling through them to empty themselves of the previous day's food. Then every day they drop a powder that burns the eyes and mouth into the hole in the ground. After enough of them have emptied themselves into the hole they dig a new one, move the bed that is not a bed to the new hole, and fill the old hole with dirt. I know these things because I know a man who has worked for the Americans digging new holes to set the bed over. Captain Phang gave us tape when we requested it from him and we used it to attach two bags of heroin to the underside of the bed, far enough from the holes cut in it that they would not become fouled by the men using the holes, but close enough that a man could reach in with an arm and pull them out."

Major Chuyen interrupted Dang's narrative with a question and was answered, "Yes, I said we were given four kilograms of heroin. Yes, the American Marine authorities only found two kilograms. That is because we divided two of them among ourselves and took it for whatever we wanted to do. I myself sold my share. The others may have done the same or they may have used it themselves. I do not know."

Major Hoang Thanh Chuyen listened carefully to Lanh Thi Dang's story and asked him only one question for the lieutenant colonel, the one about two or four kilos. After hearing the whole story he had one more question. "Why have you come forward with your story now, why did you not simply let the American Marines be punished and sent away so that Captain Phang could reclaim all that he had been doing?"

"There are two reasons. The first reason I decided to talk at this time is this man"—he indicated Lieutenant Houng—"calls these American Marines his friends. He would have killed me if I did not talk—the same as he killed Nguyen Minh, who did not talk. I do not want to die if I do not have to. The other reason is another man, one who is not an agent of Captain Phang's but wants to be, found out about the other two kilograms of heroin and threatened to go to Captain Phang and tell him about it if we did not share with him our payments from Phang. I wanted to kill him and talked a few of the others into helping me. It was easy to talk them into it. They didn't want to share with him any more than I did and were afraid of him going to Captain Phang about the other two kilograms. He hid before we could kill him. Captain Phang will learn of us stealing from him and that will be the end of our working for him. He might even have us killed. By talking to the American authorities now, perhaps I can escape before I am killed."

Major Chuyen nodded and turned to the lieutenant colonel. "I believe him," he said. "His story is too elaborate to have been made up . . . and I have heard rumors of this Captain Phang."

The lieutenant colonel thanked Major Chuyen for his assistance and promised to tell him how it worked out later. Then he said to Hasford and Houng, "That does it. As soon as

I can get a bird we'll fly up to Da Nang and get those boys sprung."

"Sir, we have a helicopter and crew on standby at Ky Ha," Hasford said.

"Let's go."

CHAPTER TWENTY-FIVE

Later the same day

The arrival in Da Nang of the lieutenant colonel, Captain Hasford, Lieutenant Houng, and Lanh Thi Dang caused a certain amount of understandable jubilation.

"Thank you, sir," a very relieved Lieutenant Burrison said to the lieutenant colonel and gratefully shook the senior officer's hand. "I told you we didn't do it," he said to Hasford, clapping the captain's right hand between both of his own. "Houng, I knew you'd come through for us," he said to the PF platoon leader and threw his arms around the smaller man and pounded on his back until other hands pulled him away. He breathed a deep sigh of relief and almost collapsed into a nearby chair. He could forget about having to convince a court-martial board he was dumb and incompetent instead of a criminal. The letter of reprimand was gone from his file without ever having been written. If he wanted to, he could think about making a career for himself in the Marine Corps.

"Where's Lily?" he croaked. He wanted to take his good buddy out and get him drunk. Hell, if he had to he'd even take Reeves and his crew and get them drunk, too. Well, maybe not Reeves's crew. Navy officers had a reputation of being able to drink everyone else under the table and want more before they even started to get tipsy.

Sergeant Bell and the corporals crowded around the lieutenant colonel, Hasford, and Houng.

"My small amigo," Ruizique said to Houng, pumping his hand, "now we can go back and kill boo-coo Vee Cee, yes? We kill them dead, all that Uncle Ho wants to send our way."

"Captain," Slover said in his best parade-ground voice, and he had the chest and lung power to have a very good parade-ground voice, "I'm going to have to come up with a nickname for you. You spent so much time with us and done so much in the past month it's like you are one of us. You need a nickname." Slover was the official giver of nicknames to the Marines of Tango Niner and renamed everybody who didn't already have a nickname better than anything they could come up with.

"Colonel," Randall said and threw his arm around the lieutenant colonel's shoulders—he forgot for a moment that lieutenant colonels in the Marine Corps are to be treated with the highest respect and humility, in view of the fact they sit a mere couple of chairs away from the right hand of God the Father. Real reverence is reserved for full colonels and generals, who actually do sit at the right hand of God—"this is the best damn thing to happen in our part of Eye Corps since Tango Niner was activated. We're going to go back out there and kick ass on Charlie so hard you're going to hear him yelling uncle all the way back here in Da Nang."

"I want those sailors," Zeitvogel said. "I want them to come out to Camp Apache and let's throw them one bodacious party."

"Colonel, sir," McEntire asked, "can we go bust Phang our-own-damn-selves? I want to see his face when he finds out he fucked up bad." Like Randall, he forgot how high up Marine lieutenant colonels are.

"Yo, Silver Leaves," Slover shouted across the room.

"You got a nickname, man?" He wanted to give a nick-name for the lieutenant colonel too. "We just got to have something down and dirty to call you. You don't have a nickname I'll give you one; be the best nickname any lieutenant colonel in this Bad Green Machine. What do the other lieutenant colonels call you when you go to the O-Club, get drunk as a skunk?"

The lieutenant colonel fought to keep from smiling. The junior men's exuberance was contagious, but he had his dignity to think of. And he was amused at the remark about getting drunk at the officers' club. Slover couldn't know it, ut the last time he had gotten drunk was ten years earlier, one night when he went out with a few other captains to celebrate his pending promotion to major. His antics that night had delayed his promotion for two years, and he owed his promotion to lieutenant colonel to the war. "They call me Tornado, Lance Corporal," he said, "because that's the way I go through people."

Slover started to correct the lieutenant colonel about his rank, then suddenly realized he was being told to show respect. At least he hoped it was a warning and not an actual bust. But the way the corners of the lieutenant colonel's eyes crinkled told him it wasn't real, yet—just be careful. "Yessir," he said and grinned. "I understand fully, sir. Thank you, Lieutenant Colonel Tornado, sir!"

The noise level in the room abated as the others realized they had been taking too many liberties with the high-ranking officer and backed off.

"I'm going to order a box of sirloin steaks and a couple cases of beer for you boys," Lieutenant Colonel Tornado said. "You can have a party on the beach tonight and return to Camp Apache in the morning. If there's anyone at Da Nang you want to have join you, give Captain Hasford their names and units so he can make arrangements for them to join you. That's all for now." He left them.

Most of them had come from the same battalion of the Seventh Marines, which was at Chu Lai, so the only people any of them knew at Da Nang were Ensign Lily, Lieutenant (jg) Reeves, and Bobbie Harder. Now that Randall was a free man again he couldn't wait to get away to see her.

"Get some, Tex," the others shouted after him. "Ask if she's got a girlfriend for me." "Fuck you, numbnuts. Tex, ask if she's got friends for all of us." "Ride 'em, cowboy!" "Tell her you need one full size for me. I'm tired of only going out with girls who can give me a blow job standing up." "Can I have sloppy seconds?" And so it went until he was out of earshot. His face would have been bright red from the catcalls—if the color could have shown through the tropic bronze of his tan. He only got lost twice looking for the building Bobbie Harder worked in.

The gunnery sergeant looked up from the papers in his hands and glanced out his window. A beefy paw picked the half-smoked cigar from the elephant's foot ashtray on his desk and stuck it between his teeth. He rolled the cigar to the corner of his mouth before speaking. "Looks like that boy you're sweet on is headed this way."

"Tex?" Bobbie Harder squealed and half jumped out of her chair.

"Unless there's more than one boy you're sweet on, that's the one," the gunnery sergeant drawled.

"Gunny, I've told you a hundred times," she said, reaching the gate in the slatted rail fence that separated the desk area of the office from the waiting area, "he's not a boy. He's a twenty-year-old Marine corporal."

"Ah-yup," he said. "That's what I said a hundred times. You gonna tell him about the dirt we got on Phang?" he called after her and returned to his papers.

The door to the office flew open at the instant she reached it. "Tex!" She threw her arms around his neck and kissed him. "Your Lieutenant Houng got the proof." There was no other way he could be here: proof of his innocence had been found and he was freed.

"How did you know," Randall stammered. "It just happened a little while ago. I came here as soon as I could get away after they told us." His blush did show this time.

Her face beamed at him and she shook her head. She

still couldn't get over how a woman could make these Marines blush through their sun-baked tans. "It's the only way you could be here now—unless you broke out of jail." He turned even redder and she leaned back and said, "You didn't break out of jail, did you?" just because she liked seeing the effect she had on him. He turned so red she was afraid capillaries would burst on his face. "Of course you didn't break out of jail, I was just teasing."

The gunnery sergeant rolled his cigar to the other corner of his mouth and peered at the papers in his hands. He mumbled something about "slobbery snot-nosed kids" and tried to ignore them.

The door flew open again and a lanky man wearing an open-neck white shirt and a tropical-weight suit bustled in, bumping into Randall and Bobbie. Wire-rimmed bifocals perched on the end of his nose. He pushed them back and started talking to Bobbie as though they were already in a conversation. "It took me a little while to work out how to crunch all the different ways the data could be analyzed, but once I did, everything was there just like you said it would be." He gestured with the sheaf of computer printout paper in his hand. "It's all right here and I think it's past time we pulled the plug on that guy. Hello," he said to Randall, noticing him at last. Then he continued, "Once you look at everything it becomes perfectly clear that it's impossible for all these claims to be valid. As a matter of fact, this evidence demonstrates that a very large majority of the claims have to be fraudulent. With that many being false one can make a reasonable assumption that perhaps all of them are. My recommendation is no more indemnities are paid to him until each claim has been independently investigated."

"What in the hell are you talking about in my shop?" the gunny roared. "And who the hell are you, anyway?"

The lanky man blinked through his bifocals and gaped at the heavyset gunnery sergeant who was bulling past the desks on his way to him. "What?"

"That's what I said. And don't forget who."

Bobbie was momentarily flustered, but got over it quickly and made the introductions and gave an explanation. Most of the information the Marines had collected on their own, friendly and enemy activities and property, was fed into computers. The data bases and spread sheets were capable of correlating all this information in almost every way imaginable but there hadn't been, and probably never would be, enough time to actually do all of it in all possible ways.

She had gathered every bit of information she could find about Captain Phang's indemnity claims and claims that mentioned Tango Niner. She took the information to a civilian computer expert she had met at a colonel's reception and asked him to run it through his computer to see what he could come up with. He fed it in and ran a search for any other data that involved Phang, Tango Niner, and indemnities regarding either. He found twice as much information as Bobbie gave him. Then he correlated against all known air strikes, artillery missions, combat operations, and small-unit patrols in the areas of the claimed incidents.

"Look here," he said. The computer printout was spread on a desk and his finger traced rapid lines on it. "On the twenty-fourth of last month Phang claimed two incidents with H and I rounds. In both cases the only artillery units near enough to the places he said were hit were involved in fire support missions for grunt outfits in the opposite direction at the time he says they happened. And here"—he pointed out a different line—"where he says a platoon from the Third Battalion, Twenty-sixth Marines, burnt down three hootches. That whole battalion was north of Phu Bai on that day. Here, your Tango Niner is supposed to have pulled platoon-size raids on two different villages ten miles apart on the same evening and killed livestock in both of them. He says they came in by helicopter on one of those raids! Impossible. This man must think we never check our own records to see if what he claims could have happened at all."

"Looks like he was right up until now," Randall said.

"Well . . ."

"That's enough," Bobbie said. "We can do something about this now, can't we, Gunny."

The gunnery sergeant chewed on his cigar for a moment. "You bet your sweet bippy we can." He went back to his desk and picked up the phone. "I never did like that squinty-eyed Marvin the Arvin nohow."

And so the wheels had started rolling. It turned out to be too late to do anything about the problem with Phang, but maybe it was something that would prove to be useful later on with other corrupt officials.

The party the lieutenant colonel supplied food and drink for that night was a success—partly because Bobbie did have some girlfriends who loved the idea of a party with a few real Marine field grunts. She had more friends who were aghast at the idea of partying with Marine field grunts, who thought anyone within sniffing distance of a Marine field grunt would be overcome by his body odor and be taken advantage of while unconscious.

But enough of Bobbie's girlfriends, civilian and Navy, showed up that all four of the other corporals, Sergeant Bell, Lieutenant Burrison, Ensign Lily, and Lieutenant (jg) Reeves were able to pair off. Captain Hasford and Lieutenant Houng flew back to Camp Apache before dark. The former prisoners boogalooed till dawn. A few even managed to sneak a good-night kiss. The biggest hit with everyone except Randall—who had eyes only for Bobbie —and Zeitvogel was an Air Force first lieutenant. She danced, talked, and drank with all comers and didn't seem impressed with her own rank. All the Marines understood why the Air Force first lieutenant wasn't a hit with Randall, but Zeitvogel had to explain to them why he wasn't entranced. He pointed out to them that, no matter how beautiful and friendly she was, she was noticeably shorter than five foot ten. "She looks like a damn midget next to me," he said. "I'd have to get down on my knees to slow dance with her. You ever try to slow dance on your knees, man? Fucks your rhythm up something fierce."

No one had too bad a hangover when they returned to Camp Apache the next morning.

CHAPTER TWENTY-SIX

Another party at the same time

Collard Green's distant relative by marriage through his mother-in-law squatted in the dimness of a hootch lit by only one small candle. Her fingers absently caressed the blade of a hoe she had spent many hours sharpening with an old file. Many other people squatted in the hootch with her, so many they squatted shoulder to shoulder, haunch to haunch, knee to spine. Vien Phoung's second youngest son was there. Candlelight shimmered dully off the machete he clutched. Nguyen Yen and her father, Nguyen Thi Chinh, crowded into a corner of the room, his arms draped around her shoulders. An ancient, rusted French rifle leaned against his side; she held an equally ancient, rusted bayonet to her breast. Tan was near the middle of the room. He had tested the ammunition that was now in his carbine and knew it was good. A man with one hand used that one hand to grip a well-oiled K-bar a Marine had given him.

His other hand had gone to Phang for the effrontery of trying to take back what he believed to be his. The one eye of a woman who had been beautiful before her face was scarred in becoming one-eyed stared hard at each person in the room, as though it could see into their souls. She had become one-eyed when Phang took that eye because she refused to give him her body.

All the people in the hootch were armed in motley manner. They had one thing in common: Captain Phang had harmed them all. They were joined together on this night to end the pain.

"Phang is evil," one of the people said.

"The Vietcong have promised to rid our land of all who are like Phang," said another.

"If that was their intention they could have done it by now," said a third.

"They are not murderers like he is," said a fourth, defending the second speaker.

"They want to rid us of Phang only so they can have his power," rejoined the third.

"Enough of politics," said Collard Green's distant relative by marriage through his mother-in-law. "We are not here tonight to discuss which robber side will steal from us less than the other. We are here to decide exactly how to rid ourselves of Phang." By tacit agreement they did not grant Captain Phang the honor of referring to him by title.

"Phang is evil, as someone said. The only way to rid oneself of an evil is to expel it, to kill that evil."

"If he is to be killed it must be within the law."

"Or else we are murderers and thieves as he is."

"His killing must not be wanton. It must stand as a teaching to others of what can happen to them if they murder, steal, and hurt as does Phang."

"As did Phang," someone corrected.

"It must be done in such a way that his spirit cannot return to do us any further harm."

"How do we kill him within the law if we are not a court of law?"

"Has everyone in this room been harmed by Phang?"

"You know it."

"Are we here to judge him?"

"We are."

"And pass sentence?"

"Of course."

"Has he committed crimes against us, crimes a fair court of law would convict him of?"

"He has."

"Then we are a court of law."

"Does anyone here doubt Phang has done to each of us what we say he has?"

None denied it.

"Or that he has committed other, similarly grievous hurts to people who are not with us tonight?"

"Some of them cannot be with us tonight because the grievous hurt Phang did to them was their deaths."

"Then he is guilty as charged on all counts."

"He is."

"Does anyone speak for Phang? Is there naught that might alleviate the heinousness of what he has done?"

"He is a man," someone adopted the role of defender, "he has family to support."

"Does he not receive payment from the government for the work he does?" asked another, taking the role of prosecutor.

"But it is a small amount."

"It is more than any of us earns," spoke someone who was not the prosecutor.

"Irrelevant. A man in his position needs more in order to fulfill his duties."

"All officials need more than they are paid. To make up the difference they are all paid small bribes. That is well understood. Why are the common bribes not enough for Phang?"

There was a silence while the defender tried to think of a reason why the common bribes paid to all bureaucrats was not enough. Finally he said the truth. "Because they will not make him rich."

"Is a desire for riches a just reason for theft?" someone asked.

"No."

"Is it a lawful reason to aid others in ignoring the legal cap on rents?" asked a farmer.

"No."

"Does it justify rape?" asked Nguyen Yen.

"No."

"Is it lawful cause to maim and disfigure?" asked the man with one hand.

"No."

"Is it just cause for murder?" asked Collard Green's distant relative by marriage through his mother-in-law.

"No."

"Does it make legal the selling of weapons to the enemy?" asked Tan.

"No."

"Has he another defense?"

"None."

"We are agreed to his guilt. Do we agree on sentence?"

One at a time each said, "Phang must die."

"How do we make sure his spirit will not come back to do us further harm?"

"How do we lead him to the gibbet?"

Phang tapped his driver's arm with his swagger stick. The driver brought the jeep to a stop next to a beautiful girl who looked at the ARVN official with what appeared to be adoring eyes.

"Yen, lovely Yen," Phang said to the girl. His smile was a smirk.

Yen smiled, stuck a folded piece of paper in Phang's hand, and ran.

"What a lovely child," he said. "A pity she is too awe-struck to speak."

It was not from awe that Yen did not speak.

A short time later in his office, Phang unfolded the piece of paper and read what Yen had written in her painstaking schoolgirl hand.

Captain Phang,

Our last meeting was a most memorable experience for me, one I have relived in my mind many times since. I wish to see you about it once more. Please meet me tonight, the man who was my first lover. There is an abandoned woodcutter's house a quarter hour's walk west of Duc Nhuan. I will be there one hour after sunset. I will have my own sheet.

She did not sign the note.

Phang smiled. So formal a note, he thought, so sweet a child. One taste of a real man and she can't get enough. If she is more active in pleasing me tonight I may lower her father's taxes and rent by more than the token reduction I already gave.

Alone, Phang parked his jeep in front of the abandoned woodcutter's house at the appointed hour and approached the door of the hut. The interior was lit by the warm glow of an oil lamp. He stopped in the doorway. Directly in front of him was a wooden bed. Yen sat cross-legged on the bed, a sheet spread beneath her. Her tunic was unbuttoned except for the one button between her breasts. He smirked and stepped toward the bed. Before he could reach it his air was violently cut off by a cord around his neck and he was thrown roughly to the dirt floor. A mass of bodies landed on him, pinned him down, made his struggles meaningless. Cords were tightly wrapped around him, binding his arms to his sides and his legs together. A smelly, foul-tasting cloth was crammed into his mouth before the cord was released from his throat. Many hands grabbed at him and threw him onto the bed Yen had risen from.

Wild-eyed, he looked around the room, his head darting from side to side. He should not have been so foolish as to come alone. He struggled with the gag, tried to spit it out. These people must be robbers, they must not know who he was. If he could speak he would get them to release him with his promise to let them go without fear of punishment. Then he would hunt them down and see them all die. But the gag wouldn't come loose.

The hands grabbed him again and tied him to the bed, stilling his struggles even more. Then he saw who the hands belonged to and sweat popped out on his forehead and ran in rivulets from his armpits and his crotch.

A middle-aged woman stepped into his view. She said, "Phang, you have been convicted of crimes against the people. Every person in this room has been your victim. Every person here has found you guilty, and sentence has been passed: death times ten thousand." She leaned forward. A rice knife was in her hand. He squirmed but it did no good. The middle-aged woman cut his shirt open and laid his chest and belly bare; she cut his belt and sliced open the front of his trousers as far as mid-thigh. Then she stepped aside.

A one-eyed woman who had once been beautiful stepped to the side of the bed. A dirty spoon was in her hand. While two men held his head still she tore one of his eyes from its socket with that spoon. A muffled howl blundered its way through the gag.

Yen knelt on the bed with a sharp knife in her hand. Her other hand yanked his testicles up from where they cowered between his thighs. Yen made one slash that went halfway through his scrotum. Phang's agony was so great at first he didn't notice Yen hand the knife to another woman who was kneeling on his other side. She finished castrating him. A third woman straddled his knees and took the knife. She grasped his flaccid penis and slowly cut through its base. At the first cut it gorged with blood and started to come erect. When the woman finished cutting, blood sprayed out and splattered the front of her tunic. Phang passed out from the pain. A bucket of urine splashed over his face woke him.

A man with one hand put down his K-bar and picked up a small ax. Another man held Phang's hand out to the side while the one-handed man swung the ax. It took him three chops to sever the hand. Warm blood spurted over the hands of the man holding the severed hand. Phang started growing cold. His life was ebbing with the blood that gushed from the three massive wounds. A tourniquet was tied around his wrist stump and a pressure bandage was slapped onto his empty groin to slow the bleeding. It wouldn't do for the criminal to die before his punishment was over. . .

A gruesome package greeted Major Tran Duc Y when he entered his office the next morning. A blood-stained bundle of butcher paper sat in the middle of his desk. A message was written on the outside of the paper. It read:

> To Major Tran Duc Y, District Chief,
>   The corrupt career of your assistant district chief is over. Parts of him are in this package. Other parts will be found in other places. Let this be a lesson to all who would steal from, rape, or murder the people.

Major Y sat at his desk and eyed the package curiously. After a moment he took a bronze letter opener shaped like a cavalry saber and slit the package open. It contained a hand, a penis, an eyeball, and an empty scrotum. Major Y sipped green tea from a fine china cup while he prodded the package's contents with his letter opener. When he was satisfied that they were real human remains and not clever constructs, he picked up the package, taking care not to let any blood drip on his uniform, and dropped it into the wastebasket by his desk. If the objects were actually from Phang's body, no matter. The captain had been far too greedy anyway—he demanded too large a cut of the side revenues garnered by the district chief and his assistant. Major Y would simply find a new assistant who would not want as much. But whoever was on duty last night, whoever it was who failed to prevent this offal's being dropped on his desk, that man would be lucky if he saw the morrow with life and limb intact.

As promised in the note, other parts of Phang's body were found in other places. A Chinese landlord almost fainted when he left his home and walked into a leg dangling from the lintel of his front door.

The other leg was found in the duty office of one of the Regional Forces barracks; blood dripping from it had coagulated on papers in the filing cabinet it was laid on.

The other RF barracks had one arm hanging in its shower room.

A red cord dangled over the side of the main well used by the cooks of the district headquarters. An enterprising young cook drew the cord out without bothering to first notify anyone it was there. The handless arm was on the other end of the cord. Initially no one believed the cook when he showed them the arm and said where he found it. When word of Phang's dismemberment reached the cooks, the fellow was reported and it took several days for him to clear himself of suspicion of having been in on the killing.

Phang's torso was mounted in the market square. A sign was nailed to its chest explaining whose torso it was and why he had been treated that way. Soldiers removed the torso and the sign, but not before a hundred or so people had seen it and read the sign.

When the priest of the town's main Catholic church entered his sanctuary to celebrate early morning mass he found a carefully arranged mound of intestines with an eyeball mounted on its peak sitting inside the tabernacle in place of the gold chalice he expected to find there. There was a small stirring among his small congregation as the weekday churchgoers wondered why their priest was retching.

They never found Phang's head. It was buried at a crossroads, with the testicles from the empty scrotum replacing the missing eyeballs in their sockets. The rest of his body could come together again, but without the head Phang's soul would wander lost for all eternity. His spirit could not come back to cause further harm to any whom he had injured in life.

CHAPTER TWENTY-SEVEN

November 15, 1966

The United States Marine Corps prides itself on being an all-volunteer organization. The grinding harshness of Boot Camp and the relentless discipline and physical rigorousness that continue in the infantry and other combat units are worthy of the most elite military units in the world. Marines pride themselves on being the best of the best. The regimen is so demanding that enlisted Marines claim it to be inhuman, even going so far as to say no one has the right to treat another human being the way they are treated. Unless the human being treated that way volunteered for it. No matter how much a young Marine sounds like he thinks he made a mistake when he says he enlisted because "It seemed like a good idea at the time," or how rueful he sounds when he says, "It's nobody's fault but mine. No one told me I had to do this. I went to that recruiting sergeant and said 'I want to sign up' on my own and nobody was holding a gun to my head," he feels pride when he says these things. Being a Marine turned out to be much harder than he imagined it would, but he is proud of the fact that not only could he take it, he is always ready to take more.

But Marines live with a rarely mentioned embarrassment. For a while during World War II, and again during the Vietnam war, when enlistments weren't keeping up with the demands of beefing up the Corps to a wartime footing, the Marine Corps accepted a limited number of draftees. Marines seldom mention this to each other and rarely admit to themselves that it has happened. After all, they really do believe, "I enlisted, so it's my own damn fault I'm here. But, by God, nobody has the right to tell anybody else he has to go through the kind of shit I'm in."

PFC Lawrence R. Dodd constantly looked like he didn't know where he was or care why he was there. He performed well but always looked like he was lost. No matter how long he served with any group of Marines he seemed to be a stranger intruding in a tightly knit group. He kept largely to himself, seldom talking to the others. But the Marines of Tango Niner could not afford to have a stranger in their ranks. They drew him out, they wanted to make him one of them.

"Say what?" Lewis suddenly demanded mid-morning of the day after the smuggling charges had been cleared.

"Bullshit," Wells declared.

"Man, I've heard some wild sea stories before," Hempen said, "but that don't even sound like any part of it could be true."

"It's true," Dodd said. "They drafted me."

Big Red Robertson stared hard at Dodd before saying, "I like sea stories and I've been known to tell a few of my own. Bullshit artists are okay, they can tell some mighty fine stories. Even seagoing lawyers have a place in the Crotch." He shook his head sadly. "But there's no room for liars in this man's Marine Corps."

"I'm not a liar," Dodd said emotionlessly. "And I can prove it." He dropped the front of the ammo crate table that had belonged to Wildman Eastham and withdrew a tattered and stained envelope. He took two dog-eared sheets of paper from the envelope and stared at them for a moment with droopy eyes. He sighed deeply and handed one of them to Lewis. It was an induction notice. Lewis read it and passed it on to Hempen. He took the second sheet from Dodd. It was a letter from his draft board informing him he had passed his physical and told him when he was to report back for transportation to the Marine Corps Recruit Depot, San Diego, California.

"You're not shitting me," Lewis said.

Dodd shook his head glumly.

"I heard they were drafting people into the Marines," Hempen said, "but I thought they'd get pogue jobs. I didn't think a draftee would get stuck in the grunts."

"I'm here, ain't I," Dodd said.

"Goddamn," Wells whispered.

"Hey, 'pano, I'm sorry about what I said," Robertson said. "I didn't know."

"It's okay, it's not your fault," Dodd said and sighed deeply again. After nearly a year in the Marine Corps he still couldn't quite believe they had drafted him.

They looked at each other, all except Dodd. His eyes seemed to be focused on something beneath the duckboard floor of the tent, something only he could see. None of them knew how to respond to the news that Dodd was a draftee. One thing they all agreed on without having to say anything was it was flat wrong that he was drafted. And worse that they put him in the infantry.

"Son of a bitch," Lewis swore softly.

"You poor mo-dicker," Hempen said.

Wells shook his head. He was too stunned to say anything.

"They can't do this to you," Robertson said. He was beginning to think about becoming a seagoing lawyer.

Dodd didn't say anything. He had heard it all before. And before that he had thought it all himself.

A silence grew among the Marines in the tent, became awkward, then strained. Strained for everyone but Dodd. He had been through this too many times in the past. Every time other Marines found out he was drafted. All it did any more was add a little bit to his feeling of not being part of where he was, of not being wanted. The others would start drifting away in a few minutes, Dodd knew that. He could guess who would go first—he made a bet with himself about it—and what, if anything, any of them would say when leaving.

Wells stood up and Dodd started to tell himself he won that part of his bet when Wells said, "Can anybody make out what Swearin' Swarnes is saying?"

They listened for Swarnes to repeat his message, then jumped to their feet and ran to the command hootch. Except for Dodd. He didn't know anyone at Camp Apache well enough to get enthusiastic about any of the same things they did, other than trying to stay alive in a firefight.

Swarnes yelled again, "They're coming the fuck back. That cherry-popping bird's on its way and it'll be here in ten goddamn minutes."

In less than ten minutes Hasford had the men of the mortar team manning their tube, the machine gun covering the north side of the hill, and the men of the rifle squad spread out on the hill's other three sides. Swarnes was on his radios and the two corpsmen were with the captain as a greeting party. Pennell stood at the edge of the helipad facing into the wind with Slover's orange pingpong paddles in his hands. Willard, the new grenadier, took his place on the perimeter with Webster and Neissi.

"Hey, Fast Talking Man," Wells called, "you're supposed to take your shirt off you gonna do that."

Pennell didn't yell back, but the look he gave Wells asked which one of them he thought was crazier. Big Louie could bring in helicopters without wearing a shirt if he wanted to, but Pennell was damned if he was going to risk losing his skin to the debris thrown up by the chopper's downwash.

Two helicopters were growing in the east, one was at a middle altitude and the other higher. When they closed to a half kilometer from the hill the mid-altitude bird swooped down and made a wide circle of the hill about two hundred meters above it. When the gunship completed its first orbit the other bird pointed its nose at Pennell, lined up with the paddles he held out to his sides, and dropped down onto the helipad. Seven men, holding rifles in one hand and clutching bush hats to their heads with the other, bolted off it and ducked under the helicopter's spinning rotor blades. The pilot and Hasford exchanged thumbs-up and the bird took off immediately. All it and its escort were doing was making a quick dropoff on their way to another mission. They headed north.

In less than a minute Burrison, Bell, and the corporals were surrounded by their men. Swarnes even dared to desert his radios for a few minutes. "If it's important they'll call back," he told himself.

They partied. Over the course of an hour all of the PFs of the platoon wandered onto the hill as word of the return reached them. The Marines and their PFs partied hard and loud, but they drank far more soda than beer and rice wine. There may have been reason to celebrate, but there were also patrols to run and a perimeter to guard that night and no one could afford to get drunk. Collard Green was the last to arrive. He came with a middle-aged woman who he introduced as his distant relative by marriage through his mother-in-law. The party was interrupted while she squatted and told a tale to the Marines and PFs of Tango Niner. Houng translated for the Marines. Hasford kept silent and listened carefully to the woman's words.

"Captain Phang," Houng translated, "him dead. Some people him hurt take him. One woman him take eye from, take eye from him. Three woman him boom-boom, them not want him boom-boom them, they cut off, . . ." He paused, groping for words he did not know; finally he cupped his hand over his crotch. "Me not know how say. Them cut off here. One man Phang cut off him hand, cut off Phang hand. More people, what Phang do them, them do him. When done, some people take knife, stab Phang. Some man take gun, shoot Phang. Phang dead. No more Phang," he finished softly and shook his head.

Collard Green's relative looked with unseeing eyes into the distance when she was through telling her story. Some of the PFs talked quietly, repeating details to each other. After a long moment Zeitvogel was the first Marine to speak.

"What'd I say," he said. "I said his own people would get him."

Then Hasford asked the woman a question in rapid Vietnamese. She slowly turned her head toward him and looked long at this foreigner who spoke the language so well before answering him. "Did you help kill him?" Houng translated. "It does not matter. Phang hurt people. People who he hurt killed him. Phang is dead. That is all that matters."

The middle-aged woman levered herself out of her crouch and started her long walk home without another word.

After their hot evening meal was eaten, before any of the patrols went out, Sergeant Bell and his three corporals, Zeitvogel, Randall, and Ruizique, stood on the west side of their hill watching the sun drop down to the tops of the mountains.

"Charlie's over there," Bell said. "And he's in the other direction as well. We're in the middle of his fucking path from one place to the other."

"We put such a hurting on his ass every time he comes through here I don't know why he doesn't find another path," Randall said.

"He can't find another path," Zeitvogel said. "He's got something important over there and this is the only way from there to where he wants to go."

"Amigos," Ruizique said, "I think we should pay Mister Charles a visit and find out what it is he has over there that is so important." Blood lust showed in the Dominican's grim visage.

"You can't do that," another voice said from behind the quartet. "It's outside your area of operations." They turned and saw Captain Hasford. He had come up unnoticed while they were talking.

"I know that," Bell answered him. "But it would be nice to know what's happening over there. Do you think Force Recon or Division Recon has patrols out there and we could find out what they learned?"

"I don't know, but I can find out."

CHAPTER TWENTY-EIGHT

November 16, 1966

"Oo-ee, would you look at that," Stilts Zeitvogel said, looking toward the east.

"What do you have, compano?" Ruizique asked. His upper lip was dark with unshaven whiskers. In the days since they had been cleared of the heroin-smuggling charges he had started growing a mustache. He now constantly wore, crossed on his chest, the two bandoleers his uncle had sent, every loop holding a 7.62mm round. He looked to where Zeitvogel pointed.

Two small motorcycles with light machine guns mounted on their handlebars roared slowly abreast on low throttle along the bulldozed road from Hou Dau. An American half-track with Vietnamese markings followed the motorcycles. Two deuce-and-a-half trucks with .50-caliber machine guns trailed the half-track. A jeep carrying an M-60 machine gun mounted on its hood and a .50-caliber machine gun on a roll bar brought up the rear of the small convoy.

"What the fuck? Over," Randall asked, joining them.

Lieutenant Burrison, walking back to his command hootch from the piss tubes, saw them standing near the northeast corner of the compound and wondered what they were looking at. He might have ignored them for the moment except for the small dust cloud he saw rising from the road beyond them. "Jay Cee," he shouted, "let's check it out." He was wearing dull buffed boots, neatly repaired, faded utility trousers, a tee shirt, pistol belt, and his bush hat.

Most of the Marines of Tango Niner and all of the PFs who were in the compound at the time were gathered between its northeast corner and the main gate watching the stately procession by the time it had covered half the distance from Hou Dau to Camp Apache. They started drifting toward the gate. The convoy could be going nowhere other than to Camp Apache.

The motorcyclists revved their mufflerless bikes to maintain their speed up the hill. They wheeled inside and spun around to stop at either side of the gate, facing the roadway. The half-track followed the motorcycles and ground to a stop a few yards inside. The other vehicles remained below the hill.

A Vietnamese officer stood in the passenger seat of the half-track. He was resplendent in a dress uniform with many rows of colorful ribbons and badges over his left breast pocket. The silver plum blossoms of an ARVIN major glittered on his collar. He wore white gloves and mirror sunglasses, and a white scarf was artfully thrown around his neck. The sun reflected fiercely from the highly polished holster which held a chrome-plated Walther PPK on his belt. His ensemble was completed by a Sam Browne belt and the biggest, gaudiest swagger stick any of the Marines had ever seen. His head swiveled and his upper lip curled slightly with disdain at the ragged warriors he saw. When he stepped out of the half-track his paratrooper boots glinted sunlight as harshly as his holster.

Burrison, with Bell a pace to his left and rear, approached the Vietnamese officer.

"Who is in command here," demanded the parade-ground apparition, looking past Burrison. He spoke English with a British clip.

"I am," Burrison said. His voice was neutrally polite. "Second Lieutenant Burrison, USMC. Who are you, sir?"

He's catching on, Bell thought. As soon as he learns to say "Who the fuck are you, sir?" he'll have it right.

The Vietnamese officer tilted his head back so he could look down his nose at the young American lieutenant. He wordlessly held his look long enough to cause the beginnings of disquiet, then said, "I am Major Tran Duc Y, District Chief." He spun slowly on his heel, taking in the sights of Camp Apache: the squad tents with their sides rolled up revealing cots piled with gear, ammo box tables with miscellany stacked on and under them, clothing hanging from rafters and tent poles; the wall-less four-holer starting to list to one side as it settled over its hole; the navy blue jeep that was in bad need of washing; the open-air shower; the scattered tables and chairs made from discarded ammo crates and a comm wire spool. But mostly he saw the Marines, none of whom was wearing what he considered to be a proper uniform—the few wearing headgear were even wearing those terrible camouflage bush hats the PFs wore. He made no effort to conceal his contempt for the ragtag crew. His survey completed, he pointed the reflecting lenses of his sunglasses at Burrison.

"By now even you must have heard of the dastardly attack the Vietcong made on my district headquarters two days ago," Major Y said, "the attack in which my assistant district chief was killed."

Burrison blinked. "I heard about Captain Phang getting killed," he said, "but this is the first I heard about a Vee Cee attack on your headquarters."

"Fortunately only one other man was killed before we repulsed them with heavy losses," Y said.

Burrison knew enough of what had happened to know the district chief was lying.

"What that unfortunate incident clearly shows is the need for me to increase security at my district head-quarters," Y continued. "To do that I am going to add the best-trained, most successful fighters under my command to the defenses of my district headquarters."

All the Marines who heard Y felt a sinking in the pits of their stomachs. They knew who the best Cong killers in the district were.

"I am taking the Popular Forces platoon from Bun Hou to be my first line of defense."

"You can't do that," Bell blurted.

Y turned his sunglasses in Bell's direction. He guessed this man standing next to the American Marine commander must be his second in command. "Sergeant, all of the Regional and Popular Forces in the district are under my command. I can assign them anywhere I want. If they do not go where I tell them to, they are guilty of desertion and subject to the full force of military law. I can take them, and I am taking them." He turned and nodded to his driver, who stood up and signaled the vehicles at the foot of the hill. The two deuce-and-a-halfs and the gun jeep drove into Camp Apache, circled around, and drove back down to the roadway, pointed back the way they had come.

An hour later a tearful Lieutenant Houng boarded the last of his PFs onto the trucks. Mayor Y's half-track honked its horn and the two motorcycles started their slow, roaring journey back to the district town.

"Don't worry, Houng," Bell shouted after the departing trucks, "we'll get this straightened out in a skosh bit."

"We'll get you back here most ricky-tick," Burrison added.

"You can't," Houng called back. "There is nothing you can do about it."

The other Marines stood dejected, staring after their PFs, their home boys. They kept watching long after the small convoy disappeared into the forest south of Hou Dau hill.

ABOUT THE AUTHOR

David Sherman served as a Marine in Vietnam in 1966, stationed, among other places, in a CAP unit on Ky Hoa Island. He holds the Combat Action Ribbon, Presidential Unit Citation, Navy Unit Commendation, Vietnamese Cross of Gallantry, and the Vietnamese Civic Action Unit Citation. He left the Marines a corporal, and after his return to the World, worked as a library clerk, antiquarian bookstore retail manager, deputy director of a federally funded community crime prevention program, manager of the University of Pennsylvania's Mail Service Department, and a sculptor.